D0667687

TAGGED FOR MURDER

TAGGED FOR MURDER

A Dek Elstrom Mystery

Jack Fredrickson

This first world edition published 2018
in Great Britain and 2018 in the USA by
SEVERN HOUSE PUBLISHERS LTD of
Eardley House, 4 Uxbridge Street, London W8 7SY.
Trade paperback edition first published
in Great Britain and the USA 2018 by
SEVERN HOUSE PUBLISHERS LTD.

British Library Cataloguing in Publication Data
A CIP catalogue record for this title is available from the British Library.

ISBN-13: 978-0-7278-8772-6 (cased)
ISBN-13: 978-1-84751-887-3 (trade paper)
ISBN-13: 978-1-78010-949-7 (e-book)

All Severn House titles are printed on acid-free paper.

Severn House Publishers support the Forest Stewardship Council™ [FSC™],
the leading international forest certification organisation.
All our titles that are printed on FSC certified paper carry the FSC logo.

Typeset by Palimpsest Book Production Ltd.,
Falkirk, Stirlingshire, Scotland.
Printed and bound in Great Britain by
TJ International, Padstow, Cornwall.

For Susan

ACKNOWLEDGMENTS

As always, I have been blessed by the best of overseers: Kate Lyall Grant and Sara Porter of Severn House, and Susan Fredrickson of everything else.

ONE

O nly Keller, of the gamy *Argus-Observer,* thought to write that the man found dead on top of the railcar, the end of that February, had died in a leap year. Chicago's more responsible newspapers were more circumspect and more precise. Likely, the murdered man spotted from a traffic helicopter hadn't leapt at all. He'd been dropped, thrown or pushed, found splayed spread-eagled on the roof of a blue boxcar, legs out, face down, victim of blunt trauma to the head and torso. Dead as a June bug, come July.

Corpses found lying about the Windy City haven't been a rarity since well before Capone. Chicagoans expect news of fresh ones to come with their granolas, *chilaquiles* and *kielbasas* every morning. This victim, though, wasn't the usual greased-up gang-banger dead from a drive-by shooting or worse, some innocent kid caught by a stray bullet while hopscotching or bouncing a ball in a park. The man found at the abandoned Central Works was somewhere between thirty and forty, dressed expensively in a two-thousand-dollar suit and a finely woven white shirt. Fine attire, and confusing. The duds didn't match his mouth. Half his teeth were rotted down to nubs. And his skin was bad, marked by the bites and nicks of someone homeless, though that could have come from lying too long neglected on top of a boxcar.

Nobody knew who he was. He had no wallet and he fit no report of a missing person. Nor could anyone be sure how he'd ended up on the top of the railcar. There was no ladder mounted to its side, and the car was at the end of a rusted rail spur, a hundred yards from the only building from where he might have been dropped. The cops had to wonder if he'd even died there. The railcar had been on that spur for days, but the corpse could have perished elsewhere and been carried, frozen to the top of the boxcar by the snow and the rain of a frigid February, to the derelict old Central Works.

It was a muddle. The cops said that their investigation was ongoing, but those were the knee-jerk words cops learn to say in

Chicago. New murders demanding new attention would come in multiples the next day and the day after and all the days after that. Even if there were enough cops to deal with them all, there would be few, if any, witnesses willing to risk their lives by coming forward. That February was at the start of what already promised to be a record year for killings, following the previous new record set the year before. That February, in Chicago, folks didn't so much want to talk to cops as scream at them.

For a man found dead on a railcar, dressed fine but probably in cast-off clothes and likely homeless, it meant oblivion. He'd be forgotten soon enough.

Or so the thinking went.

TWO

A guy whose fast voice I couldn't quite place called at ten o'clock the morning after the man on the boxcar was discovered.

'Dek,' he said.

'Indeed, this is Dek Elstrom,' I answered agreeably, because I am most agreeable when there's been a doughnut, even one so stale, for breakfast.

'Herb Sunheim.'

Herbie Sunshine, most called him, not because he was a sunny-seeming fellow but because he was exactly the opposite, a morose man in a worn shiny suit, suited to gloom. The man's clothing fit his enterprise. He ran a tiny commercial real estate brokerage, catering to small businesses looking to grab or to unload distressed properties at distressed prices. He occasionally tossed me background investigation work on his clients when he couldn't find anyone to work cheaper. Nickels mattered to Herbie.

'Long time,' I said.

'Got a job. Accident.'

Herbie always spoke in a sort of thug-staccato, like each word cost him a dollar he didn't have, but that morning he sounded anxious to fire them out even faster than usual.

'You OK, Herbie?' I asked.

'Right away on this.'

'Great,' I said. I was between jobs, as had been my norm for too many years, and was primed to pounce on anything that would cough up a buck.

'Just property photos,' he said.

'No backgrounds, no write-ups?'

'Pictures only.'

'Give me the address.'

'Central Works. Boxcar in back.'

'Where they found that stiff yesterday?'

'Views of the building, boxcar, vicinity neighborhood. Pays half a large.'

'There are pictures online,' I said, despite my poverty. It didn't make sense for a nickel-rubber like Herbie to pay five hundred dollars for pictures he could download for free.

'Pronto, confidential, to me only,' he said, instead of answering my question.

I let it go, thinking he must be representing deep-pocketed property owners, paranoid that their negligence had contributed to the victim being dropped, splat, on top of the railcar. Nowadays, people sued everybody for everything, and any lawsuit could impede a development, slow a sale, or even wipe out an owner's equity. Spending large for an investigator to take photos might well have been an owner's way of showing partners and lawyers he was doing all he could to avoid disaster.

I was happy to comply. I told Herbie to write the check because I was already headed out the door.

Along with killers and corpses, Chicago has always been chock-full of pie-eyed, commercial real estate optimists. Seemingly blind to the gang wars stacking stiffs in record numbers, massive municipal pensions demanding ever-increasing property taxes, and the city's tanking financial status, developers seemed to be scraping and building faster than ever that February, frenzied as if to suck the last of the loot out of Chicago before the whole caboodle collapsed.

The bit of blight on the west side where the boxcar man was found was typical of the times. It was the former site of the Central States Electric Works, a once-huge manufacturing complex that produced telephones back in the day when folks used such things to talk mouth-to-ear and not to play games, thumb texts, or watch movies. Most west side Chicagoans had a relative or two who'd worked at the Central Works.

Its vast acreage sat on the northeast corner of a six-lane highway to the south and a four-lane street to the west, and had once held a dozen sooty brown brick factory and office buildings. All of those buildings, except one, were now bulldozed away, no doubt in preparation for redevelopment. Just a mile to the east, closer to the city, several new ten- and twelve-story apartment buildings had already sprouted up. Slab-sided in beige precast concrete, black windowed to mute the absence of anything green growing outside, hundreds of units beckoned hundreds of hipsters. A new micro-brewery was plopped in the center of the residential canyon, a simple crawl to even the farthest of the apartments. It was idyllic, for those that enjoyed cement.

Except occasional gunfire could be heard there. Just a mile to the north or south were blocks of weed-choked, disintegrated sidewalks and burned-out buildings, worthless bloody turf where gangs shot at each other over disrespect and imagined slights because there was nothing else left to fight over. They'd lost their monopoly on marijuana, those bangers. Weed, it was joked, was now being sold cheap by grandmothers in lacy living rooms who got their stashes with medical cards. And the gangs had been edged out of the rougher trades as well. Big operators from outside the country had taken over the peddling of crack cocaine, heroin and the burgeoning synthetic concoctions markets, considering Chicago prime not only for its immense population, but also for its location. It was a convenient way station for breaking down big loads for reshipment to the east coast. Those operators, from Mexico, Central America and other places, used their own people to sell and ship; they didn't want to risk control by hiring local. And so it went. Chicago's once-mighty big gangs crumbled, devolving into smaller and smaller groups, until at last they fragmented into block-based, murderous little boys' clubs, having nothing much to do except shoot at each other.

I parked along the highway and walked north across two hundred yards of sparkling shards of glass, damp dirt and shallow puddles of snowmelt, snapping phone pictures as I went. The blue boxcar rested at the west end of a spur of rusted tracks that ran at the back of the last standing building. It was wrapped once around with yellow cop tape and appeared to be exactly where it had been when photographed by news photographers.

Two of Chicago's finest sat in a squad car parked on the side street a hundred yards west. I couldn't imagine what they were watching for, a day after the body had been discovered and removed, and decided they were simply taking a break. There'd been much press recently about bad-acting Chicago police, real and those falsely accused. That resulted, many said, in cops going fetal, responding only to calls that could not be avoided, and only when there was certainty they'd come out alive. So, more and more, cops were sitting in cars idling on safe streets, maybe like the ones to my left. I couldn't quite blame them for that.

The news reports had been accurate. There was no ladder mounted on the side of the boxcar. The victim must have fallen, or been dropped, or he'd jumped from some place higher up.

I snapped more pictures of the railcar and the surrounding area, the wasteland Herbie called the 'neighborhood vicinity,' concentrating on the spatial relationships of everything surrounding the railcar. The only building that remained on the property, a boarded-up, four-story former factory, lay on that same rail spur, a hundred yards to the east. The likeliest scenario was that the body had come out of one of its windows, and that the railcar was then moved to the end of the spur. That would not offer comfort to Herbie or his client.

Still, there'd been rain and snow and freezing temperatures earlier that February. I'd text Herbie with the pictures, telling him his client's best shot was to contact the railroad in the hope that the boxcar had been shuttled about enough times to make it possible that the victim had ridden in from somewhere else, stuck frozen to the top.

I walked along the tracks and around to the front of the building. In the style of old Chicago factories, the main entrance was ornate. Fluted beige cement pillars, striped black with soot from back when Chicago's factories made things, surrounded the entryway, as if in testament to the importance of the work that was to be performed inside. The building's massive doors, likely ripped away decades before, had been replaced by the same thick, weathered plywood that covered all the windows.

One of the window boards was loose enough to pull back and see inside. A fast glance revealed a place likely popular with drug users and dealers. They were the only ones who'd have the stoned

courage to linger in such a place long enough to smoke the hundreds
of cigarette butts that lay crushed on the scorched floor. Some of
the stubbed-out smokes looked fresh, and that explained the loose
board. Almost certainly, the building, like many vacant properties
in Chicago, was still thriving as a dusk-to-dawn drug hostel for
teens driving in from the suburbs.

'Hey!' A younger man with slick, gelled dark hair had come
up behind me. He was lean and fit, about five foot ten, and wore
a carefully knotted narrow red necktie. His charcoal suit looked
to be as fine as the one worn by the man found dead on the railcar,
though likely the young man had better teeth.

'You can't read?' he asked. He pointed to the blue-and-white
but mostly rusty No Trespassing sign attached to the bricks.

'Who are you?'

'Not your business,' he said.

'Then smile,' I said, taking a picture of him pointing to the
sign.

He didn't smile. 'What are you doing here?'

I held up my phone. 'Taking pictures,' I said, enunciating slowly
as though for an idiot.

'News or insurance?' he snapped.

I had a deliciously evil thought. 'I'm stringing for Keller at the
Argus-Observer.' I'd hated that columnist since he trashed me and,
by association, my ex-wife Amanda, in his fish wrapper of a scandal
sheet several years before.

'The sign says "No Trespassing,"' the gelled man shot back.

'I did notice that,' I said, and took another picture of his scowl.
I asked if he'd like it for his mom, but that only made him scowl
even more. He yelled for me to leave.

I had enough pictures. I left.

THREE

'**B**ut it's not Thursday,' Amanda said mock-seriously, coming
up to the table I'd snagged by the window.
'Thursdays, schmursdays,' I said, standing to give her a
kiss. Thursdays were our designated days to rebuild our relationship,

but lately we'd been bending the protocol, seeing each other two and even three times some weeks. We were mattering again, more and more.

I'd called her office from the Central Works grounds, suggesting a late lunch because I was momentarily employed and soon to become momentarily flush. We arranged to meet at a trendy grocery in Chicago's Loop, owned by a New York chef who sold his own spaghetti sauce for the price of perfume. The grocery had been all the rage for hipsters and wannabes for over a year because it also offered what were termed 'multiple dining options.' Until I'd become hip to the new lingo, 'multiple dining options' meant, to me, a KFC, a McDonald's and a Taco Bell strung close along the same potholed street.

'You look splendid,' I said, and she did, even in a conservatively cut blue business suit and small-collared white blouse.

'You look, ah . . .'

'Usual?' I suggested, because I always did, dressed usually in khakis and blue button-collared shirt.

She laughed, kissed my cheek, and we sat down. The chairs were clear plastic and undulated – unwise seating, I thought, for a place that encouraged copious consumptions of pasta.

The windows were also clear and overlooked Erie Street. It was a mesmerizing perch for observing one of the city's newest and most ingenious kill zones, the newly reconfigured traffic lanes down below. The two center lanes had been left as traditional stretches for automobiles. But now, running on either side of them, were newly striped lanes for cyclists, some of whom wore helmets. Others, less veteran, merely adorned their heads with the confused grins of the soon-to-be-dead, for the outermost stretches of pavement, along the curbs, remained reserved for automobile parking, as always.

Thus was mayhem ensured.

A car driver desiring to park would stop, as usual, in his center automobile lane. But now he'd have to angle back across a new bicycle lane to get to the curb. If, by some miracle, he struck no cyclist charging up from behind, he was afforded a second chance when he swung open his car door to get out. Looking down at the swerving and horn honking along Erie Street, I could only marvel at how Chicago's ruling class kept coming up with ways to thin their herds.

'Dek?' Amanda prodded.

I turned away from the impending carnage below and offered the world's loveliest woman a smile.

'You've got work?' she asked.

I told her about Herbie Sunheim's assignment to photograph the Central Works grounds.

'Isn't five hundred excessive for snapping phone pictures?' asked one of Chicago's richest women.

'Particularly for a mega-tightwad like Herbie. I can only think that both he and his client are too petrified to go near the grounds themselves, for fear of being spotted showing concern.'

'If that's true, their reasoning is thin.'

'For five hundred dollars, I can cater to the thinnest of reasoning.'

She managed only a small laugh.

'And you, today?' I asked. 'What are you catering to?'

'I've been thinking about kids killing kids,' she said.

'Ouch,' I said.

'Chicago,' she said.

I waited.

'I've come to what you always call an "inspiration,"' she said. 'I think people like me can do something about it. No . . .' She shook her head. 'People like me *must* do something about it.'

'Now we're on familiar turf.'

The Amanda I'd fallen in love with viewed teaching others to appreciate fine art as her life's mission. She'd lived in an almost totally unfurnished multimillion dollar mansion in a gated community solely to safeguard the valuable artwork she'd inherited from her grandfather's estate. She loved art. She loved curating it and writing about it in large books. But teaching classes at Chicago's Art Institute, preaching the gospels of Matisse, Monet and Manet – that was her purpose, her life.

Until her long-estranged father, the CEO and majority shareholder of Chicago's largest electric utility company, had made her an offer she couldn't refuse. He'd offered to appoint her to direct philanthropy in his company's name. She'd accepted. It was an offer to do good things on an enormous scale.

It did not last because her father did not last. Within months, Wendell Phelps was dead and Amanda, his sole heir, became principal shareholder of the utility company and, nominally, its CEO. Overnight, she became one of Chicago's most influential executives. And one of its most obligated, on behalf of the corporation and her late father, to a large number of political, philanthropic and social commitments. So, while simultaneously excited by her new challenges and humbled by her lack of business training, her life became one of short attentions, bouncing from commitment to commitment, never landing long enough to honor any of them really well.

'Jobs,' she said now. 'I'm trying to focus on jobs. Jobs for kids. Benchwork, hand assembly, low-skill work.'

'Jobs that you could create through your company?'

'It's said that jobs can stop bullets.'

'Some on your board of directors will accuse you of ignoring the company's core business.'

'Dek, I'm the CEO in name only, there because I own a ton of stock. I don't understand the utility business. But this little idea I can wrap my arms around. I'm going to pitch it as being beneficial for the company. Not only might bringing jobs to the worst of Chicago's neighborhoods tip the tide against the killing, it will burnish our company's reputation. We'd get glorious press.'

'Your company would go it alone?'

'No. I want to build a coalition. Ask other Chicago companies to join us. That way nobody's balance sheet will be hurt too much and the plan will take on the aura of a movement. Chicago's corporations rising up, united and all that.'

'Giving back?' I asked.

Down below, brakes screeched and horns blared; another near miss. She paid it no mind.

She shook her head, perhaps angrily. '*Taking* back, damn it. Seizing what was taken away. Taking back lives that have been relinquished, taking back futures stolen from kids in Englewood and Austin and all the other nightmare neighborhoods.' Her eyes glistened.

'How much?' I asked. 'That's what your directors are going to ask first.'

'At the absolute most, and that would be down the road, capital costs would be ten million dollars to rehab some old factory for production. Then fifteen bucks an hour, six hundred a week, per kid. For a hundred kids, that makes sixty grand a week, plus medical and payroll taxes. Call it a hundred grand a week with utilities. Here's the beauty of it: if ten big companies participate, it costs each one only ten thousand a week, or a half a million a year. Companies the size of ours spend way more than that on PR and advertising now, and this would get them far better press.'

'And that's just outlay?'

'Exactly! We'd offset that with income from whatever we are assembling. Granted, it might not be enough to pay for all the expense, but bottom line? This could be a cheapie for all concerned.'

'It sounds so simple. Why hasn't it been done before?'

'The feudal fiefdom mentalities of our corporations, my own included. Each wants sole credit for accomplishments; no one wants to share.' She sighed. 'Maybe I'm being naive, but I'm also going to push the mayor for free city college tuition for the workers, and free books and free passes for bus and rail transportation to get to those schools.'

I thought for a moment. 'The mayor wants prominence, a role in Washington. He might go for this if he thinks it will help his national reputation.'

'I'm going to suggest he create enterprise zones on those south and west sides. Tax breaks to rehab deserted old factories might spur big development in the city's worst neighborhoods, like maybe what you're saying is going on at the Central Works site.'

'All the buildings have been bulldozed away except the one in the middle.'

'Perhaps for parking, or lots of greenery, or for new construction,' she said.

'They must have big plans for such a large site. Certainly, there is a lot of redevelopment going on in the city right now.'

'So it would appear, but some think it's already slowing, thanks to Chicago's reputation as the killing and taxing capital of the country. Add in the fact that Illinois is the worst state in the country, financially, and you wonder how the mayor can get any businesses to invest here.'

It was a lot to mull, and we sat for a moment in relative silence, save for a new round of squealing brakes and blaring horns coming from down below.

She checked her watch. 'I've got to get back,' she said.

I glanced across the room. One of her ever-present guards, a bulked-up fellow in a dark suit, put down the jar of ten-dollar marinara he'd been pretending to examine for the past half hour. For sure, he hadn't risked trying one of the undulating, clear plastic chairs.

We went to the escalator. Only when we got outside did we realize we'd not gone to the counters to enjoy multiple dining opportunities.

That didn't seem so important that afternoon.

FOUR

The tapping woke me again, just before dawn. It had been happening on and off for a week, always in the dark and always higher up, faint against the turret's river side. I'd been figuring it for a bird, perhaps a deranged woodpecker unable to discern glass and limestone from wood or, more fitting for Rivertown, a crow or even a vulture, a scavenger, searching for something to snatch.

That morning, the tapping seemed to sound more sternly, as if nagging me to remember something I'd overlooked. I'd gone to bed vaguely bothered by the thought that I'd not taken the right pictures at the Central Works.

I got out of bed, cranked open the narrow slit window that faced the river, and looked up. Like always, by the time I opened the window, the tapping had stopped. I heard only silence and saw only moonlight. Down below, there was only more moonlight, glinting off the debris in the Willahock River as it rippled toward the cleaner towns to the west. Upriver, the recycler was recycling.

I closed the window, knowing that I'd never get back to sleep. I'd lie awake, tensed for the tapping to start up again – tapping that never did. And this night, I'd lay tensed as well by whatever it was at the Central Works that I couldn't remember.

I slipped on jeans, a sweatshirt and my peacoat, and went down to the kitchen to run hot water through yesterday's coffee grounds, then took my travel mug up the stairs and the ladders to the roof. I eased the hatch open as silently as I could, on the chance the tapper had returned, and climbed up into the night. I went to the balustrade that faced the river.

The air was still. There was no flap of wings, no caw of a hunter. The crazed creature that had been nipping at the turret was gone.

I keep a lawn chair on the roof, for restless nights, hot or cold. This one was cold. I sat down anyway and did what everyone seems to do when the mind defaults to vacancy. I thumbed my phone into life.

Herbie Sunheim had texted me during the night, thanking me for the photos and promising swift payment. I answered by offering to work my way through the railroad's departments to see where the railcar had been previously, on the chance that previous stops might blur the dead man's link to the windows at the Central Works. I did not end by noting that his five hundred dollars was unlikely to ease my long-term prospect of remaining broke, and that I was desperate for more work.

By now, the sun was beginning to rise. I leaned back and watched the workday traffic start to stutter along Thompson Avenue. Unlike the parade of johns that slow-cruised Thompson after sunset, daytime drivers always tried to hurry through Rivertown, as if worried they'd get stained by just passing through.

They could hurry no more. The lizards that ran Rivertown had installed four new traffic signals along Thompson Avenue, slowing traffic to a crawl twenty-four hours a day. Spaced in short succession and timed to stay mostly red, they'd been intended to give nighttime visitors adequate opportunity to survey the meat aligned along the crumbling curbs, and the girls, themselves crumbling beneath clumps of mascara and caked rouge, time to describe the delights that could be enjoyed by generous gentlemen.

An instant hit with the ladies of the curb, the long reds proved to be popular with the town's treasurer as well. Daytime drivers, used to speeding through Rivertown on their way to and from work, were now trapped along Thompson Avenue. Desperate for escape, they began running the red lights, only to get stopped by Rivertown cops issuing hundred-dollar traffic tickets. Thousands of new dollars, mostly in cash, began pouring into the city's coffers at city hall every day. The lizards called it serendipity.

To me, restless on the roof that morning, the impatient tapping of brake lights along Thompson Avenue only made whatever I couldn't think to remember about Central Works pulse harder. I was too edgy to stay on the roof. I went downstairs and out to the back of the turret, to see if my tapping visitor had left traces of white on my yellow limestone.

When I'd moved into the beginnings of my grandfather's

lunatic castle dream years before, the long-abandoned turret had been streaked so white, inside and out, that a solid week of power washing had been needed to remove it all. Ever since, I'd worried that the descendants of the pigeons I'd evicted, imprinted with the strafing needs of their ancestors, would return, bent on splattering what would be, for them, a fresh canvas. But that morning, all was well. The tapper had left no fresh whiteness on the limestone.

I'd just turned to walk up the rise to the front of the turret when my foot got caught by a half-buried, rusty old soup can that some wino from the health center across town must have dropped weeks, or maybe years, before. They do that, those winos – leave bits of bottles and other junk when they stagger down to my stretch of the Willahock to nurse pints and watch the rubbish drift by.

But at that moment, I wasn't thinking winos. I was seeing rust. Rust lying unnoticed on the ground; rust that had been trying to trigger my subconscious.

I went inside for cold coffee and clearer thinking. And then I went out to the Jeep.

The Central Works had been tagged.

Two men in rubber coveralls were up on a scaffold, power washing the side of the building that faced the railroad spur, removing the graffiti that had been painted there overnight. A third man worked the compressor and water tank on the ground.

I supposed it was no surprise. The old factory had become news with the discovery of the corpse on the railcar, and that must have presented an irresistible target to some daring wall artist. Taggers had been crawling up into the undersides of Chicago's viaducts and on to the sides of its buildings for decades. Most left crude gang memorials – monochromatic, semi-literate testaments in gangsta lingo to fallen comrades, done in funereal blacks or blues – but, scattered around the town occasionally, were also impressive bits of art.

What little had not yet been washed off the Central Works looked to be of quality, a rendering of what might have been part of a window surrounding some snatches of color. Glistening in bright reds, blues, yellows and beiges, the rendering must have taken some time and presented some risk to the tagger, having to hang partway out of a third-floor window to complete.

I took distance photos from the highway and more as I moved up across the field; freebies for Herbie to nudge him into considering me for more work.

Something else was new on the old factory besides the graffiti. New, large red and white No Trespassing signs were screwed to both corners of the building's rail side. Herbie and the property's owner were worried about the legibility of the rusted sign by the front entrance, and had hurried to put up more legible ones, as if that would keep out undesirables. It was a panicked, stupid response, too late and too little to offer any protection from a legal judgment.

'Washing the whole building?' I asked the man working the water tank and the compressor.

'Nah. Rush job. Just the tag,' he said.

'Won't that leave the building looking splotchy if only part of it is clean?' It didn't figure, if the building was about to be rehabbed into something upscale. All four walls should have been washed.

He shrugged. 'Guy called this morning, offering to pay double to get it removed fast. The paint's fresh, a bitch to get off.'

I snapped another dozen photos of the wall and walked down to the railcar at the end of the spur, paying particular attention to the rust on the steel tracks. It was where my subconscious had been trying to direct me earlier.

Fresh scrapes of bright steel showed through the rust on the rails. The railcar had very recently been moved to the end of the spur. Unfortunately for Herbie and his owner, the fresh scratches probably confirmed that the railcar had recently been directly beneath a window on the factory.

More confirmation of that lay in the mud beyond the end of the spur. Two deep, wide tire ruts had been cut into the ground. They, too, were fresh, uncluttered by debris or the beginnings of weeds. The boxcar had obviously been towed to the spur's end by a vehicle with large tires very recently. And that meant the unknown man had come out of a window at the Central Works.

To be sure, I followed the tracks back to the building and a little beyond. As I'd expected, the scratches on the rails past the building were significantly duller than those from the building to the end of the spur. The railcar had been delivered to the building and left to sit there for some time before it was towed to the end of the spur. I took more pictures that were sure to make Herbie unhappy.

I started back toward the Jeep, but didn't spot him until I was halfway across the field. The well-dressed, gelled man who'd confronted me the day before was standing close to the edge of the highway, leaning against the fender of a partially visible black car. He was watching the men wash the building. And, I supposed, he was watching me.

He'd shown no ID the day before. He'd offered no explanation of who he was, or what he was doing there. Like yesterday, I could only figure him for an owner's representative.

I waved. He didn't wave back.

Back in Rivertown, stopped by the first of the long-timed traffic lights along Thompson Avenue, I happened to glance down the street that ran alongside the bowling alley. The front end of an ancient orange Ford Maverick was jutting out from the curb, as though either parking or leaving. I knew that Maverick.

It didn't move. It remained angled out, immobile. Alarmed, I swung onto the side street and pulled up alongside. The driver was slumped over the steering wheel.

I jumped out. 'Hey, Benny!' I yelled, thinking of a sugar-and-lard-induced heart attack as I tugged his door open.

Mercifully, his eyes opened. 'Oh, hiya, Mr E,' he mumbled. But then his eyes widened and he jerked to an upright position. 'Oh, jeez, Mr E,' he then blurted. Apparently, I'd frightened him awake.

Like most Rivertown residents, I'd known Benny since his second – or perhaps it was his third – junior year of high school, when he became the town's part-time parking enforcement officer. The job paid little but it came with the creaky Maverick and a daily dozen of municipally subsidized doughnuts. That was fine with Benny, because the doughnuts were always fresh and because everything was always fine with Benny. He was known for his laid-back, happy disposition. And he surely brightened the disposition of the town's treasurer as well, for Benny rarely waited for a violation to actually occur. He had only to suppose that a meter was about to expire before writing a ticket. Like the almost perpetually red lights that would come later, Benny became a fine source of cash almost instantly. So fine, in fact, that when Benny reported to the treasurer that he was likely to repeat his junior year yet again, the treasurer supposedly hurried to reach a cash agreement with the high school principal to graduate Benny before the start of the next school year. The principal was happy; Benny's teachers, who'd gotten to know him too well, were happy, and Benny himself was happy. But it was Rivertown's treasurer who was the happiest of all, for now Benny would be ticketing meters, expired or not, full-time.

Despite his frequent infusions of powdered sugar, Benny had a metabolism that ticked at the rate that oaks grew, and so he required frequent naps. That was fine with the lizards that ran Rivertown. Frequent snoozing was perfectly acceptable so long as it didn't interrupt his revenue stream, and folks around town were used to seeing him asleep in his Maverick, mouth agape, at all hours of the day.

Never, though, had I ever seen him fall asleep in the midst of parking his car. Even more worrisome was the partially full box of doughnuts sitting on the seat beside him. Benny rarely rested until the entire day's dozen was consumed.

'You feeling all right, Benny?' I asked, leaning in the open door for a better look. The skin around his mouth was its familiar hue, pale white from the usual dusting of powdered sugar trapped in his unshaved stubble of whiskers, but now his entire head had turned almost the same shade of white.

'Just need some . . . just need some . . . sleep . . .' he stammered.

'Tuck the nose of your car closer to the curb, Benny,' I said, shutting his door and leaving him to his rest.

At the turret, I uploaded the pictures I'd just taken onto my computer. The photos clearly showed that the scratches on the rusty rails between the building and the end of the rail spur were shinier than those on the tracks between the building and the main rail line. I made a note to tell Herbie that someone had moved the railcar very recently, and that he'd better hope it had not been his property owner attempting to tamper with evidence.

I forwarded to the new pictures of the building that I'd taken that morning. Even partially obscured by the workmen on the scaffold, they confirmed what the photos I'd taken yesterday showed. The body could have dropped directly onto the top of the boxcar from any of the windows above the spur.

I leaned closer. I hadn't paid much attention to the graffiti that was being power washed away when I was taking the photos, other than recognizing it as colorful and part of a larger picture. Now, though, there was something about the bits and specks left of the rendering that was troubling.

I printed several of the clearest images on plain paper and then, with a soft lead pencil, spent the next hours sketching in my guess as to what had been removed before I'd gotten there. By late afternoon, I was sure. I emailed my sketches to Herbie, and then called him.

'You've got a bigger problem than incriminating scratches on rusted rails, but maybe that will give you an opportunity,' I said.

FIVE

Herbie didn't call. So, after two hours, I called him again, and again got routed to voicemail.

'My sketches might show something big-time serious, Herbie,' I began. 'I think a tagger painted a head on your building, set inside what appears to be an open window, and it might be horrifying. The head is low; and there's a hand on what might be the head's shoulder, perhaps tossing the man out the window. You've got a witness to a body dump and maybe even a murder: that tagger. I'm also guessing your owner has panicked, towing that boxcar away from the building, and then hiring power washers to obliterate the art. Your best shot is to tell your owner to calm down, and to try to find that tagger. He'd be able to testify that the victim didn't simply fall because of owner negligence, but was deliberately pitched out. And since the old building looks to have been securely boarded up for some time, your owner wasn't keeping an attractive public nuisance, open to anyone looking to do bad things—' The voice messaging shut off.

I called back to finish. 'I'm guessing your owner, or at least his representative, is the well-dressed young guy I photographed by the No Trespassing sign yesterday, back again this morning to make sure the tagger's message got scrubbed away. Talk to your owner, Herbie. Find that tagger.'

And that, of course, meant hiring me.

I drove to Leo's ma's house. Leo Brumsky has been my pal since seventh grade. He makes upward of a half-million dollars a year as a provenance consultant for most of the major auction houses, authenticating the age and history of items put up for sale, wears designer suits for work and outrageous, discount Hawaiian duds for play, and drives a hundred-thousand-dollar Porsche road-ster that he changes every year and a half or so. He spends half of his time at his ex-model girlfriend's Chicago condo and the other half at his mother's brick bungalow in Rivertown, where he keeps his office. He's smarter than anyone I've ever known and certainly more patient with disjointed thinking than anyone I will ever meet.

None of that had anything to do with why I drove over to his mother's place that day. I wanted to see him because he makes me laugh.

'Yah?' Ma Brumsky called out, muffled from somewhere inside, after I knocked.

'It's me, Mrs Brumsky. Dek.'

'Yah?'

'Dek!' I shouted.

The lacework fluttered behind the window to the right of the door. A moment later, three sets of chains slid back and the door opened only a crack, restrained by the remaining two. One rheumy eye appeared in the gap. 'Vat you doink here, Dekkie?'

I couldn't be sure because of the narrowness of the door opening, but it looked like Ma Brumsky was done up in some sort of fifties' costume, judging by what I could see of part of a white felt poodle's head that was stitched on an inappropriately short pink skirt. Not far enough below it, I saw more wattled leg flesh than any considerate septuagenarian should flash.

'Looking for Leo,' I managed, trying to accept that any skirt on Ma Brumsky, no matter how short, was an improvement of sorts. Not that many months before, Ma and her friends had been arrested for co-ed skinny dipping in Rivertown's health center pool and carted off, in towels, to the police station. She was a marvelously free-spirited woman and a constant burden to her son.

'Hot dog, Dekkie,' she said.

'Hot dogs? He went out to get hot dogs?'

She laughed and closed the door. Chains slipped back in place.

There was only one reasonable place for hot dogs in Rivertown, and that was Kutz's peeling wood trailer beside the Willahock River. Beginning toward the end of every February, Leo began anticipating the wienie wagon's season opening the way other Chicagoans anticipated opening day at Wrigley Field, Sox Park or the Bears' Soldier Field. Swinging down to Kutz's clearing to be sure of when the irascible old crank was set to slide back his greasy plastic window and declare his lukewarm, partially contaminant-free lunch fare available for ingestion was a ritual for Leo, reaffirmation of a rite he'd been practicing since we were kids. But always, toward the end of every February, Leo kept me apprised of the status of the forthcoming grand event so I might accompany him to be among the season's very first to pounce on Kutz's gristly fare. That, too, was tradition. But that day, leaving Ma Brumsky's bungalow, I realized Leo hadn't peeped once in anticipation of Kutz's reopening.

I headed to the outskirts of town, turned onto the road that led down to the viaduct. And then I slammed on my brakes.

An enormous new, black-on-white sign stood alongside the road.

KUTZ'S WIENIE WAGON REOPENING SOON!
SAME FOOD!
TABLE SERVICE!
THOROGHBRED RACING MAYBE!
ICE CREAM TOO!

As if all those excited exclamation points weren't shocking enough – Kutz never got excited, he merely swore softly, mostly at his customers – a bulldozer was directly ahead, sending out great black clouds of diesel smoke as it labored to smooth the rutted, occasionally graveled ground that Kutz offered as a parking lot. Kutz never concerned himself with smooth, either – not in his behavior, and certainly not on his land. I parked at the very edge of the clearing where, I hoped, the odds were better that the Jeep would not get flattened by a dozer operating blind in black smoke.

Leo walked into view from behind the trailer and stopped. 'Ah, jeez,' he said, flashing only half of his oversized, bright white teeth into a tentative smile. 'I wanted to surprise you most of all.'

Leo's outlandish costume for the day consisted of blaze-orange slacks, a neon-green ski jacket and yellow high-topped canvas sneakers. All usual stuff, but that day he was adorned with something new.

'What's that on your head?' I inquired of the rumpled white cloth cylinder rising above his pale head like a rippled chimney. It extended his five foot six inches by another full foot.

'A toque.'

'A chef's hat.'

'People of refinement know it as a toque.'

'You're not a chef, and no one of refinement would be caught anywhere near this hot dog trailer.'

'Didn't you read the sign?'

'Yes. Ice cream is coming to join Kutz's normal, flammable fare. But table service and thoroughbred racing? Never. Also, I can't help but notice that as well,' I said, pointing to the bulldozer spewing noxious black smoke. 'Kutz is making changes, and you're actually helping?'

The place had remained especially sacred ground for Leo and me precisely because it had never changed since we were kids. The pigeon-splattered picnic tables were the same ones we'd eaten on; what little white paint still clung to the trailer was the same as when we were kids, only there was less of it. The wood menu hanging in front was also mostly unchanged, though Kutz did paint on price increases whenever he could. And he did serve up something different, occasionally. His most recent offering was barbecue cheese French fries, a gelatinous mingling of red ooze and orange ooze and dissolved potatoes.

We reveled in it all, particularly Leo. He was a great believer in the propriety of tradition.

'Kutz has found love,' he said.

'In spending money?' I asked, incredulous.

'He's run off with the girl of his dreams, a spry seventy-something in need of financial stability.'

'Kutz?' I laughed.

'They're rocking a trailer he bought in Sarasota.'

Mercifully, a new realization pushed the rocking thought away before it could stick, intractable, like the man's barbecue cheese fries. 'Kutz's bundle of love, the one seeking financial stability, somehow heard that you make big money and that you love this place?'

'Actually, it was Kutz who called me, offering a ten-year lease on his operation,' he said evasively.

'Kutz is in his upper eighties,' I said, and then realized more. 'Ah, but though his sweetie is only a few years younger, you said she is spry. She's breathing new life into him, of a fashion?'

'Perhaps not breathing, exactly.'

'Who picked up your check?'

'She did, but who can know about affairs of the . . . heart?' he said, letting the delicately phrased thought trail away. He didn't want to let the thought of Kutz rocking a trailer in Sarasota linger, either.

'Speaking of affairs of the heart, you're giving up more than half a million a year in provenance work just to sell hot dogs here?'

'Now you're talking about the real beauty of this enterprise,' he said, adjusting his toque to be sure it still stuck straight up. 'Ma and her friends are going to operate the establishment.'

'No,' I said, but it was more to the two flashbacks that had just collided in my mind. One was of the new sign at the front of the clearing, advertising table service. The second, more horribly, was of the glimpse I'd gotten of Ma Brumsky's too-short, pink poodle skirt.

'No,' I said again, because such thoughts needed to be banished twice. 'Not Ma and the ladies, not table service. Oh, please, not poodles.'

His furred eyebrows arched high on his pale forehead. 'You stopped by the house?'

I could only nod.

'The girls are making their own costumes,' he said, actually beaming.

'You've seen them, then,' I said.

'Better than the stripper outfits from a few years ago,' he offered up. 'Better than the health club, too,' he said of the skinny dipping just months before. 'Those ladies need to be busied with things that require full clothing.'

My mind wandered for a moment, as it is prone to do, to wonder if some sort of lustful rejuvenation was spreading across the elder community of Rivertown. First, Ma and her friends had been caught frolicking naked with a man at the health center pool, and now Kutz and his sweetie had taken off to tango in Sarasota. I pushed the thought away; I didn't want to imagine walking down to the river some night to find eighty-year-olds rutting on my lawn.

'Where did you find that bulldozer?' I said, pointing to the dark cloud. It was turning toward the river, as though lost.

'City of Rivertown insisted I use their approved contractor.'

'He's going in circles, or at least in one circle,' I said.

Leo just grinned.

I looked past him, noticing for the first time a small square of ground that had been fenced off, just past the trailer. 'And that?' I asked, pointing to it.

He only grinned wider.

'Thoroughbred racing . . . maybe?'

'Things will be revealed in due time, my son,' he said, nodding as gravely as he could with that white thing stuck to his head.

Change was flying too fast at that clearing. I pointed to the trailer. 'You'll keep this the same,' I said, to steer the conversation to calmer ground.

'Peeling paint and all, but I'm changing the water,' he said, almost sadly. Word was Kutz never changed the water he used to cook his hot dogs from year to year. Nobody questioned it, because that was preferable to him scooping fresh from between whatever was floating in the Willahock. 'What are you doing this afternoon?' he asked.

'Apparently, not a thing,' I said, because I had a client that wouldn't return my calls.

Pointing to a pile of precut lumber alongside the trailer, he asked, 'Care to put together a wood enclosure in back? Pa's tools are in the trailer.'

'An enclosure for what?'

'Ah, that would be a surprise, but there'll be a free hot dog in it for you, sometime in the future.'

The black cloud had just passed between the trailer and the Willahock, and the air back there would soon clear.

'A hot dog made with fresh, pure, non-river water?'

'I surely hope the new taste won't disappoint the regulars,' he said.

I'd worked plenty of afternoons for less than the value of a hot dog, but what sealed the deal was the chance to busy my hands and maybe my brain without spinning puzzles about why Herbie Sunheim wasn't returning my calls.

SIX

I t made no sense.

Herbie didn't call that evening, demanding to hear exactly what I knew about the tagger that witnessed the murder at the Central Works – a tagger who might save his property owner from a negligence lawsuit.

What began to make better sense was the likelihood that the tagger had seen that his work had been scrubbed away – work he'd risked coming to a crime scene to put up just hours after the body had been discovered. Taggers are gamesmen. I was hoping he'd dare to return to repaint his story.

I drove to the Central Works at ten that night. This time, I parked four blocks west and came up along the highway on foot, staying close to the buildings and out of range of the car headlamps speeding by and the bright patches beneath the street lamps. I wore my black jeans, black running shoes speckled even blacker from when I painted the turret's slit windows, and a brand-new black sweatshirt lightened only by the bright red image of Spiderman that Leo had given me because he said my wardrobe needed flair.

There was but a stingy slice of moon, leaving the Central Works grounds in a milky darkness. I turned and crossed the four-lane side street in line with the railcar, moving low across the bulldozed ground and stepping gingerly to minimize any loud crunches from broken glass. It took ten minutes to creep to the end of the rail spur.

I moved along the side of the boxcar to the end closest to the building. Looking up, I could see nothing in the darkness. The night was quiet; no noise came from the old bricks. I sat down, close to one of the railcar's big steel wheels, thinking to wait one hour to see if the tagger showed up.

It didn't take that long. A faint creak sounded thirty minutes later, high up in the old factory. A soft thud, like something had been set down, followed. A piece of the window board-up was being removed. The soft brush of clothing against bricks came next.

I stood carefully to look up past the end of the boxcar. The black shape of someone only faintly darker than the building behind him leaned out of the open third-floor window, holding on tight with his right arm while his left arm was extended out toward the bricks. An aerosol can began hissing paint.

And then the world went bright white, lighting the ground, the boxcar, the building.

And the tagger, hanging out of the window. And me.

Quick as a cat, the tagger dropped into the building and was gone.

I spun around as a huge engine, loud and throaty, rumbled to life down by the highway. An enormous wall of blinding lights – some roof-mounted, others lower, driving lights and headlamps – lurched up onto the grounds, lighting me even brighter, and began charging toward me.

I turned from the glare. A last glance up at the building showed the tagger had left only a faint tangle of lines against the bricks. He'd already be out of a front window by now, running away from the other side of the building.

I ran for the four-lane road to the west, the lights bucking up and dropping behind me, growing brighter as what was surely a massive off-roader bore down, closing the distance between us. It would have a high, hard bumper, that beast. The men inside would have guns.

I wanted to scream, I wanted to yell, to get the attention of the cars passing by in front of me, but they were late-night cars, kids and drunks and workers getting off second shifts, speeding along too noisily to hear.

The engine grew deafening behind me. I could hear its tires crunching broken glass.

I got to the curb and ran into the street, willing the speeding drivers to see me. A horn blared; another car shot past, just inches away, hands reaching out to flip me off.

Brakes squealed from the other direction. I didn't look; I could only run straight. More horns blared; a pair of headlamps swerved. A mass of metal brushed my arm.

And then I was across.

I chanced a fast look around. The Central Works grounds were dark, but that meant nothing. They could have switched off their massive rows of lights. And the traffic speeding by would mask any rumbling of the big engine.

An auto body shop was closest. I ran between the building and a chain-link fence, back into its storage lot. A dozen wrecked cars were lined up in a row, bleached colorless in the bluish glare of two security lights.

I climbed the six foot fence and dropped into the rear lot of the plumbing supply next door. A driveway was on the other side. I came up along its shadows to the front sidewalk.

The Central Works grounds were still dark. The off-roader might still be there, idling dark, or the driver could have come across the street on foot.

Or he could have driven down the street, to wait.

The plumbing supply was at the corner of a residential block. My best chance was to escape into the blackness of the houses. I sprinted out into the glow of a street lamp, then raced around the corner and into a block of bungalows. I ran through the darkness at the middle, through the light at the next intersection and into the dark past that. At the end of that block I turned and ran south.

The highway was thick with passing cars. I saw no vehicles with roof-mounted lights but that didn't mean they weren't there, parked out of sight along the highway.

The Jeep was only fifty feet away. I ran to it, jumped in and sped away. I got back to the turret twenty minutes later. After barring myself safely inside, I violated the very first rule I made when I first moved in. I poured wine.

Ever since I'd moved into the pigeon-infested turret, drunk and broke, I'd kept a gallon of red Gallo on the unfinished floor of my kitchen as both temptation and resolution. Temptation, because I needed to be reminded how far I'd once slid. Resolution, because I'd arrested that skid. The dusty old jug had rarely been opened, and then only to share, sparingly.

That night, I granted myself a waiver, a solitary splash to calm my shaking hands. I poured two inches into my travel mug and took it up to the roof to stand in the cold and watch the lust and the lights sputter along Thompson Avenue. And to try to figure out what I'd just escaped at the old Central Works.

There was no knowing for sure, but as I stood at the balustrade, I first tried out the hope that I'd simply overreacted to kids tooling around in some daddy's over-lamped off-roader – punks who'd spotted fun in scaring someone skulking along those ruined grounds that would make for good posturing the next day at school.

But that hope depended too much on roaming teens just happening by and choosing those old grounds for some sport. A man had been pitched to his death there, a murder that a tagger had witnessed and had returned to paint, twice. Far more probably, the driver waiting in the monstrous off-roader was watching out for the same tagger I'd come looking for, to make sure that scene never got depicted again.

The agile tagger had gotten away. I almost hadn't.

The familiar tapping jerked me from these thoughts, sounding down on the river side of the turret much earlier than ever before. I crossed the roof and looked down. Clouds had covered the moon. I could see nothing along the limestone or on the ground.

But the tapping was still coming, hard and sharp, rising up the side of the turret. But something else rustled beneath it, closer to the ground.

I hurried to open the trap door, but it is heavy and it fell closed with a bang behind me as I clambered down the ladder to the fifth floor. I raced down the next ladder and the wrought-iron stairs to the door and ran around to the river.

I was too late. Whatever had come to rustle on the ground and peck at the turret was gone. I stood motionless out in the night for a moment anyway, straining to listen, and thought of Herbie's forthcoming check for five hundred dollars. I decided I'd spend some of it on those little solar-charged lights people stick in their yards to show nighttime passers-by where their landscape needs weeding. Such little lights wouldn't deter the occasional wino from staggering down to the Willahock to relieve himself before a night's slumber on the bench, but they might scare off a crazed bird from disturbing my own rest.

I was tired enough now to sleep. I doubted any more tapping would come; it seemed to happen only once a night. But there would be nagging, whether I was awake or dreaming, about why a man had come to be tossed from the old Central Works, and how a tagger had come to see it, and who had come to chase me away.

And, most of all, why Herbie Sunheim still hadn't called.

SEVEN

I'd set my alarm for six o'clock the next morning and got to the Central Works before any power washers could show up. The memory of the bank of lights that charged at me was still strong, as was the possibility that someone might be around, watching. So I slowed only long enough, coming off the highway, to snap a quick photo of the new graffiti before turning up the side street to park two blocks north of the Central Works site.

I brought up the photo before I got out of the Jeep. Snapping that quick picture had been enough.

The tagger had left only eight straight white lines. The front four formed a simple rectangle – an opening. Drawn inside them, angled back in perspective, was another rectangle.

Eight straight lines, precise and effective. It was a door swung open, inviting someone to take a look inside.

I hurried south to the front of the factory building, quickly pulled back the loose plywood panel I'd peeked through earlier and crawled inside. As I'd seen before, the pipes and wiring bundles had been ripped out for saleable scrap, leaving only ragged holes. Now, though, I noticed that two fresh wood wall studs surrounded a shiny, new industrial-sized electrical conduit that ran from floor to ceiling – evidence that the building was going to be renovated.

I passed several large reddish-brown stains on the floor, crossing to the rail side of the building. They were patches of dried blood spill. Like torn-out wiring and cigarette burns, they were no rarity in Chicago's deserted buildings.

There had been stairs at the back, but they'd been ripped out, too. Similarly, cut-outs for a long-gone elevator yawed open above me like a string of black holes, all the way up to the top floor. Grateful there'd only been a single sugar cookie for breakfast, I went up the tagger's way – and perhaps the victim's and the murderers', though I couldn't imagine why they'd climb just to kill – chimpanzee-like, cross-stud after cross-stud, up through the cut-out to the second floor.

Nothing there was out of the ordinary, just more punched-out walls, empty old electrical boxes and a continuation of the shiny new electrical pipe I'd noticed on the first floor.

The third floor would have been the same as the first two, gutted except for that shiny new electric conduit, save for the open window where the tagger had leaned out the night before. The plywood he'd unscrewed was propped alongside it. I wondered if this was the window from which the homeless man had been pitched.

Footsteps crunched on the gravel along the rail siding below. Two men's voices sounded up through the open window.

'You're sure that's his?' one asked, barely above a whisper. They must have been directly below. I eased farther away from the open window.

'How many red Jeeps have a green top?' the other said, just as quietly. "I'm telling you, it belongs to the guy who's been snooping around.'

'It's parked a half-mile north. It could belong to someone in the neighborhood.'

'It's his. He's being careful.'

'We go in the building?'

'No need,' the other one whispered. 'The building looks securely boarded up, except for that one window up there. He's not here yet. I'll stay here in back and listen for him coming along. You go watch that Jeep but stay out of sight. Whoever sees him first calls the other. Oh, and get the license plate number so we can find out who he is.'

One man waiting by the door, the other keeping watch on the Jeep – neither sounding like they were interested in casual conversation – and me, a rat in a box.

Unless . . .

I had an inspiration. I padded quietly across to the opposite wall and texted Leo, my pal of pals. With luck, he was in town. *You around?*

What's shakin'? he texted right back.

Still got Jeep key?

Not that many months before, he'd demanded a duplicate of my ignition key after discovering a corpse in my Jeep. Leo, a worrier, called it a time-saver, saying it had taken him unnecessary anxious seconds to unlock my turret with his key, go up to the kitchen and snag the spare to the Jeep from the hook. I called it a needless precaution because, so far, there'd only been the one stiff. Nonetheless, I relented. Now that I was trapped inside the Central Works, it appeared giving Leo his own Jeep key might save me anxious seconds this time around.

Que? he asked back, in Spanish, I believed, though it is a language that neither I, nor he, knew.

In trouble. Hurry. Need you drive up street west of Central Works. Pass Jeep half mile up, park farther north, leave your key under mat, walk south, drive Jeep to your house.

Que?

There was no time to explain. *Text when you're away.*

I clicked off. He'd do it, and quickly.

There were no voices down below. They'd split up.

Even from across the floor, the open window above the rail spur made me feel exposed. I eased to the back again and took care to climb silently up to the top floor, as if the extra distance from the ground would make me safer.

And saw what the tagger had invited me to see.

Driving home. Raspberry cheese, Leo texted, forty long minutes later.

I photographed what I'd been staring at and climbed gently down to the third floor so I could hear my watchers outside. With luck, one of them had seen Leo driving away in the Jeep, and would now leave themselves.

Five minutes later, a voice directly below called out to someone farther away. 'No luck?'

'It wasn't his,' the other voice answered, from a distance. Gravel crunched as he walked up.

'You're sure?'

'It belongs to a tiny bald guy, dressed like a parrot, which figures. He just drove away.'

'What do you mean – "dressed like a parrot"?'

'Jungle colors. Reds and blues and greens on the shirt, bright orange pants. And yellow shoes. I've never seen a grown man dressed like that, except at a circus, though even clowns show more restraint. The guy was exactly the sort of oddball who'd drive a red Jeep with a green roof, all done up like Christmas. He must live or work around here.'

'Did you get his license plate?'

'No need. It wasn't the guy who came around here to take pictures.'

'There can't be two Jeeps like that,' the man who'd stayed by the building said. I was sure about his voice now. He was the gelled man who'd come up to me the first day, demanding to know what I was up to. And the man who'd been around the next day as well, watching. 'It would be nice to know who he was, just in case,' he said.

'What about that fresh paint up there?' the one who'd gone to watch the Jeep asked.

I pressed against the wall, holding my breath. If it occurred to them that the tagger had drawn an open door, an invitation, they'd find their way inside. And find me.

'I'd like to know who the tagger is, and what it means.'

I exhaled more easily. They hadn't seen the tag as an open door.

Their voices faded. I didn't dare get close to the window the tagger left open. A sliver of sunlight showed at the edge of one of the plywood board-ups farther down. I edged over to it and peered through the crack. The two men were crossing the field, walking south toward the highway. They were both dressed in dark suits, both moved lightly and both had shiny hair. From the back, either could have been the one who'd confronted me by the No Trespassing sign the first day I'd come to take pictures, or the one leaning against the fender of the partially visible black car when I'd come back. Cops, thugs, or owners' men; there was no way of knowing what they were.

I climbed down to the first floor, slipped out through the loose plywood and hurried to the sidewalk I'd run across the night before when I'd been fleeing from an over-lit, off-road vehicle. Turning right, I walked quickly north until I found Leo's ride. It was not the Porsche I was expecting, but rather the white van he used to cart Ma Brumsky and her septuagenarian friends around. Oddly, for Leo was no handyman, the back two rows of seats had been pulled out and the space was loaded with lumber.

I called him once I was safely a mile away. 'I wanted the Porsche, not your van. And what's with the wood?'

'Careful, or else I'll make you drive Ma and the lovelies next time they want to go bowling,' he said.

'They'll have to sit on the wood.'

'You're making conversation. Your voice sounds shaky.'

'The past few hours have been a shaky,' I said.

'Bring raspberry cheese,' he said. 'We'll sit on the front stoop and you can tell me about the latest mess you've gotten into.'

I told him I'd be there in thirty minutes.

'Raspberry cheese,' he said.

EIGHT

'Jungle colors,' I said, trying to nod wisely at Leo's assault of fire engine reds, neon greens and blaze oranges when he came to the bungalow's front door.

He motioned with the hand holding the knife for me to open the door. His other hand carried coffee in two of the chipped china mugs Ma Brumsky had liberated from a Walgreen's lunch counter, back when drug stores had lunch counters and no video surveillance.

'You have the gall to suggest I clash with your rusting red-and-green Jeep?' he asked, carefully stepping out onto the concrete stoop.

'No, it was the observation of a man I was hiding from, watching you get in the Jeep. There was nothing wrong with his eyes.'

'A man I rescued you from,' he said, bending to set the coffee down on the cement.

We sat on the steps we'd been roosting on together since seventh grade and I tore open the long white bag holding the Danish.

'No cheese,' he observed.

'Nothing wrong with your eyes, either,' I said, leaving his formidable intelligence to conclude that the bakery didn't have his favorite combination.

He sighed, and cut the Danish five times. He set down the knife and took a slice. He'd eat the biggest four of the six slices, and none would add an ounce to his 140 pounds, adding further proof that life was unfair.

'So, what's the latest intrigue?' he asked.

'From the beginning,' I said, clicking on my phone and bringing up one of the pictures I'd taken the first morning I'd gone to the Central Works.

He took the phone with his free hand. 'A railroad car and, farther away, a boarded-up old factory,' he said. He turned to me and arched his formidable eyebrows. 'Seems to me I saw this scene recently, on the news.'

'A realtor representing the building's owner hired me to take pictures the day after the body was found on top of that boxcar.'

'Negligence liability concerns?'

'That made the most sense.'

He nodded, and thumbed forward. 'Now we have an unhappy, stylishly dressed younger man with shiny hair pointing angrily to a No Trespassing sign,' he said. 'He was not charmed by your presence?'

'I thought he might be a representative of the building's owner that first day, but there is that slight bulge beneath his suit jacket, at the left hip.'

He squinted and nodded. 'He's packing. A cop?'

'He didn't flash a badge. I saw him again yesterday, and then this morning, only today he was with another guy. I could hear them talking. I don't know what they were doing there, but they were interested in my identity, which made me anxious, hiding as I was upstairs in that old factory. The first one remembered my Jeep, from when I'd been there earlier. You driving it away threw them off my scent.'

'So maybe not cops, but thugs? You set me up to have thugs with guns watch me drive your Jeep away?' He took a third slice.

'Better you than me, I figured. And I did bring you a Danish as compensation.'

'Idiot,' he said. He forwarded to a new picture.

'Day two, yesterday,' I said.

He studied the picture for a long minute. 'Men are power washing away graffiti. Art added the night after the body was discovered?'

'At some risk to the tagger, not knowing who was watching the building.'

'Chancing to tag a crime scene.' He nodded admiringly. 'That's a wall artist with stones.'

I motioned for him to skip over the sketches of the head and the one hand I'd filled in roughly for Herbie, since they were no longer necessary, and told him to stop at the first picture I'd taken that morning, the one I'd snapped from the Jeep.

'All the old graffiti is gone, replaced by . . .' He paused. 'A rendering of an open door?'

'The tagger returned, this time to spray a fast invitation to see what was inside the building. I was there last night when he did it.'

'Whoa,' he said, turning to look at me.

'So were nasty people in a high-tired, off-road vehicle with a zillion lights. They must have spotted him, but he's agile as a cat, and fast. Me? Not so much. They came at me across the grounds. I lost them only by running into traffic on that side street.'

'You're nuts,' he said, forwarding to a new picture.

'That's what the tagger's open door was inviting me to see.'

He'd caught his breath, studying the next picture. 'My God,' he said finally.

'This is what the tagger first painted outside, then inside after it was scrubbed away.'

'Your client will want color prints of this for the cops,' he said, standing up.

We dropped the remains of the coffee and Danish in the kitchen, and went down to his basement workroom. It is filled with a beat-up old wood desk, a hodge-podge of mismatched file cabinets, a light table, multiple magnifiers and a color printer. And the enormous overstuffed purple chair in which his father passed away, years before.

He printed three copies of the tagged scene and then displayed the photo on the huge wall screen.

'A total of four men are drawn,' he said, as much to himself as to me as he moved to the screen. 'Three are inside the window frame. The lowest of those – the poor fellow screaming in the middle – looks about to be pitched out the window onto the railcar shown directly below by the faceless men standing on either side of him. The fourth man is the barest of shadows, pressed against the wall outside an adjacent window.'

'That's the tagger,' I said. 'I left a message for my client, saying he had a witness, someone who could testify it was murder, not negligence, that killed the man on the railcar.'

'Good news.'

'My client hasn't returned my calls since he texted me, acknow-ledging receipt of the first batch of photos.'

'Instead he, or the owner, had the tagger's outside work scrubbed away?' He shook his head. 'Makes no sense. One of them should have called the cops and said, "Looka here: a witness who can testify that it was murder, not negligence."'

I took the phone and found the pictures of the deep ruts left in the ground past the end of the rail spur. 'These ruts probably show that the owner knew there was a body on top of that railcar, and that he towed it to the end of the spur, so no one snooping around inside the building could look down and see it before the boxcar got picked up.'

'And once the boxcar was removed, there might be no telling where the body came from,' he said. 'Who's the fool tampering with evidence: your realtor, or the owner he's trying to protect?'

'The realtor hired me to go take pictures there, so it's not him.'

'But you saw too much?'

I nodded.

'That's why your realtor isn't calling you,' he said. 'You've jeopardized the owner.'

'Maybe the guy just panicked.'

'You were almost run down last night. That's more than just a panicked owner who'd tried to obliterate evidence by tugging a railcar and washing away some graffiti.'

'I need to talk to Herbie,' I said, turning for the door.

We walked through his basement, past the model train layout I'd helped him put together in seventh grade. It was still opera-tional, ready for those occasions when Leo needed to run it around its old rails. Leo kept his past close.

Outside, he said, 'You've tumbled into something that's safest in the hands of cops.'

'Right after I've talked to my client.' I motioned to his white van, parked at the curb. 'And you? What's with that load of lumber?'

His cell phone rang. 'Yes?' He listened and clicked off. 'My freezer,' he said.

'What freezer?'

'My secret freezer,' he said, heading for his van.

I let it go. I was too full of raspberry Danish and too confused about why Herbie hadn't called to want to take on another mystery.

NINE

I left three messages on Herbie's voicemail before noon that day, each saying that I'd taken important new photos that I wasn't going to send until he called. Then I phoned his office. The mouse-voiced woman who answered mumbled that Mr Sunheim was not in. I asked when he was expected. She murmured something about taking a message. I said it was personal. She hung up.

The postman came at two-fifteen, bringing me a plain white envelope with no return address. Inside were ten one-hundred-dollar bills folded in a blank sheet of white paper. The envelope was postmarked the day after I'd first gone to the Central Works, likely just hours after Herbie had texted early the next morning to say he'd received my photos.

The envelope could only have come from Herbie, but a couple of things were troubling. For starters, the money was double the already inflated amount Herbie, the nickel-hoarder, had promised. And he was paying me in cash, which might have been a tip-off that whoever owned Central Works was used to paddling in murky waters and was accustomed to paying for illicit things, like trying to run me down or tossing a guy out of a window, with untraceable greenbacks.

I called Herbie again, thanked his voicemail for paying so promptly, and added that if I didn't hear how he wanted me to earn the surplus, I'd use my own imagination.

And then I drove into the city.

I'd met with Herbie several times, but always at one of the properties he was involved with. I'd never been to his office. Builder's Complete Realty was located on the seediest fringe of the city's west side, in a red brick pile that looked old enough to have housed failing garment and shoe manufacturers at the beginning of the previous century. I parked around the corner in a two-story cement garage that was puddled outside from snow melt and inside from roof leaks and dragged-in slush. Herbie's office was on the fourth floor, at the end of a hall of green-and-black floor tiles that might have been clean or might have been dirty. It was hard to tell because half of the hanging globe light fixtures were either burned out or simply missing. No doubt Herbie had been enticed by cheap rent.

His company name was hand-lettered on cardboard taped to the frosted glass on one of the oak doors halfway down. It opened into a space not much larger than a maintenance closet. Up front, a scratched black plastic visitor's chair was jammed between the wall and a beige metal desk. The woman jammed between that desk and the one behind it was about thirty years old, had tight, purplish-brown curls, purple eyeglasses as thick as Leo's magnifiers, and wore a purple sweater. Were it not for the thick orange rouge caked on her face, the woman could have passed for a grape.

I remembered Herbie telling me his wife did his clerical work. 'Mrs Sunheim?'

'She doesn't work here anymore,' the woman said in the same mousy voice I'd strained to hear on the phone.

'Who are you?'

'Violet Krumfeld.' She held up her right hand to show me a solder-encrusted purple ring. 'Violet, see, like the flower.' Indeed, the ring had a flower, of sorts – a painted clump stuck in the middle of all the solder.

'That's a lovely ring,' I said.

'My sister made it in class.'

'What sort of class?' I asked of the lumpy thing that looked as if it had come from a welding shop.

'Jewelry arts, when we were kids,' she said, touching a finger to her eye, as if to brush away a tear.

There were no papers on her desk. Nor was there a computer – only a red IBM Selectric typewriter of the kind popular forty years earlier. I wasn't surprised Herbie hadn't spent large on technology.

The back desk was as messy as hers was neat. It was heaped with papers, as if the two filing cabinets next to it had been emptied onto it and pawed through by someone with failing eyesight. That desk must have belonged to the reclusive Herbie.

I played dumb – an easy role – and asked for Herbie as though my eyesight was failing, too, and I hadn't swept the whole of the tiny office with one glance.

She played smarter. 'You just called,' she said, batting fake lashes like push brooms behind her thick glasses. 'I told you he wasn't in.'

I dropped onto the scratched black plastic chair. 'It's important that I talk to him.'

'I could tell,' she whispered in her mouse voice.

'He's got me on retainer.'

A smile cracked the rouge on either side of her mouth, and then she laughed, sort of. 'Ret . . . ret . . .?' She sniffled. She couldn't finish the word because apparently she was laughing too hard, though it was almost inaudible – more of a series of soft convulsions that screwed up her face.

'I need direction,' I said.

'I could tell,' she murmured, opening a side drawer to extract a Kleenex to dab at the brooms behind her glasses.

'He's not returning my calls,' I said. 'Can you call him for me, Violet?'

'I've been trying. Mr Sunheim is not taking calls.'

'Call him at home,' I said.

'Where's that?' she asked.

'You don't know where your boss lives?'

'You call him at home,' she said.

The lashes beat on, up and down.

I left her my card.

Despite Violet Krumfeld's cryptic confusion about where Herbie lived, finding his address was simple. It was listed in the online white pages as being in Chicago, two miles north of Midway Airport.

Getting there was more complicated. I left the city just in time to get caught in the clog of rush-hour traffic, and got to enjoy, close-up, the eating, phoning and hygiene habits of my fellow motorists. The drive took an unbearable hour.

Parked cars, all older models but certainly newer than my Jeep, crammed Herbie's narrow street. His house was a tiny, single-story, white-frame place squeezed onto a tiny lot, identical to the other tiny wood houses on the block, except his had a For Sale By Owner sign stuck in the front yard.

Two airplanes, both Southwest Airlines 737s, darkened the yard in fast succession as I walked up the front stairs. An unsmiling, heavy-set man in gray pants and a black down jacket watched from the porch next door as I rang the bell. No one came.

'Marge is at work,' the man who kept tabs on his neighbors called over.

'How about Mr Sunheim?' I asked, ringing the bell again.

'You a friend?'

'A contractor.' It was true enough.

'For the house?'

'For his business,' I said.

'Try his office in the morning.'

'They moved?'

'Just him.'

'Where?'

'Don't know,' he said, and went inside his house.

I turned on the stoop and looked at the worn houses and the tired cars strung along the street. It wasn't hard to see Herbie, always a slump-shouldered guy, behind an eight-ball, sweating every day to make ends meet. Maybe the sweating got to be too much.

And maybe talking about anything got to be too much, too, and that's why he hadn't called. He might have just chucked his past life and taken off, though sending me an extra five hundred in greenbacks on his way out of town made no sense at all, especially for a guy so intimate with his wallet. Herbie could have squeezed a lot of life out of the extra five hundred dollars he tossed me.

A new beige Cadillac Escalade pulled to the curb as I walked down to the sidewalk. 'May I help you?' the stern-faced woman getting out demanded, implying no desire to do any such thing. She was middle-aged, dark haired and attractive enough, if one liked frown lines and hawk's eyes. She wore a pink blouse that had come untucked beneath the hem of her short brown jacket.

'I'm looking for Herbie Sunheim.'

'He moved.'

'You are?'

'The soon-to-be ex-Mrs Sunheim. And you are?'

'A business associate of Herbie's.'

Her eyes narrowed even more. 'You owe him money?'

'Just the opposite. He owes me,' I lied to those hawk's eyes. Likely the woman had hawk's talons, too, where money was involved.

'He owes me too, pal,' she said, her interest in me fading to zero. 'If you find him, remind him.'

'You don't know where he's living?'

'He's never there.'

'Let me try,' I said.

She pushed past me on her way up her walkway. She wasn't going to help anyone get to Herbie and his wallet before she could.

'Nice car,' I called after her of the big-dollar Cadillac.

She turned. 'That's something else he owes me for. He leased it, the jerk. Us? A Cadillac?'

'He must have done it out of love,' I said without laughing. More than likely, he'd done it out of spite.

'Herbie's always been small change,' she said. 'Small change for years, and then he goes and leases something like that.'

She climbed her steps and let the door slam behind her.

TEN

An automobile backfired at four-fifteen the next morning, not waking me up because I wasn't asleep.

I got out of bed and went to the window in time to see it clatter off Thompson Avenue and cut its lights and its engine on the short street that led to mine. Few cars could sputter that loudly and still move, so had it been a little earlier, I would have taken its driver to be the most frugal of the johns. They favored the dark of that short street. End-of-shift bargains could be gotten there from the hardiest of the late-night hookers that worked Thompson Avenue, Rivertown's road of lust. But four-fifteen was too late for professional ministrations, even in Rivertown. The neons and the girls had flickered out over an hour before.

Conversely, four-fifteen was too early for some overserved Rivertown cop to be bumping his car along the curb, feeling his way to the police station behind city hall. Shift change didn't happen until six. Besides, Rivertown police cars never clattered like the one that had just stopped on the short street. They were kept in tip-top shape, daytimes, by the mayor's uncle's crew over at the city garage.

I beat it up the stairs and the ladders to the balustrade in time to hear a car door open and slam, though no interior light had flashed on. A second later, another door opened and slammed.

Two sets of footsteps grew louder, running onto my street. Giggling. Kids, I figured, intent on the bench by the river, perhaps to watch the plastic debris glint as it bobbed by, or more probably to touch love.

The street went silent as the kids crossed onto the grass directly below me, and then more giggling arose, approaching the bench. My mind wandered, then, to my own old young times down by the river with a girl who was now dead. Now I would be a voyeur, and I didn't want that. I turned to go back inside.

The familiar banging and tapping began, rising up alongside the turret. The last time I'd been on the roof when it came, I'd let the trap door drop loudly behind me as I charged down the ladder, scaring the tapping thing away. This time I would wait.

The banging and tapping got louder, rising. And with that came a new sound I'd not been close enough to hear before: a soft whirring.

In the next instant, whatever was whirring whirred itself over the top of the balustrade, almost cuffing my ear as it passed by. I swung at it but I was too late. It disappeared over the opposite balustrade.

It had a small light.

I hurried to the street side to look down. The light had been extinguished and the night was too dark to see anything else, but there was no missing the sound of footsteps pounding the pavement toward the short street. The creaking car doors opened; the clattering car started up. It switched on its lights, turned around, and headed back to Thompson Avenue.

I climbed down into the turret, understanding the tapping at last. It would be simple to stop it.

But I had only the barest idea of what to do about Herbie Sunheim.

Violet Krumfeld, the Herbie Whisperer, remained evasive when I stopped in later that morning. 'I told you, I don't know where Herbie is,' she said, somewhat audibly.

'Look, he hired me to take some pictures—'

'Of what?'

'That's confidential, but he sent along a—'

'Ah, yes, that retainer,' she said, starting to sniffle at the preposterous hilarity of that.

'He's not checking in with you?'

'We discussed this. I can't help.'

'Where's he living?'

'I can't give you his home address.'

'He moved out of his home.'

She sighed. She knew. 'I don't know where he is now, and his wife pretends like she doesn't know, either.' She whispered so softly I couldn't hope to tell if she was lying.

'She knows; she just won't say. What was he working on most recently?'

She shook her head.

I called Amanda on my way over to the county recorder of deeds. 'I'm twice as flush as the last time I evaded buying you lunch.'

'How come?' she asked, but it sounded perfunctory. She was distracted.

'My client sent me double the agreed-upon amount, and in greenbacks.'

'Hold for a moment,' she said, and covered her mouthpiece. Then, coming back, she asked, 'He paid you a thousand bucks in cash for snapping phone pictures?'

'To do more, I'm almost sure.'

'You still haven't talked to him?'

'He's been incommunicado since I sent him the first photos, but a skinflint like Herbie Sunheim never overpays. Fortunately, I had an inspiration, and went back to take more photos.'

'Ah, your inspirations.'

'Let's discuss them, yours and mine, over lunch.'

'Can't. Lemon pants,' she said.

'What?'

'Sorry, that's my new shorthand. I pitch to the board this afternoon.'

'You're optimistic?'

'Guardedly; I still have selling to do. I just finished two hours with our marketing and advertising people, trying to get prepared. Raincheck on lunch?'

'You betcha,' I said, because that's what we'd learned to say to

each other since out divorce. It implied that there would be a
tomorrow, no matter what.

The county recorder's office was on Clark Street, not far from the
Art Institute where Amanda had happily worked for years. Local
news reporting had it that, even in tough budgetary times, the
county recorder had managed to create dozens of jobs, though all
of them had gone to relatives and other connected people. Such
employment practices were common in Cook County, and had
been known for forever as hiring 'somebody who somebody sent.'
Along with the killing and the corruption and the pie-eyed real
estate developers, Chicagoans accepted that thousands of such
somebodies would forever be feeding at the public trough.

Unsurprisingly, the recorder's office had the feel of a county
agency designed for such people, hushed and dimly lit for the
slow, zombie-like movement of the walking dead. Though no one
was in line, it was twenty minutes before a woman responded to
the relentless clearing of my throat, and another thirty before she
came back with the name written semi-legibly on a slip of paper.
The Central Works property was owned by a real estate trust
named Triple Time Partners. Its address was only blocks away.

It was one of the first warm days of March and the sidewalks
were filled with earnest young people escaping the tall buildings
on one pretext or another, to bustle from sunny patch to sunny
patch along the cement. Though I was only a few years older than
them, I could not recall a time when I'd ever felt like bustling, let
alone been earnest.

Triple Time's street address was in an old but stylish former
jewelers' exchange set beneath the elevated rail tracks along Wabash
Avenue. It was not listed on the first-floor directory, but the suite
number I'd gotten at the recorder's office was on the fifth floor and
belonged to something called Dace Property Management. I stepped
in.

The glassed-off reception area was tiny but stylish as well. Two
chrome and black leather chairs and one glass table sat on a bright
red rug that was almost the same color as one of Leo Brumsky's
more subdued pair of pants. A glass door set in a glass wall separated the reception area from the equally stylish young receptionist,
filing her nails. I opened the glass door and asked if I might speak
to someone about one of their properties.

A lean, middle-aged man came out into the reception area smiling. He was about forty, wore a brown, houndstooth-checked jacket, beige slacks, white shirt and a yellow bow tie that contrasted nicely with the ruddy, healthy glow of his skin. I thought about telling him that my ex-wife, Amanda, had bought me a yellow bow tie as well, but that I'd worn it only rarely, since knotting it required consulting a YouTube instruction video each time I put it on.

He introduced himself as Walter Dace and led me back to the lone private office. We sat on silver mesh chairs around a small, round glass table. With all the glass in the reception area, and now his table, I imagined the man's Windex budget was enormous.

He'd noticed me looking around the small suite as he led me back. 'You're wondering how large we are?'

I nodded.

'Large enough,' he said.

'You manage properties for multiple real estate partnerships?' I asked.

'Which property are you inquiring about?'

'The one where a man fell to his death.'

He stood up. 'Thank you for coming.'

He walked me out past the receptionist, who was still filing her nails, and held open the glass door. I went through it without yielding to the childish temptation to leave a smudge, crossed the reception area to go out the hall door and rode the elevator down to the lobby, an exit as smooth as sliding down a greased chute.

An 'El' train rumbled overhead as I stepped out onto the side-walk. Normal confidentiality concerns would have made Walter Dace reluctant to talk about any property he managed, and my asking about the one where a corpse was found certainly warranted my getting the bum's rush. But the tempo of his little enterprise nagged. I'd been in plenty of property management offices, and all were hectic with concerns about leases, janitorial issues, equipment malfunctions and such.

Dace's operation offered up none of that. Nothing seemed to be going on there. The place felt like a front, a name on a door.

It felt like a brick wall.

I'd struck out chasing the last of the leads I imagined Herbie might find productive and by now his voicemail was full. Without his permission, I couldn't take the next logical step, which was to point the cops to the mural I'd discovered on the top floor of the Central Works. So I stopped at a sporting goods store on my way back to Rivertown and then swung down the river road to Kutz's clearing.

Leo's white van was parked alongside the wienie wagon with its rear doors open. Only a little of the lumber I'd seen inside remained. Most of it was now stuck upright in the ground around the oval that had been graded into the clearing. They were fence posts, like those surrounding the small clearing to the side of the trailer that I'd noticed the last time I'd stopped by.

Leo was marching along inside the graded oval. He waved and came up as I parked.

The day's outfit was the usual medley of colors so outrageous they'd clash in a pitch-black cave. And once again he was topped by his chimney-like chef's toque that, because it was white, almost looked normal. But that day, Leo had embellished his wardrobe even more bizarrely. He wore a carpenter's tool belt. It was obviously new; there wasn't a smudge on its gold faux suede. Nor did it look like it would get dirty soon, for the belt held no tools. No hammer hung from its loop, no nails, tape measure, screws, screwdrivers or any other thing bounced in any of the heavy-duty pockets.

'Why are you wearing a tool belt?' I quite naturally asked.

'It's just like yours.'

'Identical to mine, in fact, when it was new.'

He nodded, as if my question had been answered.

'I ask again: why are you wearing a tool belt?'

'Look around,' he said. 'There's much work to be done.'

'But you have no tools.'

'I have Pa's, remember? You used them to put together the enclosure behind the trailer.'

'I remember you wouldn't say what the enclosure I built was for.'

'That will now be revealed.'

'And Pa's tools? Where are they?'

'In the trailer,' he said, starting to lead me around to the back of the trailer.

'Why wear a tool belt if you're not going to carry tools?'

'I'm no good with tools,' he said.

It was nonsensical dialogue. I gave it up and followed him around to the back of the trailer.

A glossy white freezer the size of a fat man's coffin had been set inside the hinged, slatted enclosure I'd built. He raised the wood lid and opened the freezer. 'We're going to offer six flavors of ice cream.'

'Magnificent,' I said of the freezer that looked just like every other large freezer I'd seen. 'Now, what's with the fence posts surrounding what's obviously a track of some sort?'

'That's still a secret,' he said.

'You're advertising thoroughbred racing on your sign,' I said, reminding him.

Ever since we were kids, Leo could not keep a secret from me. Every time he'd tell me he was keeping a secret, I'd feign indifference. That made him turn purple, and always he'd spill within a minute. Not this time. There was no purple; there was no spill. Leo pursed his lips, staying mum about whatever he was planning to set loose to run in circles within his oval.

'Speaking of secrets, how are you getting on with your case?' he asked.

I told him I'd still not heard from Herbie Sunheim, and had struck out with Herbie's wife and his office assistant about where he was living.

'You don't suppose something bad has happened to him?' he asked.

'I'm hoping he's just taking a breather from life, living some-where else because he's on the outs with his wife. I'm going to try and chill.'

He laughed. 'You never let anything chill. You'll pick at it, over and over, until you find out why Mister Sunshine isn't calling, and why he sent you the extra five large.'

I told him I'd checked on the ownership of the Central Works and gone to see its property manager, who'd thrown me out.

'You've been thrown out of plenty of places,' he said, accurately.

It was true enough. We walked to the Jeep.

'What's with the big fish net?' he asked, pointing to my sporting goods purchase, visible through the clear plastic curtain on my new green top.

'That's for night fishing,' I said.

ELEVEN

'Where's Herbie living?' I asked Violet Krumfeld on the phone first thing the next morning. Nothing had come tapping in the night and I'd slept straight through. Now I was rested, at my sharpest and convinced that the woman knew more behind her mask of purple ditz than she'd been revealing.

'I don't know,' she murmured.

'Why don't you call the cops, report Herbie missing?'

'I've been telling that to his wife,' she said.

'What does she say?'

'She wants his checkbook.'

'Like I told you the last time we spoke, she knows where he is but she's not telling,' I said. 'She's afraid others will get to his money before she can.'

'She calls here twice a day, crazy about that checkbook.'

'It's not there?' I asked.

'If you're thinking he ran off to the Bahamas or somewhere with the corporate cash, forget it. Herbie's too morose, and his clothes are so shiny they'd blind anyone on a beach.' She paused, I thought, to sneeze, but then I remembered she made such a sound when convulsed with hilarity. Her own wit had cracked her up.

'This operation's a shoestring, a shiny shoestring,' she finally managed.

'Did Herbie ever talk about getting a Cadillac?'

She started taking short, fast breaths, succumbing to riotous laughter again.

'Herb . . . Herb . . . Herbie buying a Cadillac?' she finally whispered. 'Herbie won't spend for a new shirt.'

'He leased a new Escalade for his wife. Escalades are big money.'

'I don't believe it.'

'I don't believe you don't know where he is,' I said.

'How about you telling me the truth?' she countered.

'About what?'

'About you getting a retainer. I looked through the checkbook. Herbie cut no payment to you.'

'So you do have the checkbook.'

'Of course it's here, but I'm not letting that witch near it. So, how did he pay you a retainer, Mr Elstrom?'

'Obviously with other funds,' I said, not adding that Herbie had sent me greenbacks.

'Yeah? Like Herbie had a secret stash?' Again she sniffled faintly. 'Listen, if Herbie had money, he'd hide it, for sure. But like I said, the man barely gets by from what we get here. No way could he build up a stash.'

'Call the cops.'

'Call the cops yourself, Mr Elstrom,' she said and hung up, which she was becoming so prone to doing.

So I did.

Surprisingly, two Chicago detectives knocked on the turret door just after noon.

'Elstrom?' the heavier one asked as they showed badges. Gray-haired, he was in his middle fifties and had a gut large enough to keep his belt dry in the worst of downpours. His name was Bruno Kopek, which was an accurate name for a Chicago cop, and the tie bar clipping his unfashionably wide gray tie to his patterned white shirt sported a White Sox logo which, in Cubs-crazy Chicago, made him for a south-sider, and defiant about it.

'I'm Elstrom,' I said.

He held up a small white bag, the kind that came from bakeries, like he was dangling bait. 'The Vlodek Elstrom that phoned in asking if an unidentified corpse had been found in the past few days?'

'Welcome,' I said, which is what I always say to folks dangling bakery bags, as bait or not.

His partner, barely thirty and short and lean, was named Henry Jacks. They stepped in.

I offered them the two plastic lawn chairs and took the empty orange roof tar can for myself. The can is acceptable seating for short conversations, and the orange color goes well with the new beige furnace I'd hooked up but had yet to enclose.

'Nice table saw,' Jacks said, gesturing at the room's only other adornment.

'I'll be moving it up to the fourth floor when I figure out what to do with the fourth floor,' I said. Finding a purpose to any room on a fourth floor was tricky stuff because reasons to climb so many stairs were always in short supply.

Kopek opened the bakery bag and extracted an apricot *kolachky*, square and folded in at the corners, as authentically Bohemian as the cop himself. 'Your first name –Vlodek – it's Czech,' he said, passing the bag to me.

'A guy who understands *kolachkys* would certainly know that,' I said, snagging an apricot *kolach* for myself. 'My father supposedly was Norwegian, my mother Bohemian.'

'Half-breed,' Kopek said, with no malice.

They took out identical small blue wirebound notebooks, no doubt to record identical thoughts. 'So, this man you inquired about,' Kopek began.

I passed the bag to the lean Jacks, who passed it on to Kopek without extraction. It figured.

'Non-black, non-kid, non-gang affiliated, obviously non-identified middle-aged male, not found on top of a railcar at Central Works,' I said. 'That should narrow it down.'

I took a bite. The *kolachky* was marvelous. Pure Bohemian for sure.

'Name of Herbert Sunheim, which narrows it down to zero,' he said. 'He's not been reported missing.'

'You could call his wife or his assistant at work. They'll tell you he's not around.'

He shrugged, chewing, more enthused about the *kolachky* than my answer. 'You told our desk officer that Sunheim was a realtor, perhaps representing the owner of the Central Works.'

'Central Works is why you're here in record time for a non-missing persons case.'

'No,' he corrected. 'First we stopped for *kolach*.' He reached in the bag for another, this time cheese-filled. 'According to the information you gave our officer, Sunheim hired you to take photos of the railcar and the abandoned factory at Central Works the day after the body was found.'

'Yes.'

Kopek passed me the bakery bag. In fishing out the cheese

kolach on top, I noticed that three of the remaining four pastries were prune-filled.

'Prune?' I asked Kopek.

He shrugged. 'It's traditional.'

For me, prune was the most marginally enjoyable of Bohemian fillings; not for nothing were sour people termed prune-faced. I reached back in the bag for the last of the non-prunes – mercifully an apricot – in case the rest of the interview did not go well, and passed back the bag.

Kopek smiled at my discernment. 'You said you went back the next day to take even more pictures?'

'There were power washers there,' I said, to see his reaction.

Neither of their faces gave notice that they knew of the tagger.

'I went back because I'd not photographed the tracks in usable detail,' I added.

'Don't be coy, Elstrom.'

'I wanted to see if the scratches on the rails at the end of the spur were fresher than those leading from the main line to the building.'

'Signifying that the boxcar had been moved away from the building? We already figured that.'

I brought out my cell phone and showed him a picture. 'I was looking for some clue as to who moved it.'

'Tire ruts. Big deal.' He looked in the bag, saw the darkness of prune and closed it back up. Only briefly did his eyes flicker to the apricot I was holding in reserve.

'Look, Elstrom, I get it that the building owner might have been inside his property, looked down and saw the corpse. I get it that he found a way of tugging that boxcar to the end of the spur, hoping there'd be a snow or something and it wouldn't get noticed before the rail carrier came to take it away. We're not interested in going after the owner for that. You can tell Mister Sunheim to tell his owner they got nothing to worry about, negligence liability-wise.'

'I can't tell Herbie anything. He's disappeared, remember?'

'Maybe he's got a tootsie.'

'You know this?' I asked.

'Call it an educated guess,' Kopek said, looking at his watch, as if about to get up.

'There's more,' I hurried to say. 'Remember that power-washing crew I saw at the Central Works when I went back the second day? The day I photographed the rails and the ruts?'

'Sure,' he said.

'The building had been freshly tagged.' I pulled up the photos of the scrubbing crew. 'I went back again that night—'

'Your third visit to the Central Works,' Jacks interrupted. It was the first time he'd spoken since his crack about the table saw. 'You like crime scenes, Elstrom?'

'I went back to see if the tagger had returned to replace what had been scrubbed away.'

'Now why the hell would he do that?' Kopek asked, making a show of adding another fold to the top of the closed bakery bag. He was ready to leave.

'The tagger had a story to show. He was there the night the victim got pitched out the window. He risked coming back right after the corpse was discovered, to paint what he'd seen.'

'Which got power-washed away?' Kopek grimaced. 'Damned shame; the picture, the tagger, both gone.'

'No. He brought his paints back again, late in the night after his first rendering was scrubbed away. As I said, I was there. I got chased away by some huge vehicle with big tires.'

'Tires you're saying could have made those ruts you photographed?'

'I don't know,' I said quickly, needing to find Herbie but unsure how far I should back away from any linkage to his client. 'What I do know is that the tagger was there for a second time. He sprayed this on the outside.' I brought up the photo of the eight straight lines.

'Means nothing,' Kopek said.

'Means plenty,' I said, 'because the tagger had wised up. He painted an open door on the outside, inviting you, the cops, to see what he'd left inside, where the power washers couldn't obliterate it so easily.'

'Do you always work so hard to force a theory?' Jacks asked.

'Alas, only when I'm at my very sharpest,' I said. I took no offense; life was often a slog.

I forwarded to the mural I'd found on the top floor. 'This is what the tagger left for you.'

Both Kopek and Jacks leaned forward. After a moment, Kopek said, 'This is certainly graphic.'

'He shows himself as being outside, clinging to the bricks at the side of the next window down. Notice that the railcar is directly below the window in the picture. See the two sets of hands, one pair on either side of the body that's being aimed out the window? There were two killers. See the dead man's face? His mouth is open. Your homeless man is screaming as he is being thrown out.'

For a long moment, nobody spoke. Then Kopek said, 'He wasn't homeless. His name was Rickey Means. That name mean anything to you?'

'No.'

'You're sure?' His eyes were intent on mine.

'I don't know the name.'

'He was a case chaser at the county courthouse.'

'A lawyer?'

'The lowest of the breed, living on whatever bones assigning judges threw at him. He had a degree from a defunct school in Indiana and scraped by with DUIs, shoplifters and junior gangbangers.'

'The news said he had bite marks.'

'He'd been lying outside, maybe for some time. He was making a living. He wasn't homeless.'

'One newspaper said he was wearing a good suit.'

'But he had bad teeth?' Kopek said. 'We wondered about that, too, but we're thinking maybe he wasn't the original owner of the suit.' He put away his notebook. 'As for your mural, there's no proving it was at the Central Works.'

'Go look for yourself. Top floor.'

'The building burned down last night,' Kopek said. 'There's nothing left.'

'Arson?'

'Probably. That site, besides attracting whoever gave Rickey Means a toss, is drawing other sorts of weirdoes. The off-roader driver who chased you away for one, last night's torch for another. Nut jobs come out to crime scenes at night, looking for some fun.'

'That arson was convenient. There must be clues as to who lit it up.'

'Maybe for the fire department but not for us. Our interest is the Means investigation.'

They both stood up.

'What about Herbie Sunheim?' I asked, standing, too.

'After we got notified of your call, we didn't just stop for *kolach*,' Kopek said. 'We called Sunheim's office and spoke with some woman who sounded like she was talking through a box of Kleenex.

We could hardly hear her. She says Sunheim is often gone for extended periods, and she doesn't worry about where he is so long as he comes back to pay her. She told us about the party goods store where Mrs Sunheim works, so we called the wife there. They're separated, Sunheim and his missus. Sunheim moved out. She said he's never at the room he rented.'

'You believe her?'

'She said she doesn't care where he is so long as he makes the payments on their Escalade and shows up in court to finalize their divorce. She gave us the address of his room. We swung by on our way here. Sunheim's landlady said what the wife said: Sunheim's not around much. She thinks he has a traveling job. And, she said, he owes her for back rent.' He sighed. 'Maybe he just said the hell with it and took off. He's got no one in his life except women looking for money.' He grinned. 'Unless, of course, there's that tootsie.'

'What was in his room?'

'Not much. Maybe he took his good stuff and vamoosed.'

'He didn't have any good stuff.'

Kopek shrugged, and said nothing.

The obvious, ugly thought had formed. 'You're sure there was no body in the rubble at Central Works?' I asked, as we stepped outside.

'The fire department is still there. So far, they've found nothing.'

'Will you?' I asked.

'Find anything?' Kopek shook his head. 'Probably not. The killing of a courthouse cockroach like Rickey Means doesn't pack heat. He's just another scumbag lawyer nobody's going to miss.'

Kopek eyed the apricot *kolachky* that was still in my hand. I'd forgotten about it.

He handed me the bakery bag.

'I hate prunes,' he said.

TWELVE

I drove to the old Central Works to see what surely was no coincidence.

Kopek was right. The building was gone. It was now only smoking rubble. A uniformed fire captain was watching two firemen train hoses on the smoldering ruin. I handed him my business card, which shows me as an insurance investigator.

'Nothing here for you,' he said, handing it back. 'We already called the property manager to check out the potential that financial lightning was involved. He shut that notion down fast. He said there was no insurance on the building, so I don't know why you're here.'

'Being thorough.' I made a show of sniffing the air. The rubble stunk of accelerant and maybe an explosive. 'This is more than simple arson.'

'You bet your ass. Fuses on timers set to blow simultaneously on all four floors – a professional job. But why anyone would bother to hire professionals to destroy an old derelict structure when there's no insurance payout is beyond me. A few cans of gasoline, some soaked rigs and a slow-burning cigarette would have done the job for fifty bucks, tops. So why are you here?'

'We like to look out for all of Dace's properties,' I said. 'It was Mister Dace you talked to about this place being uninsured, right?'

'Yeah.'

'I hope he doesn't come back at us and say we let this building slip through the cracks uninsured,' I said, needing to be sure.

'Relax. I asked Dace twice about insurance. He said the building was slated for demolition like the others that were here. They just want the grounds.'

'Dace did the bulldozing?'

'That's what he implied.'

'Then he should have done them all at once,' I said.

'Done what?' he asked, confused.

'Bulldozed all of them all at once, instead of leaving one to be bulldozed standing later.' I pointed to the smoking heap. 'Would have saved you all this trouble.'

'We'll send them a bill,' he said. 'A whopper.'

I thought back to the new electrical piping I'd seen inside but said nothing. 'So, you won't be investigating this?' I asked instead.

He shook his head. 'The owners are unperturbed, so I'm unperturbed. I think some arsonist got the wrong location.'

I took a detour on the way back to Rivertown because the soon-to-be ex-Mrs Herbie Sunheim wasn't nagging right. She should have been pestering Violet Krumfeld for more than just

Herbie's checkbook. She should have been pestering her to get ahold of him to dump that unaffordable Escalade.

According to the Internet, Ronald's Happy Parties was the closest party goods store to Herbie's house. It was located less than a mile away, stuck to the end of a strip mall that held a dry cleaners and a tattoo parlor. Ronald's clear front window displayed a colorful array of pastel party goods and, farther back, a portly balding man, presumably Ronald himself. He was standing behind a counter, entirely too close to the right of the woman I recognized as the soon-to-be ex-Mrs Herbie Sunheim. They both appeared to be looking straight out the front window. Their heads did not meet; their lips most certainly did not touch, but Marge Sunheim's right shoulder was rising up and down with some exertion.

Such a spectacle, with Herbie Sunheim so recently vanished, was lacking in grace. I got the phone number from the Internet and called.

The man answered the counter phone with his right hand, the left having dropped behind the counter somewhere. 'Ronald's hap . . . happy parties,' he managed, sounding out of breath.

'Oh, hi,' I said. 'I'm wondering if you have happy paper party plates?'

'Oh, oh, yes,' he managed, presumably to me but, then again, he might have been speaking to the laboring soon-to-be ex-Mrs Sunheim.

'Pardon me?'

'Yes! Yes!' he said, almost shouting.

'Do you have happy paper party plates in pink?' I inquired, quite reasonably.

'Pink, yes!'

'Plenty in pink?'

'Plenty what?' he demanded, somewhat rudely, though in fairness, he sounded like he was losing his breath, perhaps in approach of some modest goal.

'Plenty of happy paper party plates in pink?' I said.

'Yes, oh, yes!' he screamed. Through the glass, Marge Sunheim had become a blur.

'Purple!' I then said. 'Do you have plenty of happy paper party plates in purple?'

He hung up. Through the window, I saw him throw his head back and turn to the soon-to-be ex-Mrs Herbie Sunheim, likely in some relief.

I'd been prepared to continue, and ask what he had in periwinkle, but I'd seen enough.

Marge Sunheim had moved on, and maybe it was more convenient for her if Herbie did not.

THIRTEEN

I'd gone to grammar and high school with Weasel Wurder. I'd heard he was still in town, though I hadn't run across him in at least five years. Under normal circumstances, that wouldn't have been long enough, but Weasel chased cases in the halls of the Cook County courthouse, as had the late, airborne Rickey Means.

Weasel lived in the basement of his mother's house at the edge of Rivertown's abandoned factory district. Leo Brumsky once joked that they had that in common, except Leo only worked in the basement of his boyhood home. He slept upstairs, like when he was a kid, except when he slept at the lovely Endora's condo, close to Lake Michigan, as he'd begun doing more and more now that he was very much grown up.

Weasel's was one of five houses on the block, and the only one that had not been gutted by fire. He didn't need to live in the basement; his mother had been dead for years. But those of us who'd known him in school knew he preferred to live below grade. It was partly how he'd gotten his nickname.

Five of the eight steps leading up to his front door were missing, and the remaining three looked to have been feasted upon by carpenter ants, so I skipped any thought of knocking and tapped on the front basement window instead. Weasel's face, long and narrow and very much resembling a weasel's, appeared like an unwashed ghost behind the grit on the glass. I rubbed enough of it away so he could see me.

He grinned, pointed to the front of the house, and disappeared. I walked around to the base of the partial front steps but stayed well back in case any lurking carpenter ants might mistake me for wood. The door opened and Weasel appeared.

'Dek!' he shouted down, as if enthused.

'Weasel!' I pretended, in kind.

He looked the same. Tall and emaciated, with yellow skin that matched what remained of his teeth. His upper lip was coated with a film of milk.

He didn't invite me in, which was a relief, since thousands of ants were no doubt partying inside. As he began stepping gingerly down what remained of the stairs, I had the thought he might like to dance his feet when he got to the bottom, to rid himself of any free-riders that had tagged along. I stepped back enough to give him room for a full Irish jig, if he so desired.

'You still working the courthouse, Weasel?' I asked, when he got down to the cement.

Surprisingly, he didn't dance at all – merely stomped one leg down hard, but that might have been merely to jam a foot more securely into one of his stained, blue suede running shoes.

'Just heading there, in fact,' he said, and indeed, along with the shoes, the rest of his wardrobe looked proper for a day of Cook County justice. He wore black khakis, a green shirt with a frayed collar and a greasy black tie that hung perfectly straight, as if weighted by the dried remains of previous lunches.

'Getting good cases, are you?' I asked, to make conversation.

'The usual – retail theft, burglary, and of course, assault. Got to chase real hard these days to even get those. Younger guys in their twenties, more spry, are always coming along.'

'You know Rickey Means?'

'A regular, like me. Why do you want to know?'

'Checking something for a friend. Do you see him much?'

'Better times have befallen him.'

His choice of the word intrigued. 'What do you mean, "befallen"?'

'Talk is he's tumbled onto a retainer client, though nobody knows for sure. He's not around as much. He's dressing nice, gonna get his teeth fixed, mostly files papers these days. Fell into some sweet doo, word is.'

'What kind of papers?' There was no point in telling Weasel that the doo Rickey Means had fallen into was hard and terminal, not sweet.

'Could be it's still the usual gang stuff and he's leaving the actual court work to others, but one guy said he's doing real estate, of all things. Whatever he's up to, he's keeping the source of his good fortune close to his vest.'

'Has he ever worked for the big gangs here?' I asked, thinking of outfits large enough to want to pitch a lawyer out of a window and then blow up the window and the building around it to obliterate any evidence.

'Nah, guys like us never did get those kind of cases. The big locals used to hire the slicks at the fancy downtown firms, but they've been put out of business by bigger operators from points south. Guys like me, we get the snot-noses we always got.'

'But not Rickey Means?' I asked, as though Rickey Means was still in the present tense.

'Nicer clothes, like I said, and better teeth on the horizon. Good times for him, I guess.'

'Who knows exactly what he's up to these days?'

He didn't ask me why, he just held out his palm.

'Someone who really knows something,' I said, to clarify.

His palm stayed steady, and open. 'Hundred for me, hundred for whoever knows,' he said. 'Bargain rate, because we knew each other in school.'

'At the meet, Weasel,' I said, because we knew each other in school.

Weasel showed up at the turret that evening, about nine o'clock. With a kid.

The kid was barely five feet tall, but the faint fuzz on his chin made him look sixteen or even older. He wore black jeans, a black T-shirt and immaculate, two-hundred-dollar, shiny red basketball shoes speckled artily by a faint Milky Way of other colors. Weasel wore dirty blue jeans, literally dirty and literally blue. His low-cut white canvas sneakers might have been immaculate once, but now they were dirty, too. He wore the same smear of milk on his upper lip that I'd seen earlier, though I supposed the milk was fresher. For sure, it was whiter than his shoes.

The kid had cautious, darting eyes and shot a hundred glances at me. He seemed interested in the turret but wouldn't come inside, so we walked down to the river. Weasel made a rubbing gesture with his thumb and forefinger, the signal that cash had to be exchanged before any information got passed. I handed each a C-note, as agreed.

'What's your name?' I asked the kid.

'No name,' Weasel said.

'Mister Shade,' the kid said.

'Tell me about Rickey Means,' I said.

'He's—'

I shushed Weasel and turned to the kid. 'I want it straight, and from you.'

After palming the hundred fast into his jeans, the kid had kept staring down at his red high-tops. 'He hire me for stuff sometimes.'

'What stuff?'

'Dropping off papers, getting coffee and burgers.' He looked up at me. His eyes were steady now, intent. 'Sometimes clean.'

'Clean? Like hauling out?'

'Yeah, haulin' out,' the kid said, turning to the Willahock as if mesmerized by the several plastic jugs bobbing downriver.

'Garbage?' I asked.

'Peoples,' he said to the river. 'Used to be.'

Rickey Means hadn't just hired the kid to run papers and fetch hamburgers. He'd hired him to get rid of inconvenient corpses.

'What do you mean, "used to be?"' I asked.

The kid turned back to me and shrugged.

'When's the last time you saw Rickey?' I asked.

'Been some days,' he said.

Weasel jerked both beads of his eyes to me. 'Rickey's gone? That's what this is about?'

'Been some days,' the kid said, and headed up the rise to the street.

FOURTEEN

My phone rang as I was driving into the city the next morning. 'Hello?' I quite naturally said into it.

Silence.

'Hello?' I asked again, because I do not give up easily, though I'd just spent an hour fearing I was about to do that. The kid the night before had gotten me no closer to finding Herbie Sunheim, and I was seeing no way forward to learning anything at all.

'How do you fit into things, Mr Elstrom?' the voice barely whispered. I pressed the phone hard against my ear. It was Violet Krumfeld, Herbie's assistant, calling.

'I told you. He hired me.'

'The Central Works?'

'Why do you ask that?'

'Because cops called maybe an hour after you called me yesterday.'

'Yesterday, you suggested I call the cops to find out where Herbie was. I did.'

'All they did yesterday was call, saying they got a report Herbie was missing and what did I know about that and where was he hanging out these days. But this morning they came around, not just asking about Herbie but about a property called Central Works.'

'Kopek and Jacks.'

'The names of the cops? I don't know. They opened wallets, showed me identifications or something. I didn't look closely. They were nice. They brought strudel. Apple, with raisins.'

'That was Kopek for sure. He's in his mid-fifties, gray-haired and heavy. Jacks is mid-thirties and thin.'

'The older one was very nice, like I said. The younger one had nothing to say very much.'

'You told them yesterday that Herbie is often gone for extended periods, like it was no big deal.'

'Herbie likes his privacy.'

'So today they wanted to talk about Central Works?'

'Mostly what Herbie said about that property. I said nothing. I've been looking through everything here since they left, and there's nothing on Central Works. If Herbie is working it, he's working it like he worked your retainer, out of his car or something. There's no file in the office. Then they asked if Herbie might be working with anybody else on Central Works, and of course, then I got to thinking about you, Mr Elstrom, and what you're not saying you're working on. I asked them if they knew you. They said yes, and asked what you were doing. I said I didn't know exactly, and you never asked about this Central Works, but you sure got more questions than answers.'

'I told them Herbie hired me to take pictures at the Central Works. It's true.'

'Pictures Herbie could have taken himself with his cell phone?'

'I suppose.'

'This is about the guy who flopped,' she said.

I didn't answer.

'And that retainer Herbie gave you? Was it for anything else?' This time she didn't laugh. This time she sounded scared.

'He hasn't said but it must concern the property owner's liability. You're sure Herbie never mentioned Central Works?'

'Not a word.'

It all fit with him paying me in greenbacks. Herbie didn't want anyone to know what he was up to.

'How about Triple Time Partners, or Walter Dace, or Dace Property Management?'

'Not a peep. Is Herbie hiding?' she asked.

'Maybe just from his wife. I don't know,' I said. 'Is there money in your company checking account?'

'Now you sound like his wife,' she said. 'She called again this morning. She said the cops called her like they called me, wanting to know whether Herbie was missing, and that it was real urgent they talk to him. That got her a little panicked, I think, but she really didn't want to talk to me about that. She called because she wants a check. I tell her the same thing I tell her every morning and every afternoon. I tell her I don't have the checkbook.'

'But you do.'

'I told her that besides, even if I did, I don't have signing on the account, and that part's true. She said that's OK, and to just give her the checkbook.'

'Is there money in the account?' I asked again.

'Seven thousand, two hundred and sixteen dollars and fifty-four cents. Herbie didn't run away, at least not far, because he didn't loot the account.'

'Does his wife ask you why Herbie isn't returning her calls?'

'Not once, the bitch. She wants the checkbook so she can forge his signature on a check. She says she has a right to company money because Herbie is behind on what he owes her. Apparently, he got into some goofy deal with a car dealer.'

'I told you about that.'

'That Caddy you were asking me about? I thought you were joking. Cadillacs don't sound like Herbie. She's smoked about that, because the dealer told her to make the payments if Herbie doesn't.'

'Those cops this morning – did they mention anything specific that happened at the Central Works?'

'They didn't mention the flying stiff, if that's what you mean.'
'Anything else?'
'They were nice and casual, and let me keep the rest of the strudel and all. And then I got to thinking that they really didn't say anything at all. They were full of questions and no answers, like you.'
'The Central Works was torched early this morning, professionally.'
'Oh, no,' she said.
'Why are you still there, Violet?' I asked, remembering her empty desk. 'Maybe Herbie really did take off and won't ever pay you again.'
She hung up.

Dace's receptionist had finished filing her nails since my last visit and was now applying red polish. Her face turned the same shade as the polish when she looked out through the glass wall and saw me crossing the small reception area. She yelled my name back toward the private office just as I opened the glass inner door and smiled winsomely.

Walter Dace, the fellow who'd given me the bum's rush the last time, materialized behind her in an instant. It was his face I'd come to see react.

'A green bow tie today,' I said, noticing, by way of an opening pleasantry. 'As for my yellow one, it's still draped on a nail, though other things have changed since I was last here.'

Though I remained in the open doorway, the receptionist hurried to twist the brush tightly back in the little bottle. Perhaps that was so she could listen more attentively. More likely, she'd noticed the darkening of her boss's face and was afraid he'd spill her polish, grabbing for her stapler to throw at my throat.

Mercifully, Dace moved slowly around her desk, disturbing nothing but air. 'You again,' he said, coming up to stop a short six inches away. I had six inches and fifty pounds on him, maybe more after the *kolachkys*, and stayed still in the threshold, neither in nor out.

'I thought I'd drop by to offer condolences and congratulations.' And agitation, but I figured he'd already sensed that.

'Are you nuts?' he demanded, breathing hard on my shirt collar.
'Condolences on your building. It blew up and burned.'
He worked his lips and watched my eyes, but he said nothing.

'You know, that building you didn't bother to insure? The one where a man came out of a window head first?'

'Your point?'

'Insurance requires an inspection.' I used to do that sort of thing, now and then, before I tanked my wife and my life. 'Every property manager on the planet knows that.' I smiled. 'Everyone except you, apparently.'

'The building had no value. We care about the land.'

'Then why bulldoze all the others on the site except that one? And why ready the place for new electrical service? Why race to power wash it if it was coming down?'

He leaned forward to push against me. I let him move me back a couple of inches but kept my foot in the door.

'You haven't heard the congratulations,' I said to the top of his head.

He tried to push the door closed but my foot and shoe were persistent. 'Say them and leave.'

'Congratulations on hiring a torch who was too obviously professional. He wired all four floors to destroy whatever you didn't want looked at anymore.'

'I . . . I hired nobody,' he said, stepping back. His mouth trembled, trying to stop a stutter.

'Then you know who did,' I said, 'and that might be enough to interest a fire inspector. You should have stuck with a punk toting a few gallons of gas and a matchbook. That kind of thing is much less noticeable than explosives and accelerant.'

'Bug off,' he said.

My visit had been sufficiently enjoyable. I withdrew my foot and bugged.

FIFTEEN

The inspiration for a fishing expedition came right after I left Dace's office, triggered not by crafty thinking but by remembering the pole net I had yet to remove from the Jeep. My mind often dances sideways like that, to no productive end, but this time it triggered a new thought. I needed to scoop the waters, to see what I could snag about Walter Dace. I hoofed it over to the county recorder's office.

Productivity had not invaded its dim hush since I'd last been there. With my arrival, there was one visitor: me. And there was one county worker: the same woman who'd helped me the time before. She sat at her desk eating something that smelled like a tuna sandwich and flipping the pages of the day's *Chicago Sun-Times*. Since there was no little busboy bell on the counter, all I could do was clear my throat like last time. Since this time I was in her full view, I figured I'd only have to do it once. I figured wrong. She kept chewing and flipping pages, not once looking up.

I called across to her. 'Can you help me?'

She looked up. 'It's lunchtime.'

'Who's filling in?' I asked.

'It's my turn today,' she said, like that made sense.

'You've got lunchtime counter duty today?'

'You got it.'

'Then help me,' I said.

She groaned, pushed all of herself out of her chair and ambled over. 'Like it here, do you?' she asked, with the warmth of granite.

'It's quiet and comfortable, a welcome respite from the distracting goings-on of live people,' I said. 'How can I find out all the properties owned by two particular entities?'

'It's difficult.' Words like those were the usual opening gambit in that age-old tribal custom in Chicago – the grabbing of the grease.

I patted my pocket, the second part of the age-old custom.

'We don't take bribes,' she said.

Like most in Chicagoland, I'd heard the public proclamations of clean-ups in county government and gave them the respect I give wind chimes and other things that make meaningless noises in the wind. Multimillion dollar bribing scandals had recently been uncovered at the highest levels in the city's public school administration and its red-light ticketing program, signifying that while bribes might now be forbidden to the lowest level of municipal employees, it was only so that larger numbers could be squeezed, like toothpaste from a dwindling tube, to the very top. It was the little payrollers like the tuna consumer that always got hurt first by Chicago's occasional reforms.

'Of course you don't take bribes,' I said.

She held out her hand, palm up. Once the third part of the old rite, now she wanted only names. I gave her the card on which I'd written Dace Property Management and Triple Time Partners.

Shockingly, she was back in five minutes with a computer-printed sheet. She'd found nothing for Dace, which made sense since he was just a manager, and not an owner, of real estate properties. But she'd found four properties owned by Triple Time Partners. I left her and her tuna and took the sheet out to the hall to read.

Listed with the Central Works were three other properties in old factory districts on the west and south sides of Chicago. All four parcels had been purchased in the last six months.

The printout showed additional information I hadn't thought to ask for. In all four cases, Herbie's Builders' Complete Realty had provided the initial down payments in cashier's checks, on behalf of Triple Time. That seemed unusual, but it wasn't necessarily a surprise. Realtors often forge ongoing, wide-ranging relationships with purchasers.

The lawyer representing Triple Time at every closing was Richard Means, Esquire. That might not have been a surprise, either, except for the fact that Means was a small-time case chaser, too low tier to be working on larger real estate deals. Complicating things even more, of course, was the fact that, as Triple Time's lawyer, he'd been pitched out of one of their properties.

One more nugget of information caught my eye. No mortgage banks were shown as holding mortgage liens, which meant the properties had been acquired for cash. That was most unusual. Commercial real estate was almost invariably bought on credit. Leveraging small down payments to buy big properties was the name of their game.

I called Herbie's office while driving south out of Chicago's central Loop.

'I haven't heard from him,' Violet Krumfeld might have whispered when she picked up.

'Triple Time Partners, the folks who bought Central Works through Herbie, worked with him on buying three other properties at roughly the same time.' I read her the addresses.

'I told you before, I never heard of Triple Time.'

'How about those addresses? You would have typed them on four purchase agreements in the last six months.'

'Same as with that name, Triple Time. I never heard of those addresses before. Like I also told you, Herbie must have been doing deals outside the company.'

I would have asked her to research her files for those addresses anyway, but she'd already hung up.

SIXTEEN

According to the barely legible lettering on its yellow bricks, the first of Triple Time's other three buildings was once operated by something called Bureski Auto Parts. Like the Central Works, it looked to have been vacant for quite a long time, was securely boarded up with graying plywood and sat alone in the middle of a square block otherwise leveled by bulldozers. Also like the Central Works, at least just before it exploded, new red and white No Trespassing signs had been screwed onto the building's corners. Triple Time seemed to be doing what it could to fight future negligence liability issues.

I left the Jeep and walked up to the building. None of the plywood sheets covering the window and door openings would bend enough for a peek inside. I didn't suppose that mattered.

The second of Triple Time's other three buildings was two miles farther south. Letters cast in the concrete cornice at the top of the brown brick building meant it to be forever known as the Vanderbilt Bakers Supply Company, which I took to mean it had once supplied salt, confectioners' sugar, flour and other items to local bakeries. Like the Bureski and Central Works buildings, it sat alone in the middle of a bulldozed clearing. It, too, had new No Trespassing signs, and the graying plywood covering its doors and windows looked tight.

Except for one. The screws on one of the sheets over a side door had been backed all the way out, leaving the plywood barely secured by only one screw. Anyone – a building inspector, a workman, a cop looking for a drug bust, or most likely, a dealer – could have left that plywood barely secured, intending to come back. I untwisted the screw, set the plywood on the ground and stepped inside.

The interior looked like the Central Works. Plaster had been broken away to rip out valuable copper wiring and electrical boxes for metal scrap, and old doors and windows had been torn out for chic reuse in modern buildings. There was blood on the floor, old and stained like at Central Works.

I thought, then, of the young black kid, Mister Shade, that Weasel had brought around. Rickey Means had paid him, some-times, to rid a building of a casualty – until Rickey had become a casualty himself. In Chicago, too often, the horror went round and round.

A glint in the gloom caught my eye. It was a shiny bright main conduit through which new wiring would be run. Just like at the Central Works.

Just like at the Central Works, too, the elevator had been ripped out, leaving gaping squares in the ceilings all the way up to the top floor. The Vanderbilt Supply building, though, still had its stairs, tucked into a corner.

I pulled my peacoat tighter around me, suddenly chilled. The little light seeping in through cracks in the brickwork and the edges of the plywood window covering was fading fast. The sun was sure to be down in minutes.

I wanted a fast look to see if the new conduit ran all the way up through the building and, since there were stairs, I went up to the second floor.

And found the body.

It rested, half sitting, against the base of the stairs leading up to the third floor, wrapped several times around in the milky thick plastic that cement contractors sometimes lay down before pouring basement floors. I pressed down hard on the plastic and felt below the faint scratch of beard stubble for a pulse, but that was only for the protocol of it. He was cold – long cold. Rigor had come and gone.

I undid enough of the silver tape at one end to peel back a corner of the plastic. Herbie glared back at me, sightless, unblinking, accusing.

I ran down the stairs, spooked enough to want to be out of that building before the last of the day's sunlight disappeared, and sprinted to the Jeep. Safely behind the wheel, I started the engine, revving it to speed the heater, and took out my phone to call the police. And then I stopped.

Rickey Means was a typical Chicago casualty. A small man, an unnoticeable man, he was a man of too little significance to warrant two detectives spending much time investigating his murder.

Herbie Sunheim was a small player, too. Like Means, he was a man of too little importance to warrant much police interest in his disappearance. Yet Kopek and Jacks had come out to the turret within just a few hours of my first calling the police to report his disappearance. And before they'd even gotten to me, they'd contacted Violet and the soon-to-be ex-Mrs Sunheim, and swung by Herbie's rooming house, wherever it was, to talk to his landlady. They'd acted fast and thoroughly, as if they'd already been primed to go hunting for Herbie.

Across the bulldozed field, the side door I'd left uncovered was now lost in shadow. Another night was coming, not that I imagined Herbie minded anymore. I guessed he hadn't minded tucking that thousand dollars into an envelope for me, either. He'd wanted something more than just a few cell phone photos.

The vague mist of an inspiration was forming – perhaps the most bizarre of any I'd ever had.

I took a breath, and then another, and then I made myself shut off the Jeep and hurry across the field in the darkness to slip that loose piece of board back into place.

And then I hustled back to the Jeep and drove away, hoping the drive back to Rivertown would cleanse my head of what I was thinking of doing.

SEVENTEEN

'No problem,' Leo said when I called him from the car, 'but there's no way to lock it up.'

It was much later that night, past ten o'clock. I'd had to ponder for quite some time, in part to convince myself that I wasn't going mad.

'I already stopped at the hardware store for a fine hasp, which you'll need anyway,' I said, because that, at least, was true. What I didn't say was that I'd already installed it on the wood enclosure I'd built and was now on my way back to the south side of the city.

'I still don't understand,' he said. 'Tell me again what you're doing with so much beef.'

'Meat,' I corrected, not so much to be literal but to con myself into believing I was lying as little as possible to my best friend. My first obligation was to protect Leo's option for plausible deniability if my grand plan went haywire, which it was most likely to do.

'You'll have it out before my grand opening?'

'Absolutely,' I said without asking when that was, and turned onto the street that led to the Vanderbilt Supply building.

My Jeep is ancient, red and rusty. But thanks to Booster Gibbs, a car cleanser and hot parts acquaintance working nights out of Rivertown's city garage, it now sported an almost-new green top removed from a dead man's Jeep. The new top is fine and tight but the green atop the rusted red paint draws attention because of its Christmas season colors, as it had most recently from the two men hunting me at the Central Works just days before. But more worrisome than the attention-grabbing colors, that night, was the crystalline clarity of the new plastic side and back windows that came with the green top. It was easy to see out of them, for sure, but worse, it was just as easy for others to see in. I drove away from the abandoned Vanderbilt Supply building petrified that a sudden stop or bounce over a pothole might cause my cargo to rise up, fully visible, and traumatize some closely following motorist should his headlamps be strong enough to penetrate not only my windows but the risen murky plastic as well. A phone call would summon cops. A felony arrest would be made. No explanation would keep me out of a jail; no judge would risk allowing me to live free of an institution. The worry of that, combined with driving in a frigid March night with the heater off for fear of thawing my passenger, would have been enough to make me shiver all the way back to Rivertown.

But there was a greater worry. A pair of unwavering headlamps, far back, began trailing me three blocks after I pulled away from the Vanderbilt Supply. Professionals do that – follow at such a distance, especially when it's late and the roads are clear and it's easy to watch a quarry's taillights a great distance ahead.

It took more courage than I wanted to spend to slow suddenly, going through a well-lit intersection, but I needed a glimpse of the car trailing behind me. It was dark, perhaps a deep blue, but it might have been darker. My mind skittered to black Impalas, the kind detectives like Kopek and Jacks drove.

It was then that I thought I heard my passenger moan.

I squeezed my shaking hands harder on the steering wheel. It was the wind, of course, and the horror of what I was doing. I unzipped my side curtain to hear the certifiably real sounds of my engine and my wheels, loud sounds to drown out a moaning that wasn't anywhere but inside my head.

No matter whether I sped up or slowed down, the trailing head-lamps maintained the same distance behind me, all the way to the western outskirts of Chicago.

I hit the Rivertown line. I knew the town's streets, its ruined factories, its darkest places where no one worked or lived anymore, places where the street lamps hadn't been fixed in years because no one ever went there. I cut my lights, ducking onto an unlit side road, and turned onto a side street and then another side street, zigging and zagging through blocks of derelict buildings and live bungalows and some blocks of both, driving dark, watching the rearview. No headlamps followed.

I came up behind a long-shuttered restaurant fifty feet back of Thompson Avenue and parked between it and a Dumpster that some optimist, intent on resurrecting the place, had filled years before with old stools, parts of booths and broken tabletops. The optimist couldn't get a liquor license, such licenses being available only to those with direct bloodlines to city hall, and so he gave it up. But his filled, forgotten Dumpster remained, a testament to his ruined dream.

I cut my engine and watched the traffic creep along Thompson Avenue, trapped by the long lights and the lingering ladies, but nothing that looked like an unmarked police car passed by. After fifteen minutes, I started up again, swung onto Thompson and drove to the road that led down to the trailer in the clearing by the river. I wasn't there but five minutes.

It was midnight when I got back to the turret. I'd been shivering for hours. The night was cold, and the building that had once housed Vanderbilt Supply was cold, but the dead man wrapped in the plastic shroud had been coldest of all.

I clutched the wrought-iron railing and pulled myself up the
two flights of stairs to crawl into bed; it was too cold to take off
my peacoat and my sweatshirt. At some point, perhaps after an
hour, perhaps after two, I drifted into a sleep.

But Herbie had followed me up those stairs, and into my bed,
my head and my dreams.

All night long, I heard him moan.

EIGHTEEN

I woke late the next morning and, for an instant, I was calm. And
then I remembered.

Or rather, I did not.

Almost every excruciating moment of my late-night trip came
back in that instant: the mildewed, dusty smell of the building;
the sound of my footsteps echoing across the floor and up and
down the stairs; the frigid feel of the weight in the plastic; the
relentless steadiness of the headlamps behind me; the sureness of
the electric plug fitting into the trailer's socket to set the freezer
humming; the gentle thud as I lowered the top of the wooden
freezer enclosure; and the moans, most horribly the moans, that I
imagined coming in protest from the dead man.

But I did not remember the click of the padlock snapping closed.

I was out the door in a flash, only to get stopped cold by the
maze of long lights along Thompson Avenue. It took fourteen
excruciating minutes to free myself and get down to the clearing.

Leo's white van was parked next to a much larger green van
that was emblazoned with a veterinarian's name and pictures of a
laughing horse and a grinning cow. Leo was standing with a man,
likely the animal doctor, at the back corner of the trailer, not ten
feet from the freezer enclosure that, by now, I was sure I'd left
unlocked. They were laughing, those two men, just like the animals
on the vet's van. I could only hope that meant nothing – or rather,
no one – horrifying had been discovered. Yet.

I jammed my hands into my coat pockets and made like I was
happy merely to stroll about, admiring the progress Leo had made
in the compound. And progress had indeed been made. The fence

posts surrounding the bulldozed oval were now connected by three rows of long white rails, identical to the fencing that enclosed the small area near the trailer that Leo had yet to explain.

Leo and the vet began walking to the vet's van. It was my chance. I started toward the back of the trailer but Leo intercepted me. 'Hold up for a minute, Dek,' he called out. 'We'll walk the track.'

'Ah, yes, the track,' I called back.

The vet clapped Leo on the back, got in his van and headed toward the river road.

'Aren't you just dying of curiosity?' Leo asked, coming up. Like last time, he was wearing his empty tool belt. Like all times, he was several rainbows of bright colors, except for the toque on his head, which, inexplicably, had remained white.

'Curious about what?' I asked.

'My new track.'

At that moment, I wouldn't have much cared if the ground had spontaneously erupted into flames, such was my need to be sure that I'd locked the enclosure surrounding the freezer. But I couldn't tell that to Leo.

'Surely you remember the sign?' he asked.

Some dim part of my mind – there are several – nudged me into an appropriate response. 'You mean the "thoroughbred racing, maybe" part?'

'Those would be the pertinent words,' he allowed.

'You said you would explain in due time.'

'Next week, when I'll be handing out free ice cream from my new freezer.'

'Ah, yes, let's look at that new freezer.'

'Did you catch my drift?' he asked, not moving.

'What drift?'

'That part about next week, when I'll be handing out ice cream from my new freezer?'

'You'll need that freezer next week?' I asked, trying to sound casual.

'Or sooner.'

I gave that a nod, because I was afraid to open my mouth.

'Come on, we'll go around the track.' He opened a gate in the fence. 'Counter-clockwise, like they do at all the great courses.'

We set off counter-clockwise, as would any thoroughbreds that knew great courses.

'This is going to revolutionize Rivertown.' He was walking maddeningly slowly, as if he wanted to savor the feel of his yellow canvas shoes on the flattened ground one meandering step at a time.

We passed the Jeep, but as soon as we rounded the turn to head down the short stretch toward the river, he stopped to admire the small fenced-in area.

'And that's for . . .?' I made myself ask, having to stop as well. Surely it was too small for horses.

'The thoroughbreds,' he pronounced.

'Just like your sign exclaims,' I said. I started walking, desperate now to see a padlock snapped tight on the freezer enclosure.

'Don't you want to know what kind of thoroughbreds?' he asked, catching up to me.

'Judging by the size of the paddock, I'm guessing mice,' I said. We were about to round the turn to the backstretch along the river. I was just seconds from knowing.

He jumped ahead and stopped in front of me, a courageous move for someone that weighed only a hundred and forty pounds.

'Dek!'

I stopped, just an inch before knocking him over. Maddeningly, his head, long and pale and topped with a damned-fool white cloth chimney of a hat, blocked my view of the top of the freezer enclosure fifty feet down.

'I know what's got you so preoccupied,' he said, his face solemn.

I managed a shrug and started to ease around him.

'The body,' he said.

I froze, sure now that I'd forgotten to padlock the enclosure and that he'd gotten a look inside his new freezer.

'Uh, listen . . .' I began, but then the words fell away.

'Right here,' he said, pointing to the river bank.

I exhaled. He was talking about the other corpse, the one he'd discovered bagged inside my Jeep some months before.

I might have mumbled something appropriate; I don't remember. I stepped around him. I had to see.

A new hasp – my new hasp – gleamed on top of the freezer enclosure, tightly secured by the shiny new padlock I'd remembered to snap on it after all.

I let out a breath. 'Jeez, Leo, we can't be talking about her anymore,' I said of the woman who'd gone into the river at the very spot where we were now standing. But, in truth, all I wanted to do was giggle with relief.

He pointed to the freezer. 'Let's see the beef,' he said.

'Meat,' I thought to say, but maybe after too long a pause.

He looked up at me. 'What's wrong? Your voice went weird.'

'I, uh, uh, don't have the combination here.'

'New lock?'

I nodded.

'Don't forget, I need that emptied by next week,' he said.

'I gotta go,' I said, heading back up the way we'd just walked, clockwise, the way even the dumbest of trained thoroughbreds knew not to go.

Hours were flashing by. A week didn't seem long enough to discover exactly what I'd been thinking when I'd abducted the corpse I'd dumped in his freezer.

NINETEEN

In the dark of the night before, abducting Herbie Sunheim's corpse seemed the only way to flush out his killers – at least two, shown in the tagger's mural – out into the open. His disappearance had alarmed his ex-wife, his assistant, the cops, and maybe even his landlady, all for different reasons. But only his killers might become stupid. Unlike Rickey Means, whose murder might have been a spontaneous, unthinking pitch out of a window, Herbie's killing and disposal had probably been carefully planned. Likely enough, they'd parked him inside the Vanderbilt Supply temporarily as a prelude to hiding him where he'd never be found, and where his corpse could not be probed for evidence that would identify his murderer. And so, my genius of the night before had reasoned, abducting Herbie's body before they could hide it permanently would disrupt that plan and force the killers to expose themselves trying to retrieve it.

Except that now, in the clearer light of a new day, that thinking smacked of twisted lunacy. I had no idea what next step to take to agitate Herbie's killers into sight.

Mostly to kill time until I was assaulted with intelligence, I sat at my computer and Googled the last of Triple Time's properties, the one on the west side that I'd not yet visited. Its satellite image was taken in some previous late spring or summer, when the trees were green with leaves. It showed a flat-roofed, multistoried old building like the other three Triple Time had acquired. But unlike the others, which sat by themselves in the middle of acres of cleared ground, this one stood in a congested block of other old commercial buildings.

I zoomed in for street views. At five stories, it was Triple Time's tallest building. Its windows were open holes; high weeds grew all around.

The buildings on either side, along the street, were empties, too. The whole neighborhood looked to have been deserted for years.

My cell phone rang. It was Weasel Wurder, and he was out of breath.

'Who'd you tell?' he shouted.

'About what?'

There was silence at his end of the line, and for a moment, I thought we'd lost connection.

'About what?' I said again.

'About asking me to nose around about Rickey Means?' he asked, calmer now.

'Nobody. Why do you ask?'

'That kid I brought around? Mister Shade? The kid that said Rickey was gone, meaning dead?'

'What are you saying, Weasel?'

'The kid's gone missing.'

The phone went dead.

I ground the gears, shifting fast over to Weasel's place. His heap wasn't at the curb, no bulb burned behind the filthy glass in the basement, and no amount of banging on any of his windows, front or back, roused him. He'd called from somewhere other than home.

I went back to the Jeep and tried to breathe deeply enough to reason that it wasn't me who'd caused the kid's disappearance. I watched Weasel's house for an hour, sitting in the car, calling his phone every five minutes. I only got voicemail.

I became too fidgety to just sit. I drove to Triple Time's fourth building to busy myself away from bad thoughts. All the way into the city, I kept redialing Weasel's phone, but still only got his voicemail.

Instead of the factory building I'd seen on the Internet, nestled among similar structures and trees, Triple Time's fourth building sat by itself in the middle of land bulldozed since the satellite photo had been taken.

Unlike the other locations, this one had activity. A large yellow Penske rental truck was backed up tight against the loading dock at the side, and two more identical yellow rentals idled on the wide, side driveway, waited to be unloaded.

This building had guards – at least two – standing at the corners, watching the cleared ground, the traffic passing by . . . and me if I slowed noticeably. I sped around the corner, parked on the next block and walked back up on a cross street. Half of the buildings I passed were vacant, though others were being used – one as a machine shop and three as storage facilities. I slowed up, coming up to the intersection, and pressed into the shadows of the building at the corner.

Glints from the truck being unloaded showed that shiny things were being taken off, perhaps long, stainless-steel sinks or counters. Something else sparkled across the intersection, a hundred yards beyond Triple Time's building. It was off the windshield of a car parked on the same side street that I was on. The car looked to be a black Impala. That needed to mean nothing; the world is full of black cars. Or it needed to mean that cops were staking out Triple Time's fourth property, or that the car I'd thought was tailing me belonged to what was being unloaded.

I turned, went back to the Jeep and headed for Rivertown. But five miles before the city line, something I'd already pretty much known needed confirmation. I pulled to the curb and took out my phone.

I hadn't paid much mind when the fire chief at the Central Works said it had been Dace who'd bulldozed the buildings there, other than to question why one had been left standing when, despite having been prepared to be rewired, it too was slated for demolition. I took it for the changing whim of a developer; in commercial real estate, things change.

Now I'd just finished seeing the same thing, sort of, at Triple Time's other three properties. Though satellite photos are refreshed fairly regularly, the last Triple Time property was still being shown as nestled among trees and other buildings. It meant the grounds surrounding that building had been bulldozed recently, probably by Dace as well.

I brought up the Internet on my phone and Googled the Bureski site. I needed only a glance before moving on to the Vanderbilt location. Same thing.

Triple Time Partners had bulldozed all four of their properties since acquiring them, leaving only one building standing at roughly the center of each multi-acre site. Reason told me that didn't need to be odd. Triple Time, likely a canny developer, might simply have wanted to unclutter its new sites, to provide space for parking, snappy landscaping and expensive new construction.

Still, Rickey Means, their lawyer, had been tossed from one of their buildings and Herbie Sunheim, their realtor, had been left dead in another. That was two too many dead in too many buildings for real estate developers, no matter how canny.

Something more was at play, something that Herbie Sunheim had paid an extra five hundred dollars for me to see.

Weasel banged his front wheels against his curb, killing his engine, at ten o'clock that night. I'd been waiting down the block for three hours.

It took him a full two minutes to work the car-door handle and lurch out. By then, I'd moved up on foot. I caught him as he staggered into the blackness of the gangway between his house and the burned-out shell of the one next to it. He stunk of whiskey and, oddly, of spoiled milk. He turned at the sound of my footsteps and took a roundhouse swing at me that missed by a good two feet.

'You idiot, Weasel!' I yelled, grabbing him by both shoulders. 'It's Dek!'

He tried to swing again but I had his arms pinned.

'You called me and then hung up, remember?'

'You're going to get me killed!' he shouted.

I slammed him back against his house and forced myself to speak slowly and clearly. 'Tell me about the kid, Weasel. Tell it fast, tell it all, and tell it true.'

'It's all your fault,' he said in a strange monotone. 'You're the one had me ask around for who knew Rickey.'

I shook him hard by the shoulders. He was talking gibberish. 'Make sense!'

He took a breath, but all it did was make him shudder. 'I found a lawyer who knew a guy who said there was a kid who sometimes worked for Rickey—'

I shook him again. 'Faster!'

'So it was no big deal. The kid called me. I said a friend – meaning you, Dek – wants some info on Rickey Means. No way, he said; no way was he talking about Rickey. Then say nothing for a hundred bucks, I told him. A C-note for doing nothing and saying nothing ain't bad change, so he said OK and to pick him up at a bus stop in Oak Park. I brought him to you. He told you nothing, remember? We collected our hundreds and left. He didn't rat anybody out about anything.'

I relaxed my hands on his shoulders. 'And then?'

'And then this morning,' he went on, still in a monotone, 'I'm in the hall at the courthouse, waiting to go in to snag an assignment like usual, when my phone rings.' His eyes were wild. 'It was Rickey on top of that boxcar, wasn't it? Bad teeth, expensive suit? That's what Mister Shade meant about Rickey being gone?'

'Who called this morning?'

Weasel licked his lips, missing the milk smear, and looked back toward the alley, as if someone was listening. 'The kid's mother,' he said. 'She found my phone number on a piece of paper in the kid's room, I guess. I had to tell her I'd arranged a meet between her kid and somebody. She said the kid never made it home the night I dropped him back at that bus stop in Oak Park.'

'Did she call the cops?'

He laughed. 'She and the kid live someplace on the west side, Austin. Nobody trusts the cops in Austin, and few cops go there if they can avoid it. I told her maybe you'd help.'

'I'll call her right now.'

He paused, as if struggling to remember. 'No phone. Her account got cut.'

'How'd she call, then?'

'She must have called from work.'

'Why didn't you just give her my phone number?'

There was another odd pause, and then Weasel said, 'Like I already told you, I said maybe you could help, all right.'

'For a fee, Weasel? Did you shake her for a fee?'

'Nah,' he said, quick enough for it to be true.

'Let's go see her.'

'What? Now?'

'Her kid's missing.'

'I told you, she called from her work. I don't know where she lives. I'll call her first thing in the morning, get the address.'

'Give me the number now. I'll call tomorrow morning.'

'My phone's at the courthouse.'

'This is all bullshit, Weasel.'

'I don't know her name or even the kid's. He just calls himself Mister Shade. I'll call and get the address in the morning.'

'I'll come by for you first thing.'

'It's just a kid, Dek. Maybe you ought to forget it.'

Drunk or not, I wanted to slap him, but I just grabbed at his necktie and tugged. He screamed, but there was no one to hear, not in that deserted part of town – no one but me. His panic came as music.

'Not just a kid?'

He flailed at me with both hands. I let go of his necktie to slap them away, but one flapped back against his face. Blood squirted from his nose.

'I'm telling you, better you forget the kid!'

'Tomorrow morning, first thing, Weasel.'

'I'll call you.'

'I'll find you if you don't.'

I let him break loose and take off down his gangway.

TWENTY

A black Chevy Suburban was parked in the shadows of the short street off Thompson Avenue, just before the turn onto mine. I stopped well back, about to cut my head-lamps, but then I spotted the lights on in the turret's first and second floors and the car parked directly in front of the turret. It was an old white Toyota Celica, spotted with the brown beginnings of rust.

It was Amanda's car, the one she drove when we first met, which meant the Suburban belonged to the bodyguards that began accompanying her, almost all the time, when she became CEO and major shareholder of her father's electric utility. A CEO worth hundreds of millions of dollars, batting around in an aged Toyota, offered up an enticing target for a kidnapper.

I drove past the Suburban, parked in front of the Toyota and got out slowly. Bracing a man against a wall, even one as greasy as Weasel, had caused aches. Moving too quickly in front of guards with guns might well cause more.

The timbered door was locked, which was as charming as it was unnecessary. Amanda was still adjusting to her new life. If she'd paused to think as she let herself in with her key, she would have realized she didn't need to relock the door behind her. Her guards were vigilant. They wouldn't let the president of the United States into the turret uninvited if Amanda was inside.

'Hi, honey; I'm home!' I called up to my ex-wife, like starched men did to their starched spouses on television sitcoms in the fifties when folks just hung around starched and didn't much divorce.

She stepped out from the kitchen, looked down from the landing, and screamed.

It was the blood – Weasel's from when his flailing hand backslapped his nose. I was smeared with it.

Mumbling that it was someone else's, as though that made it all right, I hobbled up past her to the third floor, dropped my clothes on the old plank floor and eased into the fiberglass shower enclosure. I had no strength left to jump around as usual in the frigid stream – I'd not as yet found funds for a serviceable water heater – and I supposed the stupid part of me needed to stand stoically beneath water as punishing as anything hosed up from the Arctic as penance for bringing hell to a kid. But the cold water offered nothing salving, and I shut it off feeling as much a bastard as before, except colder. I dressed quickly in unbloodied clothes and went down to the kitchen.

'Warm cider,' Amanda said.

'In new cups.' I sat down at the plywood table to admire the beige cups emblazoned with a picture of a bank in Dubuque.

'A quarter apiece, at an odd-lots store. I bought you four,' said the heiress who kept eleven million dollars of art in her lakefront condominium and hundreds of millions more in her investment portfolios.

'I have cups,' I said.

'Not ones picturing a bank in Dubuque. Besides, you shouldn't reuse Styrofoam,' she said, giving a nod to the ones on the counter.

I shrugged. The cider she'd warmed felt good, but her being there warmed me most of all.

'So, there's been blood?' she asked of my pre-showered self.

Always, I told Amanda everything, but knowledge of the theft and concealment of a corpse is a felony everywhere. Like Leo, she needed to be innocent of what she didn't know, so I gave her an amended version of what I'd been bumping against.

'You're going to see the child's mother?' she asked when I was done.

'Tomorrow, with Weasel, as soon as he gets me her address,' I said.

'Weasel will be of help?'

'Weasel's tongue has always been forked. Some of what he said didn't quite make sense.'

'Your morose, Nordic-Bohemian genes are thinking the boy is dead?'

'Potentially Nordic,' I corrected. 'My supposed sailor father left no trace of himself behind.'

'Except you, of course.' She smiled. 'Trust me, you have Nordic genes. They've embraced the notion that the boy is dead and that it's your fault.'

'Among other puzzles,' I said.

'All stemming from why that courthouse hustler, Rickey Means, was pitched out of a window?'

'He's the key to why Herbie overpaid me, why I got chased off the Central Works grounds, where Herbie expected to get the loot to lease a big-buck Escalade for his wife, why one building got blown up and what Triple Time intends to do with the others.'

'And whether Herbie is dead and not just missing?' Her eyes were steady on mine. 'What about him?'

I got up, took Kopek's bakery bag from behind the Styrofoam cups and sat back at the table.

'I already peeked inside,' she said. 'Nothing but prune.'

'There was cheese and apricot, but Kopek the cop and I ate the good ones, me perhaps a little more than him.'

'You're not going to tell me the rest of what you know about Herbie, are you?' asked the woman who knew my subterfuges better than anyone else.

'How is your jobs idea faring with your board of directors?'

She let it go. 'Lemon pants,' she said.

'You used that term before,' I said, understanding. 'You refer to older country club men who dare only to wear outrageous pants to play golf? Conservative men, too cautious?'

'Men who lack the stones to ripple the waters. Men who don't want to rile the mayor by inferring he doesn't have a plan. Tired men who have offered only to form a committee to study my proposal.'

She reached down to her purse on the floor and pulled out a folded front section of a *Chicago Tribune*. A picture of a shirtless boy, a couple of years younger than the kid I was worried about, took over a quarter of the page. A scar ran down the boy's bare chest and across his abdomen.

'The scar is from cutting a bullet out,' she said. 'He had to carry it for a while before the doctors said it was safe to operate.' She stared at it for a moment, and then put it back in her purse. 'It's getting late for my guards.'

'They're down the block, pretending they're not down the block.'

'So we can all pretend I'm not worth a pile if kidnapped.' She sighed. 'Our taking that one unscheduled flight in my father's jet made them crafty. They hid a GPS device on the Toyota somewhere.'

'No sense getting rid of it,' I said.

'They'd just plant another.' She stood up and headed for the stairs.

'You forgot your purse,' I said.

She nodded but started down anyway. I grabbed the purse and followed her, thinking she hadn't heard me.

At the bottom, she opened the door, but instead of stepping out, she flicked the outside light two times in fast succession. The Suburban shot up instantly. She motioned to whoever was behind the black glass on the passenger's side to come to the door. Two hundred and fifty pounds of solid beef packed in a wide suit jumped out, surprisingly agile, and came up.

'Jerry, this is Dek. Dek, this is Jerry.' Jerry gave the purse I was holding in my left hand only the briefest of glances before we shook hands.

'Jerry, step in for a moment, please,' she said.

He stepped in and Amanda closed the door. 'This, ah, structure was constructed to be historically accurate,' she said, reaching for the four foot, rough piece of wood that had hung next to the door mostly untouched, except for once when I'd shown her what it was for. She fitted it, horizontally, to the forged steel brackets bolted to the wall on either side of the door. 'Not even a battering ram can break the door down from outside now,' she said to Jerry.

He shrugged, accepting. 'What time in the morning, Miss Phelps?'

'Six sharp. I've got a meeting at eight,' she said, lifting the wood bar so he could leave.

'Nice to meet you,' he said to me now, without the slightest peek at the purse in my hand, and went out the door. No doubt, Jerry had seen much in his professional life.

She closed the door after him and fitted the bar back into the brackets.

'We'll have fire on the third floor?' she asked, of the fireplace in the bedroom.

'I'll bring up wood.'

After just the briefest lowering of her eyes, she said, 'Yes, I imagine you will.'

TWENTY-ONE

She was gone when I woke up but she'd left a note propped against one of my splendid new Dubuque bank cups. *What was that tapping outside in the middle of the night? I shook you awake. You said 'lizards,' and went right back to sleep! Surely lizards can't tap! Lovely fire. A.*

The morning was warm enough for al fresco thinking. I brought my phone, coffee and, in desperation, one of the hardening prune *kolachkys* down to the bench by the river.

I called Weasel but his phone had been set to switch immediately to voice messaging. 'Today's the day, Weasel,' I said anyway. 'We go to see the boy's mother.'

I leaned back to watch the river. The Willahock had never been pristine. From the earliest days, entrepreneurs and gangsters up and down the river had used it as a drain. But that March, there seemed to be an increase in the volume of plastic trash floating by. Some said it was a freeing of debris caught in ice jams melting upriver. More saw it as the natural result of the mayor's cousin – a man whose trucks never left Rivertown – recently being awarded the city's recycling pick-up contract.

I nibbled at the crumbling lard at the edges of the small pastry and threw the dried prune center into the river. It sank in an instant, a mercy to my eyes, though I supposed it posed a threat to the whiskered fish that probed the muck at the bottom.

I mulled over what to do about Herbie, and then I mulled some more. And then I was sure enough. I headed up to the turret, to my computer and my printer, and for the next hour I played with formats and fonts and lies. When the lies were printed sufficiently, I hurried down to the Jeep.

There was much to do to keep Herbie Sunheim alive.

Rickey Means' law practice address was an unmarked storefront sandwiched between a currency exchange and a place that sold rejuvenating skin-care products and janitorial supplies. Inside, six women wearing headsets sat behind a noisily vibrating soda-can machine.

'Rickey Means?' I inquired of the woman closest to the front. She seemed calm, despite her proximity to a compressor sounding like it was about to fire out a baseball-sized steel bearing.

Her phone rang and she held up a forefinger for silence, as if that were possible. 'Appleton Insurance,' she said loudly. And then, 'Yes,' 'No,' and 'Yes,' before hanging up. Turning to me, she said, 'Huh?'

'Rickey Means. This is his law office, right?' I asked, with what I hoped was a straight face.

'Who?' she asked, but she didn't look startled. She knew the name.

'Rickey Means, the lawyer?'

Her phone buzzed again, and again she held up a finger for silence. Answering as a towing service, she asked, 'What year?' Typing into her keyboard, she said, 'One hundred, cash.' Followed by, 'We'll be there by eleven.'

She sent off the email and looked up at me. 'You were saying?'

'Perhaps Mr Means is not in?'

'We just absorb his mail and messages.'

I handed her a business-sized envelope to absorb. 'This is information he requested.'

She looked at the return address I'd so cleverly computer-printed on the envelope. 'Thank you, Mr Sunheim.'

'Call me Herbie,' I said, and left.

Walter Dace's office went quicker because, like on my earlier visits, no phones were ringing when I stepped in. The receptionist cutie had finished with her fingernails and looked bored, at least until she recognized me. She buzzed Dace like she was stabbing a spider.

'I forgot to ask the last time I was here,' I called in, opening the glass door as he charged out of his office. 'Your bow tie . . . did you tie it yourself, or is it one of those pre-tied jobs, perhaps a clip-on?'

'Out!' he said, marching forward.

'Pre-tieds are cheating, like Velcro instead of laces on shoes,' I said, handing him another of the white letter-sized envelopes. 'I tie mine from scratch,' I prattled, 'though I have to consult that YouTube video we chatted about the last time I was here.'

'Sunheim?' he asked, looking down at the envelope. His confusion was encouraging.

'You remember Herbie, right? He considers you one of his dearest friends, I think.'

'What the hell are you talking about?'

'Herbie Sunheim, your realtor? The guy you turn to for all Triple Time's commercial real estate needs?'

He touched one of the wings of his bow tie, perhaps seeking comfort. It was another gesture I found encouraging.

'He asked that I drop it off,' I said, 'for you and the Triple Time folks. By the way, who are those folks exactly?'

His face paled. That was most encouraging of all.

'I've gotten no word from him, I told you!' Violet Krumfeld's face reddened beneath her rouge as she attempted to yell.

'Not to worry,' I said. 'I have.'

'Thank God.' She slumped back, her flush fading in relief. 'Why can't he call me? What am I supposed to tell his witch wife? She calls two, three times a day, screaming that she's a co-owner of the business, demanding that I send her the checkbook. I tell her if I could sign checks on that account, I'd write a big one for myself, for all the worry he's caused me the last few days. All she says is "What? What?" like she's hard of hearing.' She took a breath and asked, 'So where is the jerk?'

'He didn't say. He phoned me last night, said for me to drop this off and that he'd be in touch.' I handed her the white letter envelope. 'For the Triple Time file,' I said.

'There's that name again,' she said. 'I told you, we got no file for them.'

She opened the envelope. Unlike the records I dummied up with Herbie's letterhead to leave at Mean's answering service and Dace's office, listing too many visits I'd supposedly made to each Triple Time property, the sheet I made for Violet Krumfeld was an invoice on my own letterhead.

'An invoice for your time, Mister Retainer?' She contorted her face into a laugh.

'As I said, for the Triple Time file,' I said. 'That buyer you keep saying you've never heard of.'

'How come you don't ask Herbie if I've ever heard of it, huh?' She looked at me with unblinking eyes, the brushes of her eyelashes staying up high and accusing. 'And this?' she asked, holding up my phony invoice. 'I don't imagine he's going to pay you anytime soon for anything. And if he gets around to asking me, I'll tell him I don't know what you're up to except trying to find him.'

I looked past her to Herbie's desk, which was now as empty as hers. 'What do you do all day?' I asked.

'Answer dumb questions, every time you call. When is His Lordship coming to the office?'

'He didn't say.'

'When you talk to him next, ask him when I'm going to get paid. I got bills.'

I started to go, but then turned back, feeling too much like too big a crumb. 'You know what, Violet?'

Her eyes widened behind her glasses. 'What?' she whispered.

'You ought to look for another job.'

Her eyes stayed wide. 'I . . . I thought he was coming in soon.'

'He's staying away; his wife wants to take what he's got and divorce him, and you haven't been paid. You're sitting here all day with nothing to do. That's reason enough to quit.'

'There's seven grand in the checking account. He owes me.'

'Maybe he'll never pay either one of us again.'

'Ask him, will you? Ask him when he's coming in?' Her face was starting to scrunch up, like she was going to cry.

I gave her what I could manage of a smile and left.

TWENTY-TWO

Herbie's soon-to-be ex-wife's soon-to-be ex-Escalade was parked at her curb. The doors were unlocked and the key was in the ignition.

'It's almost out of gas,' a voice called from behind me. And then she said, 'Oh . . . you. I thought you were from the dealer to repo the car.'

'Have you missed any payments?'

'I called them. I want it gone. They said I have to pay because my name is on the lease. I said the bastard forged my signature and they had to talk to Herbie. They said they're not handwriting experts and since both our names were on the lease along with signatures, I was responsible, same as him. I said I'd leave the doors open and the key in the ignition.'

'They won't pick it up. There's a contract, forged signature or not. After you've missed a few payments, they'll send somebody to pick it up and then sue you for the thousands they'll say they can't recover in selling the vehicle.'

'I told them the thing's going to get stolen.'

'After you left it unlocked with the keys in the ignition? They'll say you're negligent. Best you make the payments yourself.'

'We don't have the money,' she said, her voice breaking just a little.

'Then how did Herbie get you a Cadillac?'

'He was sucking up, trying to keep things going. I told him no dice.'

I walked up and handed her the envelope. 'Herbie wanted me to drop this off here,' I said of the same dummied-up invoice that I'd left with Violet Krumfeld.

'Why bring it here?'

'It's what he said.'

She looked at me like she was looking at a liar, which was true enough. 'You're telling me you talked to him?'

'OK, maybe not about this specifically, but I need to get paid.'

'Me, too, pal.'

'The best thing for both of us is if I brace him, face-to-face.'

She shook her head, unwilling to give me the whereabouts she'd given Kopek and Jacks.

I pointed to the For Sale sign stuck in the ground. 'The house is owned jointly by you and your husband?'

'And the bank, big time. We got a mortgage.'

'You put the place up for sale after he moved out?'

'I told him that was the next step. I'm cashing out.'

'You're angry about the Escalade?' I asked, of the obvious.

'And a lot more than that.'

'You threw him out?'

'Bet your ass,' she said. 'But not just because of that damned Escalade.'

'Selling this place is going to be another pesky problem for you, and one that I can make worse,' I said. 'You need his signature for the sale to go through. Even if you forge it on a sales contract, like he did with your signature for the Escalade, I can stop you from collecting if I put a lien on his assets.' I was blowing smoke through a hat, but the lies were flowing fast out of me now, like they were greased.

I gave her a moment to mull that, and then said, 'You told the cops where he is. Tell me.'

'He's never there,' she said.

'Give me the address anyway.'

Still she held out. She didn't want me to get at Herbie before she could get her own hooks onto his wallet. And that was enough to convince me that she, along with the purple plate man, had nothing to do with Herbie's murder. The woman didn't know she'd become the Widow Sunheim.

'Maybe I can get him to sign something saying you had nothing to do with contracting for that Escalade,' I coaxed.

'Ah, hell, stucco house off Ogden Avenue in Brookfield,' the poor woman said, giving me the address she must have given Kopek.

I told her I'd be in touch and started down the block toward the Jeep.

'But he's never there,' she called out after me.
I didn't doubt that at all.

The white two-story residence in Brookfield looked to be like any
of the tens of thousands of ordinary homes in Chicagoland that
rented out a room or two without the troublesome involvement of
a tax man or a health inspector. It was on a quiet, tree-lined street,
two blocks south of a major east-west drag.

A fiftyish, gray-haired woman in a yellow floral housedress
answered the door. I gave her one of my cards, and said I'd come
to see Herbie about an insurance matter. She said he hadn't been
around for a few days, adding, 'I think he's hiding from the wife.'

'Mind if I take a look at his room?'

'Absolutely not!' she said.

'But he's owed,' I said, lying to yet another unsuspecting woman.

'He's in arrears,' she said.

'An insurance settlement might help with that,' I said, to my
shame.

'Cops were here, looking for him, too,' she said, no doubt of
Kopek and Jacks.

'That wouldn't have been about insurance,' I said.

'They said it was about parking tickets. He's owed money, you
say?'

'A large settlement. Anyone else come looking for him?' I asked,
thinking of his killer.

'I don't always answer the door myself. People come to visit
that I don't know about.'

'It would help if I could see his room. We need to find him so
we can pay.'

She shook her head, but it was slowly.

'He's in arrears, you said?' I said then.

'Just a week's rent, but still . . .'

'You could file a lien on the insurance payout.' It was indeed
a shameful day, tossing lien lies around with abandon. 'You
wouldn't even need a lawyer, just fill out a form, but first I need
to check his room for ideas as to where he might have gone.'

Once again, greed proved to be the best grease. She led me up
the stairs to the second floor. His room was at the back, on the
left. She produced keys, unlocked the door, and made to go in
ahead of me.

I quickly stepped in front of her. 'I've done this before. Best you let me look alone, so there's no liability issue. Why don't you go downstairs, write down what you're owed, and add in the next two weeks for good measure?'

She fairly skipped – or would have, if she'd been younger – down the stairs, and I went in.

The room was immaculate. The bed was wrinkle-free, there was no dust on the headboard or the dresser, and the tiny chair was properly squared to the small table. The room had been recently cleaned by an inquisitive landlady, looking for anything of value she could hold hostage for rent.

I felt through the socks and underwear in the dresser and found not even lint. The pockets were empty in the one suit hanging in the closet. Three once-white, now-yellowed dress shirts hung on hangers next to it, and two neckties, both striped, both spotted, were looped on another hanger next to them. There were no shoes, no sports clothes. The man seemed to have had nothing, and yet he'd leased his wife a Cadillac. Then again, he might have left most of his stuff back at his house, thinking his rented room days would be temporary. Perhaps he hadn't known about the man selling purple paper plates.

I felt for tape beneath the dresser drawers, and ran my hand between the box spring and the mattress. Kneeling down to look under the bed, I spotted a few specks of white paint, tiny flakes against the white baseboard, where the woman's vacuum cleaner wouldn't find them unless she moved the bed first. They were odd, those flakes, in a protected spot where they shouldn't have been chipped loose.

I pressed against the baseboard and felt it jiggle. I lay on my belly so I could see beneath the bed, and pressed again. More little specks of paint fell on the carpet.

I worked my fingers along the top of the baseboard. It loosened and came out an inch – enough to slip my fingers in deeper. A faint pull brought a four-foot section away from the wall. There were no nails holding it, but the nail holes were white and sticky. Someone, likely clever Herbie, had recently filled the nail holes with toothpaste.

The house was old, built in the days when craftsmen smoothed real plaster on slats of wood lath. Removing the baseboard exposed a gap between the bottom of the plaster and the top of the wood flooring. The cavity was filled with edges of paper, tightly crammed in. They were packets, set in length-wise. I wiggled one out. It was a packet of hundred dollar bills. Fanning it, I guessed there were a hundred bills, to make a total of ten thousand dollars.

I pulled out thirty packets before my fingers could find no more – three hundred thousand dollars in all. Or maybe there was only two hundred and ninety-nine thousand, since Herbie had likely removed ten of the hundreds to send to me.

I pressed the baseboard back in place, did what I could to brush the paint flecks up against the wall, and stood up. I jammed the cash into the inside and outside pockets of my peacoat and the pockets of my khakis. Most had to go inside my blue button-down shirt, by my belly. I sauntered downstairs clutching the front of my coat tight to my gut, opened the front door and almost made it out.

'Hey!' the landlady yelled. 'My accounting!' She thrust a sheet of paper around from behind me.

'Bad back,' I mumbled, to explain my contorted posture. I grabbed the paper fast and clutched it to my stomach.

'Find anything useful?' she asked.

I eased outside, stepping carefully down the cement stairs so that ten or twenty or thirty thousand dollars wouldn't tumble out from my coat, or my pants, or my shirt.

'Superior neatness,' I called back.

Weasel called as I was driving back to the turret.

'It's all set for ten o'clock tonight,' he said, but he said it softly, tentatively. Then again, I'd slammed him up against the side of his house when we'd last met.

'What's the address, Weasel?'

'Like I said, it's in Austin,' he said, giving me a house number on North Livermoor.

'Why so late?' Austin was one of the worst of the bad crime districts in Chicago. Lives didn't count for much there, especially at night.

'Maybe she works late.'

'She said that?'

'Ten o'clock.'

'I'll pick you up at nine-thirty.'

'Just you. I'm not feeling well.'

'We go together. The mother won't know me.'

'She don't know me either, remember? All I did was pick up her kid at a bus stop. Anyway, I described your Jeep – red and green. Make sure you park in front so she can see you.' He repeated the street number on North Livermoor.

'Nine-thirty sharp,' I said.

'I won't be here.'

'Then I'll hunt you down.'

'Nobody wants to be out in Austin that late.'

'A kid is missing. We go together tonight.'

TWENTY-THREE

Weasel's house was dark. I expected that. But his car, an aged Taurus, was parked at the curb. If I hadn't been so nervous about heading into Austin I would have laughed at him hiding in such plain sight.

I tapped on his basement window and got no response. I tapped louder. Still no response.

'I'm going to break the window and come in,' I yelled through the glass.

That got a muffled yell back and, a moment later, the slam of a rear door.

'No problem setting this up, Weasel?' I asked when he finally materialized in the gangway, coming from the back of his house.

'I told you, I'm not feeling good,' he said, mumbling. Even in the dim moonlight, I could see his face was pasty, about the same color as the milk inside the quart carton he was carrying.

We started toward the Jeep, which I'd parked behind his heap, but a sudden thought stopped me. 'The mother knows we're coming, right?'

'Why are you questioning?'

'As you said, nobody wants to go into Austin after dark. I want to make sure this is solid.'

'Solid,' he said, looking away. He opened the carton and took a swallow of the milk.

'What's with all the milk, Weasel?'

'Ulcer or something.'

I took it for understandable nervousness. He got in the passenger's seat, I got behind the wheel and we headed to Austin, where nobody wanted to be after dark.

According to Chicago's police superintendent, the Austin district on the west side was one of the toughest places to stay alive in the city. According to the news, gangbangers and innocents got shot there, in roughly equal numbers, every week. According to Amanda, who saw the link, black youth unemployment in Austin exceeded eighty percent.

We took Chicago Avenue east through Oak Park, turned south a couple of blocks and then headed east again past Leamington, LeClaire and Latrobe, passing dark block after dark block. A quarter of the houses were boarded up. Another quarter were simply gone, burned or crumbled and pushed away.

But there were signs – literally signs – put up by those who lived in the houses that still stood lit against the night. Hand-lettered, four-by-eight sheets of plywood stood at the head of many of the blocks, listing rules: no washing cars in the streets, no bare chests, no congregating on the sidewalks. No idling, no hanging around. And sure as hell, the signs read, no dealing, no dealing a damned thing. Folks who lived in those ruined blocks were attempting to take back, trying to wrest their neighborhoods from the twitchy gun fingers of the gangbangers that prowled their streets.

Weasel was growing agitated beside me. 'I don't like this at all,' he said, gulping at the milk. 'There ain't many lights.'

'It's late. Shades are pulled, drapes are drawn.'

'Houses are gone.'

We came to Livermoor. As I turned south, he said, 'Best if you walk up from the next corner. I'll keep the engine running in case we got to vamoose fast.'

I shot a glance at him. 'I don't see how that's going to help.'

'I'll leave the passenger door wide open.' He reached to touch the steering wheel.

I slammed on the brakes. 'Damn it, Weasel!'

'It's in the middle of the next block. I don't want to be waiting for you to open the damned door.'

His hand shook as he pulled it away. He was petrified. So was I.

There were too many burn-downs, too many board-ups. It was a war zone.

I took a breath. Maybe the weasel was making sense. Things could go wrong fast in that neighborhood, and the quicker I could dive into a running car, the safer I'd be. I stopped at the corner and got out. He slid behind the wheel.

The street lamp was dark, perhaps burned out, more likely shot out by young gunslingers readying themselves for livelier targets. Only the Jeep's headlamps lit the intersection.

I stayed with them, crossing the side street and into the next block. The lot on the corner was vacant; its home scraped away. The house beyond it was boarded up.

Weasel sped up. I hurried along the sidewalk, trying to keep up, but Weasel was getting too nervous. He was a hundred feet ahead now. Some lamps showed faintly behind covered windows across the street. It was not hard to imagine a hundred eyes behind them, watching my shadow, fearful, afraid or angry for the fool on foot following the Jeep, exposed. My side of the street was dark.

Weasel stopped. The house immediately ahead was boarded up, and that was wrong. From what I could tell in the dark, it had the right street number. It was where I was supposed to be.

Gunfire lit the night, fast shots fired from the street. Glass shattered as Weasel gunned the Jeep and sped down the street. I could only duck and run into the gangway alongside the boarded-up house. Car tires squealed, farther away.

The night went silent too soon, accepting. No doors banged open, no screams of outrage shouted out. Only my footsteps sounded in that black night, pounding on the crumbling gangway out to the alley in back.

I turned and ran north up the alley, parallel to the street I'd just walked up, to the side street I'd crossed just minutes before. I stopped. Weasel, if he had any fiber left in his soul, would double back around with the passenger door banging open, to find me and speed me away.

The night stayed silent.

A minute passed, and then another, and then a car engine began growing louder in the distance. I moved up to the curb. The night stayed dark; he was approaching without headlamps – smart, to avoid being seen – just as I would have done.

The engine was loud now, too loud. It was too powerful to be the Jeep's. I ran back into the alley and dropped down behind a trash barrel next to a garage a hundred feet back.

The engine rumbled up and slowed, approaching the alley. Turning in, the driver switched on his high beams, lighting it up as if it were noon. I pressed tight against the barrel and held my breath; any movement would be magnified in that glare. He stopped, his engine idling strong, a man with a gun. I dared not look.

A moment passed, and another, and then he gave it up. He backed into the street and drove slowly away. Finally, the engine grew faint enough for me to hear my own breathing. I got up from behind the trash barrel.

I felt for my phone, then realized I'd left it in the Jeep's cup holder.

There were no other motor sounds in that night. Weasel Wurder, the bastard, was likely miles away.

I'd die if I stayed in those blocks, not just from gunmen looking for me but from roving gangbangers drawn by the sound of gunfire, looking to fight, rob, or worse. I hurried north across the side street and into the next alley, half-running, half-walking, trying for silence but knowing every footfall pounded loud, like a drum beat in the silence of that night.

I crossed another side street, and then another, and then the alley dead-ended at Chicago Avenue, the main east-west drag we'd taken to Austin and the same street where Weasel had picked up the kid at a bus stop, to bring him to me. That bus stop was in Oak Park, safely to the west. A bus headed there had to be coming along at some point.

It was almost eleven o'clock. The stores that still struggled along that part of Chicago Avenue were closed up tight for the night, their recessed doorways barricaded flush by thick accordion fences. I moved west in their shadows, looking for a place to hide and wait. Two blocks up, I came to a burned-out storefront that nobody had cared enough to barricade. It would have to do. I stepped in through the smashed front window.

A car passed, heading east into Chicago, but it passed fast. No driver wanted any business with anyone out in that neighborhood after dark.

Ten, fifteen minutes went by. Two more cars sped by, one going into the city, one going west. Neither stopped for the red lights at the intersection. Not even traffic laws applied to that stretch of Chicago Avenue, come darkness.

And then I heard it – a bus coming from the east – but it was coming too fast. I jumped through the broken window just as it shot by, and I ran after it, yelling, as it lumbered into the next block. Somehow the driver heard, or saw. He stopped suddenly in the middle of the block. The door hissed open, and I ran up the two steps.

'What the hell?' the driver shouted, shutting the doors and starting up without waiting for me to get a hand safely on the rail. He was older, black, gray-haired.

I looked down the aisle. His only passenger was an old black woman halfway down, clutching a worn cloth shopping bag, sound asleep.

'Oak Park?' I asked.

'Sit the hell down behind me and stay low,' he said. 'I don't need no damned white man drawing fire into my bus.'

'How much?' I asked, dropping down behind him.

'Forget the damned fare. Just stay low.'

He drove on for a mile before he spoke. 'Damn, man, ain't nobody up to any good out in that neighborhood this late. Nobody black, sure as hell nobody white.'

'I was waiting inside a store.'

'Uh huh,' he said, nodding but not believing. 'Ain't no stores open there, this time of night.'

'This one suffered a fire.'

'That don't narrow it down.'

'There's a cab stand in Oak Park?'

'Ain't no cabs be prowlin' this late, even in fancy neighborhoods. You got a phone?'

'Left it in the car,' I said, in what surely was one of the grandest understatements in my life.

'You are one crazy man, for sure.'

We drove another block. 'You want a cab?' he asked.

'I surely do.'

He pulled out his phone, tapped a number or an app and mumbled an order for a cab to be waiting at the Harlem Avenue intersection, with the meter running, and we drove on in silence: him thinking I was crazy; me thinking I was crazy; and the old woman asleep in the back, likely thinking nothing at all, all the way to Oak Park.

*   *   *

I had the cabbie run past Weasel's place first. His Taurus was parked at the curb and my Jeep wasn't. The rat's basement windows were dark.

I was too tired to break in and look for his throat on the off-chance he was hiding inside, so I had the cabbie drive me to the turret next. That the Jeep wasn't there was no surprise, either.

My house key was dangling in the Jeep's ignition somewhere, so there were two choices for a third stop. One was Leo's ma's bungalow. He had a key to the turret but might be at his girlfriend's condo downtown. In any event, I'd likely wake his mother.

There was a surer option to get in the turret, and one that was necessary anyway. I had the cabbie drive me to the city garage across town. It was now past two o'clock in the morning, but Booster Gibbs and his crew would be in full swing, stripping cars that bore bullet holes or troublesome vehicle identification numbers, and simply cleansing others of less worrisome blood-stains or fingerprints.

I paid the cabbie and walked up to tap on the side door. The metal plate covering the small window slid back, and one of Booster's eyes appeared on the other side. He stepped outside.

As usual, he was garbed head to toe, cap to booties, in green surgical duds, purple latex surgical gloves and a full white face mask that covered his enormous beard. Booster, like his crew, took obsessive care to leave nothing of himself in the cars he was working on.

He looked down the driveway at the curb. 'Don't see that fine Jeep I topped,' he said, referring to the green top he'd installed some months earlier.

'It's elsewhere, but I don't know where, exactly. It's why I'm here.'

'Unpleasant circumstances?'

'Gunplay in Austin. Weasel Wurder was behind the wheel—'

'That creep,' he interrupted. Like me, he'd gone to school with Weasel.

'I need you to send a crew to find my Jeep.'

'Cops looking, too?' he asked, so he'd know whether to dispatch a fenced flatbed truck with a tarp, or just a car.

'Not yet, but I'm not sure.'

'What's the potential that Weasel will be inside?'

'I heard glass shattering. He could have gotten hit, but he drove away.'

'The windshield's the only glass you got besides headlamps.' Then, 'You were out of the vehicle, on foot?'

I nodded.

'That creep,' he said again. 'There's a chance he set you up . . .?'

'I'm trying not to make that a conclusion.' I told him to start on North Livermore, south of Chicago Avenue.

'Hundred bucks an hour OK?'

I gave him five hundred of Herbie's C-notes. 'If you find Weasel shot, tip the cops anonymously. If not, flatbed the Jeep back to you for a cleanse or more, depending on the nature of what you find.'

He didn't bother to ask if I had an ignition key, because Booster liked to say he found them needlessly time-consuming. He got his nickname for his prowess in hotwiring cars.

'I also need a ride from a lock man,' I said.

'Your turret keys being inside your Jeep, of course.'

Booster's man was proficient. He picked my lock and had the door open with a flourish in seconds.

I barred the door behind me, and hobbled up the stairs to the second floor and the card table I use as a desk, thinking to call Weasel. And then I remembered that I'd given up my landline months before to save expenses.

As for the next, last minutes of that night, I don't remember hobbling up the next flight of stairs to bed at all.

TWENTY-FOUR

A banging on the timbered door woke me at nine-thirty the next morning. Violet Krumfeld stood outside in the too-bright sun.

Right in front of my Jeep.

'Why don't you answer your phone?' she said, somewhat audibly.

'I didn't hear it ring,' I said, trying to look beyond her to see whether the Jeep had suffered anything incriminating, like bullet holes or a shattered windshield. Or both.

'Know why?' she asked, stepping closer to block my view.

I could only shake my head. I needed more sleep and I needed more peace, and for sure I needed to get to my Jeep, to see what it would tell. But more than anything at that moment, I wanted to step back inside the turret and bar the door, in case anyone who'd prowled about in Austin the previous night had the thought they might see me better in Rivertown in the light of the new day.

She held up her own cell phone, thumbed in a number and smiled. A phone rang behind her. It was my phone, inside my Jeep.

'What are you up to?' she asked, I thought.

I rubbed my eyes to signify that she'd woken me up.

'I tried calling you until midnight,' she said, summoning up a rouge-cracking smirk. 'Late night?'

'Working for Herbie, day and night,' I said, taking a more comfortable step back into the gloom of the turret.

'I'm sure,' I think she said, stepping forward uninvited. 'I have questions. Do you have coffee?'

For such a mouse, she was persistent. I invited her in because she was already in. After barring the door, I started to lead her up to the second-floor kitchen.

'What's with the bar on the door?' she said behind me.

'I anger people occasionally.'

She offered no objection to that, and began to follow. Then she stopped.

I turned around. She was clutching the railing on the second step. 'It's loose,' she murmured of the gently trembling wrought-iron staircase.

'For almost a century without collapsing.'

She hurried up behind me and followed me into the kitchen.

'Plywood for a table,' she said, waving the hand that sported the welded purple ring. 'Charming.'

I filled the other two cups Amanda had bought me and set them on the charming plywood.

'Aren't you going to warm the coffee in the microwave, at least?' she asked.

'My microwave leaks radiation,' I said, which was true, but mostly I wanted her and her nose gone so I could get at the Jeep. Booster's day had ended, so there was no chance to talk to him until nightfall, but it was likely Weasel's day hadn't yet begun, at home, and I wanted to slap his head.

We sat down. She didn't bother to taste the coffee, which was just as well since it was already two days old and hadn't been any good when it was fresh.

'So, working for Herbie until the wee hours?' she asked.

I nodded, lifting my cup to savor the chill of the coffee.

She sighed. 'At least he's talking to someone, even if the jerk won't call me for messages.'

'He's getting messages?' I asked, trying to sound casual.

'Which is why I had to drive out here.'

'You drove all the way out from the city to deliver Herbie's messages?'

'Just one.' She pushed her thick-lensed glasses farther up her nose. 'And to find out what's going on, but I'll start with a message. CSB called the office yesterday.'

'CSB, the railroad conglomerate?' I asked, like I hadn't triggered the call.

'A man said Herbie called, inquiring about the routing of a certain railcar. The man wouldn't say which railcar, exactly, but we sort of know, don't we, Mister Retainer Elstrom?'

'The Central Works one,' I said, because there were limits to how stupid I wanted to look.

'Of course, Central Works. The place where some unfortunate man was found dead on top of a boxcar. The place you keep asking me about. You and the cops.'

'To be fair, I've started asking you about other properties.'

'Yes! Those other places owned by that, ah . . .'

'Triple Time Partners,' I said. 'Investors you say you've never heard of.'

'Yeah, well, since Herbie seems able to talk to you and call CSB, he ought to be able to call me,' she said, watching my eyes.

'Give me the name of the CSB person.'

'You're not going to tell me anything, are you?'

'Not yet,' I said, standing up. It was time for the woman to leave.

'Then I don't have to tell you what Mrs Sunheim called me about this morning?'

I sat back down.

'She called first thing. She said two cops stopped by as she was heading out the door to go to work. She thinks one of them was the one who'd called her at work before, asking about Herbie's current living arrangements. She'd told him then that Herbie had rented a room and didn't live with her anymore, and gave him the address so he could see for himself.'

'Kopek and Jacks, your strudel friends,' I said.

'I described them to her and it was them who stopped by this morning, all right. Know what they wanted?'

'I'm hoping you'll tell me.'

'They wanted to come in her house for a look around.'

'For what?'

'For any sorts of clues as to what Herbie was mixed up in. They said they received reports that people were worried that Herbie was in trouble. She told them to go scratch, that Herbie was just dodging her so he wouldn't have to pay her anything or go through with the divorce. She said they had to have a warrant to get in her house.'

Violet gave a pronounced nod and raised her eyebrows.

'There's more?' I asked.

'Herbie's wife said an insurance guy who works for Herbie stopped by again yesterday, bugging her for what she already gave the cops.'

'Which was what?' I asked, needing the maddening woman to be precise.

'Come on, Elstrom.'

'You mean the address of Herbie's rented room? The cops had already been there, according to the landlady. Herbie wasn't there. His room was as neat as a pin.'

'You learned nothing?'

'Nothing there even points to him being alive,' I said, because technically, it was true.

She stood up, handed me a pink phone message slip and headed for the stairs. I followed her as she clutched her way down, and I walked her out the door.

A Chevy Volt was parked behind the Jeep. It had a ridiculous decal in the rear window – an index finger raised to the lips of a round cartoon head, making a shushing motion.

It made sense, her driving an electric car as noiseless as she was.

What made worse sense was the black Impala that started up behind her on Thompson Avenue, following her east toward the city.

TWENTY-FIVE

From the door, it appeared that no bullets had punctured my glass or vinyl or paint. Nor did it appear that anyone was lurking nearby. I walked out to the Jeep.

The keys were under the seat. The carpet was damp. The car had been cleansed, shampooed top to bottom, fingerprints and bloodstains – if any – scrubbed away. For sure it had been Booster's crew, and not Weasel, who'd brought the car back.

I grabbed my phone from the Jeep's cup holder, beat it back into the turret and up to the kitchen and my crummy coffee. I thumbed in Weasel's number. As I expected, it went straight to voicemail. 'How the hell did the shooters know I'd be at that address, Weasel?' I shouted, though it was to nobody at all.

Next I called the number Violet had written on the pink message slip. The man who'd called Herbie's office from CSB was named Hanson. He was in the railroad conglomerate's insurance department.

'You spoke to one of my associates yesterday, Mr Sunheim,' he said.

'He said someone else would call me back,' I said, because that, at least, was true.

'The number you called from yesterday was blocked, like today, so we found your office number and called there instead. We can't be too careful. The newspapers suggested we are a bunch of nincompoops who can't keep track of our rolling stock.'

'I'm cautious, too,' I said, though my caution came from wanting to avoid discovery as a fraud.

'You told us yesterday that you represent the buyer of the old Central Works,' he said.

'Only in the actual purchase of the property. I'm the realtor.'

'Nonetheless, I'm sure we have the same objective.'

'Limited liability,' I said. 'You don't want there to be any hint of negligence. Neither do I.'

He forced a chuckle, one empathetic negligence-avoider to another. 'How may I help you?'

'What was your railcar doing at that abandoned factory?'

'Surely your building owner told you it was routed there as per his instructions.'

'My owner has become extremely reticent, given all the publicity surrounding the discovery of the deceased,' I said. 'What was shipped there?'

'Your owner must tell you that.'

'Can you give me the name of the shipper?'

'We don't release information about our customers, but I will tell you we left it exactly where requested.'

'Directly alongside the building, so it could be unloaded.'

'Of course.'

'And then it was moved to the end of the rail spur,' I said.

'I'd planned on sending a man there to find proof that someone else had moved it without our permission, but the building burned down before he could get there. The building rubble is gone, and the ground around it and the tracks has been freshly graded. That's a shame.'

'Photos wouldn't help you,' I said.

'Our legal people think there's a chance the victim was put on top after the boxcar was moved.'

'How would that matter?'

'They're lawyers. No one understands how lawyers think, not even other lawyers.'

'The medical examiner will examine the body for signs it was dropped from higher up and they'll find them, because that building is the only one around.'

'Of course.' He sighed. 'We pay our law department big money for such obvious advice.'

'I have photos of deep tire ruts in the ground and fresh scratches on the rails. Both indicate that the boxcar was towed to the end of the spur by a fat-tired, big horsepower off-road vehicle.'

'Those might be interesting, if they help point to a perpetrator. Send them to me.'

'And so I ask again: what was in the shipment?'

'Very large, very expensive, and apparently very fragile kitchen fixtures,' he said without hesitation. 'The shipper told the purchaser that routing the boxcar directly to the rail siding would be more expensive than having the goods picked up at the rail yard and redelivered by truck, but the purchaser wanted to minimize the risk of damage from double-handling.'

'The building was slated to become a restaurant?'

'I guess so, but now that the building's been destroyed, we'll probably never know.'

'The shipment's intact, still in the railcar?' I asked.

'No. The police told us the boxcar was empty when they discovered the body. Everything must have been already loaded into the building and lost in the fire. We're waiting for the police to release our car so we can take it away.'

I didn't tell him that the shipment hadn't been lost, that I'd been in the Central Works just before the fire and that it had been empty. Nor did I mention Walter Dace saying he'd never cared about the Central Works building, that it was scheduled for demolition. Dace wasn't a clever liar. Shipping new fixtures to a building meant to go down obviously made no sense, just as scrubbing away its graffiti made no sense. I told Hanson I'd email him the pictures of the tire ruts and hung up.

I kept an eagle's eye on the rearview as I drove to Weasel's, but no one followed. I tried to think that meant the gunfire in Austin might have been ordinary night play in that neighborhood, but pushed those thoughts away. That kind of relaxed thinking could get me killed.

Weasel's car was still parked in front of his house. The basement bulb was still off. I called his phone from the Jeep, and got routed to voicemail like before.

I walked up and tapped on the glass. I got no response. I tapped harder. Still, there was no response. By all appearances, Weasel was not home, which might have been precisely the appearance he desired.

I went around back to bang on the kitchen door. He didn't answer, the weasel.

I tried the knob. It turned easily.

'Weasel?' I called in. When there was no response, I shouted it: 'Weasel!'

I went in.

Despite it being early March, the kitchen was as humid as a sweltering dog day in August. Ancient gray vinyl wallpaper curled at the tops of the walls, a likely tip that snow had melted in, and down from the roof all winter.

The plastic garbage basket in the kitchen was overflowing. A capped, half-full plastic half-gallon of milk sat on a counter stacked with dirty plates and bowls. The top plate was covered with yellow noodles. I poked at them with one of the dirty forks lying on the counter. The noodles were soft, not yet dried. They could have been that morning's breakfast, I allowed, because that's how my mind and stomach worked – anything goes at dawn. Or they could have been last night's late dinner, after he'd returned from Austin.

And that led me to wonder how, if Weasel had made it home, he'd gotten there. Seeing the Jeep returned to the turret, freshly cleansed and unmarked by bullet holes, meant not only that Booster Gibbs had found it wherever Weasel had left it, but that Weasel had not gotten caught by gunfire, at least not while driving. And that pointed to him as a delivery man, where the item to be delivered was me. He might well have set me up to approach that abandoned property on foot, in a neighborhood where a few gunshots would not arouse any real interest.

I walked through the first floor, but that wasn't where Weasel lived. It was where he stored. The living room, dining room and the two bedrooms were piled with bicycles and tricycles, small kitchen appliances, cheap wristwatches in small boxes and what seemed to be a thousand other items. Empty Amazon, Kohl's, Target, and Wal-Mart shipping cartons were strewn everywhere. All had names and addresses of people who lived in Chicago. Weasel supplemented his legal fees by cruising neighborhoods to snatch from sidewalks and doorsteps.

The basement had a washtub, but no washing machine or clothes dryer. A bedroom of sorts had been fashioned behind a partition made of wood studs and mildewed fiberboard. The single bed was unmade and filthy. The dresser looked to have been hurriedly emptied, its four open drawers containing only a couple of black T-shirts, one pair of ripped men's briefs, and two socks, one orange, one brown. A beige suit, a red shirt and a dozen empty hangers dangled from a metal clothing rack on wheels. More empty hangers lay on the cement floor, as if clothes had been tugged away in panic.

The unlocked back door, the food left out to spoil and the ripped away clothes all pointed to Weasel fleeing the house in fear.

Except that his rusted Taurus was still parked at the curb.

TWENTY-SIX

left Weasel's hovel and drove into the city, to Dace's office. Only the man fronting for the Triple Time Partners could explain how a building slated for demolition needed a boxcar full of restaurant fixtures, or why it had been fitted with new electrical conduit, or why it needed to be torched and blown away, or why the thing hadn't been pushed over in the first place, as he'd told the fire chief it was slated to be, or who was responsible for unloading the railcar before the fire.

And probably only he could say why Herbie Sunheim, his realtor, and Rickey Means, his real estate lawyer, had been killed, but I didn't expect to catch anything from him on that, either.

I opened the hall door, took one step inside, and stopped.

The glass wall lay shattered in a wide line of a thousand sparkling bits on the floor. Crazily, its glass door was still intact and leaned open against the side wall. I walked up close enough to see all the way inside.

Gunfire had done it. The receptionist had caught several bullets in the chest, likely fired from outside the glass wall, with enough force to knock her backwards, out of her chair and onto her back on the floor. Shards of glass lay on top of her and in the glistening, still-growing puddle of blood seeping out from beneath her. It hadn't happened very much earlier.

Her keyboard and screen rested on her desk, but their cords dangled unconnected. Her computer was gone.

Walter Dace had tied his last bow tie. He lay face down in his office doorway, shot multiple times in the back. It wasn't hard to imagine: he'd lurched halfway out of his office, drawn by the crash of shattering glass and perhaps the unfamiliar popping sounds of gunfire as well. Seeing his fallen receptionist, and probably the gunman, he'd tried to turn, to lunge back into his office to lock the door, but he'd understood too late.

I didn't need to step farther in. His computer would be gone too.

The office had been searched, but neatly. Several file and desk drawers had been pulled open, but no papers or file folders were tossed about. It had been eradication, simple and fast. The killers had known what they were looking for. They'd silenced Dace and his receptionist, taken their computers and their relevant papers, and left.

I backed out into the hall, wiping the doorknob, inside and out, with the tail of my shirt, then looked up at the walls and the ceiling. I'd been caught by high-mounted security cameras once, recorded as a fumbling fool, but this building was old. I saw no cameras.

I skipped the elevator and took the stairs down to the basement. There were fenced-in storage spaces there, and doors marked for furnace and utility and maintenance. Another door led up to the street. It was fitted with an old-style battery alarm meant to sound at an outside break-in. I unscrewed the cover with a dime, disconnected the battery, opened the door and wiped down what I'd touched.

I had no watch cap to tug low on my head. All I could do was raise the collar on my peacoat before climbing the stairs up to the alley. There would be security cameras mounted on some of the buildings outside, front and back, but I could do nothing about those.

I hurried, head down, along the alley, not wanting to tally the dead but unable to resist doing the count. Four, five, maybe six in total. Rickey Means, Herbie, Dace and his receptionist, all for sure. And maybe the kid, Mister Shade, that Weasel had brought around, and maybe Weasel himself.

And maybe the mouse-voiced woman; she'd make seven.

A cab would be quickest. I ran out to the street, flagged a cabbie and promised him an extra twenty if he'd speed to Herbie's office, scared Dace's killers had found her, too.

I beat it up all the stairs to Herbie's floor, unable to wait for the elevator. I ran down the hall, twisted the doorknob open and hurried in.

She was on the phone, absolutely and almost inaudibly alive. Instead of finding some way of expressing her usual mild irritation, she actually smiled.

'For you,' she murmured, and handed the phone to me.

'Elstrom,' I said, half out of breath.

'What the hell do you have to do with anything?' an enraged woman asked. I recognized her voice. She was Herbie's wife.

'Almost always, absolutely nothing,' I said.

'How'd you do with Herbie?'

'Just as you predicted, he wasn't in his room.'

'Give me back to that mosquito-voiced bitch.'

I handed the phone to Violet.

'You were saying, Mrs Sunheim?' Violet whispered into the mouthpiece. After listening for a moment, she said, 'No, Mrs Sunheim. If I had signing capability on your husband's accounts, I would have drained them of their cash, hopped a flight to the Caribbean and would be sipping a drink that comes with one of those little umbrellas you can stick in the sand to shade the bugs.'

She sneezed, which I knew now could be the beginning of her descent into convulsive laughter, but she caught it and went on in a steady enough whisper, 'Mr Elstrom is the only one who's talked to your husband recently, Mrs Sunheim. That's why I put him on the line with you but, as you heard, he's not helpful. You have his card? Wonderful. He stays up really late, drinking and behaving reprehensibly with tarnished women, so don't worry about calling him after midnight. Yes, ma'am, I'm hoping that works. Bye, now.' She hung up.

It was an amazingly aggressive performance from a woman I'd thought incapable of any such thing.

Smiling sweetly, she said, 'You seem nervous, Mr Elstrom. You're fidgeting on one foot, then the other. And you're out of breath.'

'I was in the neighborhood—'

'Jogging?' She cut me off with an impatient wave of her hand. 'Now, cut the razzle-dazzle and tell me what's brought you here when we just talked, face-to-face, a couple of hours ago at your cylindrical abode.'

No doubt the woman had swallowed gravel since she'd come to the turret that morning.

'Other than Kopek and Jacks, has anyone else stopped by or phoned, asking about Herbie, the Central Works, or any of those other three properties I told you about?'

'You mean anyone other than you?' She batted her eyelash brooms. 'Concerning something I know nothing about?'

'Something Herbie knows something about.'

'Why don't you ask him, Mr Elstrom? You're the only one he seems to be communicating with.'

'How about being followed?' I asked, remembering the black Impala that might have been tailing her after she left the turret. 'Have you noticed anyone following you?'

She took off her thick glasses to look at me with now-unblinking eyes. 'We're getting dramatic here.'

'You're sure you've not noticed any strangers milling about?'

'No one's following me. And how long exactly has it been since you talked to Herbie? I mean, *exactly*.'

When I didn't answer, she said, 'I thought so. You're not in touch with Herbie at all, are you?'

The murders of Dace and his receptionist changed everything. It was time for some truth. 'Not since the day he hired me, and then only a text, early the next morning,' I said. 'That's why I finally called the cops.'

'You think Herbie's dead?'

'I don't know who knows what's happened to Herbie,' I lied, meaning nobody but his killer. And me, who'd put him in a freezer meant for ice cream. 'Two things are important now. The first is to identify the investors in Triple Time.'

'The buyers of the Central Works and the other three properties?'

'They might know where Herbie is.'

She shook her head. 'I went through all the files after those two cops left. There's no file, no mention anywhere of them.'

'How about a realtor's commission?'

'Not for Triple Time or any of those four properties. Will you please sit down? Your fidgeting is making me nervous.' She waved the hand sporting the purple welding project at the black plastic chair squeezed between her desk and the wall.

I squeezed down onto it.

'I matched all Herbie's commissions to deposits made,' she murmured on. 'None came from anything I didn't know about. You just said there are two things important now. What's the second?'

The blood, still hot, soaking at Dace's office had stayed fresh in my mind, as had Herbie, though colder. 'As I told you before, I don't think you're ever going to see another paycheck. Lock the office and go find another job.'

'I can't just—'

I cut her off. 'I think I saw someone tailing you after you left the turret. A black sedan.'

'Police car?'

'Or a pretender.'

'I'm not being followed,' she said.

'I was followed last night, by someone who shot at me.'

Her hand went to her mouth. 'My God!'

'You're not going to get paid here anymore, Violet. There's no reason to hang around.'

'What aren't you telling me?'

'Only half-baked fears, but they're real enough. Lock up, go home.'

'Because of what I don't know?' she asked, blinking her broom lashes hard, fighting tears.

'Because of what *I* don't know,' I said.

The image of Dace's receptionist came back hard. Likely enough, she hadn't known anything either.

I got up, too fidgety to sit, stuck between the wall and her desk. 'Leave this office, Violet, and never come back.'

TWENTY-SEVEN

The fidgets remained.

I'd learned nothing of what Herbie had stepped into, other than maybe it had gotten him three hundred thousand in cash, and for sure it had gotten him dead. Secreting away Herbie's corpse and waving faked documents had agitated no one out into the open except perhaps a man or two with guns who'd come looking for me in Austin. All I was seeing now was Walter Dace and his receptionist lying sticky in still-drying blood.

I thought, then, of Kutz's clearing – one of my old refuges when I was a kid – and how peaceful it would be to sit at a picnic table and ignore what I'd stuffed in Leo's ice cream freezer and watch the river and not think of much of anything at all until it was time to head to the city garage to ask the nocturnal Booster Gibbs what his crew had encountered, finding my Jeep.

Leo's white van was parked, as usual, next to the wienie wagon. The veterinarian's big green van was also there, backed against the opened gate to the paddock.

Ordinarily, the scene might well have been soothing. But that day, calm was not to be found at Kutz's clearing. It was a madhouse.

There were goats – four of them. One goat was pure white, two were pure brown. The fourth and largest of them was a mix of brown and white.

They were jumping about inside the fenced-in paddock, bleating in high-pitched falsettos like they were being accosted by hooded people with hatchets. But they were not. Only the veterinarian darted among them, attempting to soothe them with pats on the head. The man must have been a long-view optimist, for none of his patting was slowing the goats at all. They bleated and kept jumping all around him in a sort of hysterical ballet. Besides the courage to remain among so many leaping hooves, the man was surely blessed with deafness and a nose clogged solid with cement to have chauffeured four such agitated creatures to the clearing in an enclosed van.

There was other movement there as well. Five gray heads bobbed slowly along the oval's main straightaway. Ma Brumsky and three of her friends, septuagenarians all, formed a ragged sort of line at the front. They were waving long branches out ahead of them, side to side, like prairie farm hustlers used to do, dowsing for the presence of water. Except instead of forked ends, these ladies' branches all had silver bells jangling on red velvet ribbons at their ends.

Mrs Roshiska, Ma Brumsky's largest and oldest friend, pushed her wheeled aluminum walker closely behind the four ladies in front. She wore her usual outfit of a pink sweatshirt and pink sweatpants, but waved no stick.

'Amazing, right?' Leo asked. For all the hysteria coming from the goat paddock, I hadn't heard him sidle up beside me. Again, he wore his white chef's toque and empty tool belt.

'You like that hat, don't you?' I said.

'Toque.'

'Toque,' I said. 'What on earth is going on here? You've brought in agitated goats and you've given sticks with bells to Ma and her friends.'

'A sort of wrangle,' he said.

'A wrangle?'

'Or a jockeying, if you prefer.'

'Ma and her friends . . .?'

'Jockeys, of a kind.'

'You consider goats to be thoroughbreds?' I asked of the creatures shrieking fifty yards away.

'Just arrived. They're excited to be here.'

'To race,' I said.

'Exactly.'

'Goat racing,' I said, to be even more precise.

'It's become popular, from time to time.' He stuck his hands into the pouches on either side of the tool belt that were meant for nails or screws.

'Where?'

'Iowa, among other places.'

'Corn is popular in Iowa, but you've not planted any here.'

'Laugh if you must.'

And so I did. I laughed, long and loud and with some relief. There'd been so much death.

'And now goat racing is poised to take off here?' I asked finally.

'On opening day, which is in just a few days . . .' He faked a cough, and pointed to the back of the trailer.

My laughter died. 'You'll be needing your freezer?'

'Ice cream is set to be delivered soon.'

And that, too, was a relief of sorts. It established an end point, a time when I must give it all up. 'I'll remove the meat,' I said.

I left then, because there was always the chance that, if I hung around in too close a proximity to what I'd left in his freezer, I might become as hysterical as the goats.

I drove over to the city garage at ten that night, well past dark. Booster Gibbs came out, smiling, and handed me three of the five C-notes I'd given him to find the Jeep and bring it back to Rivertown.

'Including the cleanse?' I asked, surprised. Two hundred dollars for his crew was too cheap.

He shrugged. 'I sent two guys in a tilt flatbed. They never made it as far as Austin. They spotted your Jeep on a side street just off Chicago Avenue, in Oak Park. Your keys were in the ignition, your phone in the cup holder. They drove it back.'

'Let me guess. It was close to the bus stop.'

'A half-mile away, but yeah,' he said. 'It was dumb luck my guys spotted it at all.'

It was close enough to where Weasel had picked up Mister Shade, the kid who may, or may not, have gone missing. Weasel could have caught a bus west toward Rivertown from that bus stop, or caught a cab.

'Let me get this straight, Dek,' Booster went on. 'It was Weasel you were afraid we'd find shot dead in your Jeep, in Austin?'

'It was a concern, yes. Bullets were flying everywhere.'

'You were close to the Jeep when the gunfire erupted?'

'The Jeep had stopped, I think. I was between it and the house I was looking for.'

'Easy targets, you on foot and Weasel in the Jeep. He survived, right? Not only survived, but for all the gunfire you heard, not a single bullet hit you or your Jeep?'

'Yes again,' I said. He was saying what I'd just about come to believe.

'And then, unmolested, he drove your Jeep to Oak Park, left it with the keys in the ignition and the cell phone in plain sight . . .?' He let the question trail off, so I could answer it.

'Where maybe it could be stolen after he walked to the bus stop,' I said, becoming smarter by the minute.

'What a crafty guy, that Weasel,' he said. 'He was hoping the Jeep would vanish, making it look like he was a victim, too, pulled from the car and having to escape on foot from the guys who came after you.'

'I was set up to be scared, but not to be killed,' I said, sure of it now, and relieved.

'Except by random gangbangers, passing by.'

'For sure, but the intension was to have me scared away, stranded, without a car to keep nosing around in.'

'Weasel's not crafty enough to set something like that up by himself.' He laughed. 'He got scared, too, even though he knew what was about to come down. The interior was drenched with milk. He'd splattered almost a whole quart speeding away, the rat. And since I always figure it's best to cleanse, even for things we can't see, we washed it out.'

'That bastard,' I said.

'I beat him up in fourth grade for stealing my baseball glove.'

'Did it feel good?'

'Only until the next day, when he stole it again. I never did find that glove.'

'What did you do?'

He shrugged. 'Only thing I could do. I beat him up again.'

TWENTY-EIGHT

I was up on the roof at nine the next morning when the black Impala pulled to the curb. A huge thunderstorm had just passed over, the first of the approaching spring, and I'd gone up to make sure the pole net I'd left there, at the ready, hadn't been blown away.

I bent over the balustrade as the rumpled Kopek and the unwrinkled Jacks eased out of the Impala and started for the turret.

'I'll be right there, gents,' I called down.

Both looked up, but only Kopek shook his head.

'Been busy, Elstrom?' he asked, when I opened the door.

His hands were empty. He'd not brought a bakery bag, and that was a disappointment, for I'd finished the pastry surrounds of the last prune *kolachky* the night before, outside on the bench by the river. The prune filling itself I'd tossed to a duck, which was otherwise floating peacefully along the Willahock. He was a wise duck. He let it sink.

'There are always things to do,' I said.

'Herbert Sunheim,' he said.

'Any word?' I asked, pretending.

'You went to Rickey Means' answering service to drop off a report on Sunheim's behalf.'

'That was agitation,' I said.

'Once we'd identified Means as the victim, we asked his service to notify us of anyone trying to contact him. Clever, you going there, pretending you didn't know Means was dead.'

'And passing yourself off as Sunheim,' the almost always reticent Jacks added.

'Agitation, as I said. I wanted to see if anyone would call Herbie's office, acting on behalf of Means,' I said. 'Alas, I don't think anyone did.'

'We would have let it go, but then we received these.' He pulled out his phone and showed me a picture.

'Tire ruts, artfully photographed,' I said. 'I sent them to an insurance guy at CSB.'

'Again, passing yourself off as Sunheim.'

'More agitation.'

'CSB's man, a Mr Hanson, wants us to believe these pictures prove his rail line isn't responsible for anything, since the photos seem to show someone else pulled the railcar to the end of the spur.'

'His lawyers want to think that,' I said, 'but it doesn't matter who tugged the railcar. It's those who tossed Rickey Means out the window that you want.'

'You dangled the pictures in front of Hanson, to learn what the shipment contained,' he said.

'Restaurant fixtures of some sort, he said.'

'Where is Sunheim?'

'This isn't just about a body on a boxcar, is it? Or my reporting Sunheim missing?'

'Where is Sunheim?'

'You tell me. You talked to his landlady in Brookfield, right?'

'Twice. The second time, she told us an insurance man had come looking for Sunheim. She showed us your card.'

'I had to pose as myself, since she already knew Sunheim.'

Jacks groaned. Kopek didn't smile. 'You led that woman on. You told her she could recover rent by filing a claim against insurance proceeds,' he said.

'That was a sort of dangling, too.'

'She left you alone in Sunheim's room.'

'There was nothing there, as you saw for yourselves. I'm guessing the landlady gave it a good scrubbing, looking for something to hold in lieu of past due rent. He's not been there for some time, she said.'

'Maybe you missed something, or maybe not,' Kopek said.

I put confusion on my face.

'Paint flecks under the bed,' he said.

'What?' I asked, like I hadn't tried to sweep the damned things away.

'Paint flecks,' he said again. 'We noticed a few under the bed the first time we visited. We didn't think they were important. But when we went back the second time – this being after you'd been there – we noticed that there were more scattered beneath the headboard. Plus, several had made it well past the mattress, like someone had tried to brush them away.'

'What do paint flecks have to do with anything?' I asked, because it was expected.

'That's what we wanted to know, so Jacks here crawled under the bed, that second visit. Want to know what he found?'

'More paint flecks, like you said.'

'A loose baseboard,' he said, watching my face.

'Meaning the landlady had bumped it with her vacuum cleaner?'

'The nails had been removed so it could be pulled away from the wall. That loosened the paint, scattering those few little flecks we noticed the first time. The nail holes were filled with white toothpaste to disguise the fact that the nails were missing.'

I had to play along. 'You think more flecks mean someone removed the baseboard between your visits?'

'Got any thoughts on who that might have been?'

'The landlady told me visitors come and go for all her tenants.'

'She told us the only one she saw was you.'

'She told me she doesn't see all the visitors. What was behind the baseboard?'

'Nothing except an empty hiding place.'

'I saw no paint specks, no loose baseboard, so I saw no secret hiding place.'

'You work for Sunheim, Elstrom. What's he trying to hide?'

'No idea.'

'When's the last time you spoke to him?' he asked.

'We've been over this. The morning he hired me to take photos at the Central Works. And then he texted me early the following morning, thanking me for the pictures.'

'So why keep working this, if Sunheim's gone?'

'He sent me twice the agreed-upon fee. For a guy who loved every nickel he didn't have to spend, paying double meant he wanted more, but he never got around – I mean, he hasn't yet gotten around – to telling me what else he wants me to do. After he returned none of my calls, I contacted the police.'

'Sunheim's assistant told us you've been agitating her, too.'

'And Sunheim's wife,' I said, skipping past Violet Krumfeld. 'Mrs Sunheim is angry, interested only in divorce and getting out from under a Cadillac lease. At first, I thought she wasn't concerned enough about his disappearance, but then I realized she doesn't want to talk to him; she just wants some checks. I said my finding Herbie might get her those checks, and that's why she ought to give me his new address. I think she's innocent in whatever's gone wrong with Herbie, but have you checked out whether there is life insurance on Herbie?'

'Small stuff. They have a hundred grand policies on each other. But we are interested in that fancy car she drives.'

'As I said, it's a lease. He didn't fork down the big money to buy it outright.'

'He must have been anticipating good times, financially, to have leased the thing?'

I had the thought, then, that he knew exactly what was no longer behind Herbie's baseboard. I shrugged, said nothing.

He gave it up. 'Who else have you agitated?'

'Walter Dace,' I said, still surprised he hadn't learned it already from a security camera video.

'The property manager for Triple Time Partners,' Kopek said.

'And that answers the question you ducked earlier. You're investigating everybody involved with the Central Works. Why?'

'It's bothersome, finding a corpse on top of a railcar. Now, about a question you ducked. Violet Krumfeld? How much did you agitate her?'

'I gave her a dummied report, too. She doesn't know anything about Herbie's dealings with Central Works.'

'How recently did you talk to her?'

'She ran Hanson's name out to me yesterday morning,' I said, mindful of the black Impala, perhaps Kopek's, that had followed her away.

'Why?'

'I'd misplaced my phone. And then I dropped in on her later in the day.'

'Why?'

'To press her one last time about anything she knew about Central Works. I'm trying everything I can to find Herbie.'

'You drove all the way into the city to press her? You couldn't have called?'

'I was hoping to have lunch with my ex-wife. She wasn't available.'

Jacks nodded. 'Miss Phelps' assistant says she gets tied up a lot, and often can't be reached.'

'You called Amanda?'

'We tried. We never got past her assistant.' He made it sound casual, but they'd begun keeping tabs on me, building a file.

'This isn't just about a body on a boxcar, is it? Or a missing person I reported?'

Kopek just smiled. 'Have you heard from Violet Krumfeld recently?'

'You mean since midday, yesterday, when I saw her?'

'She's not answering the phone at Sunheim's office.'

'She might have followed my advice and quit. I told her I doubted Herbie would ever write her another paycheck.'

'Because he's disappeared?'

'Missing men don't often write checks. Get her phone number; she'll tell you what I said.'

'We've found no record of a cell phone, or a landline, or even where she lives.'

'She knows nothing,' I said, again.

'How was the prune?' Kopek asked.

'In desperation, necessary,' I said. 'I threw the filling of the last one at a duck.'

'What did the duck do?'

'Ducked,' I said, because I could think of nothing smarter to say.

Kopek nodded at that, and they walked to their car and drove away. They'd come about paint flecks and a baseboard cavity.

What I couldn't tell was what they'd taken away.

TWENTY-NINE

It started raining black Impalas. Another one showed up that afternoon. Two men got out. Both were in their early thirties, wore well-cut dark suits, and had even better cut, gelled dark hair.

'No trespassing,' I said to the one holding up a badge, coming up to my door.

He didn't smile, just like he hadn't smiled when I'd snapped his picture next to the No Trespassing sign the first morning I'd gone to Central Works.

'Interesting color combination,' the other one, the driver, called out. He walked over to the Jeep. Making a show of looking at my license plate, he pulled out his phone and murmured into it.

I recognized him, too, by his voice, from the day I'd hidden from them both inside the Central Works. He was the one who'd gone to watch my Jeep.

According to the ID that went with the badge, the cop who'd come up was named Raines. 'Green top on a red paint job,' he called back, arching his eyebrows.

'People might consider it too Christmassy,' the driver said, still holding the phone to his ear. 'You never see those two colors combined on the same vehicle.'

'Almost never,' Raines said. 'But we saw it recently, didn't we? Parked up the street from an abandoned factory?' He turned to look squarely at me. 'Different driver, though.'

'The other guy was more colorful, dressed like a parrot,' the driver said, putting his phone in his pocket as he came forward to join Raines. His ID said his name was Cuthbert.

'Jungle colors, you called it,' Raines said, reminding him. Reminding me, too, though I hoped they didn't know I'd overheard.

'Your interest in my ride speaks well of your ability to appreciate innovation,' I said.

'So, who the hell is this guy?' Raines asked the driver, Cuthbert.

'How did you find your way here if you didn't know who I was?' I asked.

'Vlodek Elstrom, according to his license plate registration,' Cuthbert said. '*Vlodek?*'

'An ancestral name I never use. I'm called Dek,' I said. 'You were just passing by and spotted my Jeep?'

Cuthbert turned and started back to the Jeep. 'Mind?' he asked, over his shoulder.

'I have a choice?'

Cuthbert took that as acquiescence, opened the driver's door and leaned in for a look. He only took a minute. Coming back, he said, 'You keep a clean car, Elstrom. The carpet's damp with shampoo.'

'I am manic about some things,' I said.

'Just washed?'

I nodded, thinking they'd gotten tipped to my being in Austin two nights before, and wondering who might have told them. A bigger wonder was how they knew when Kopek and Jacks did not.

I decided not to ask. It didn't seem to be a morning for candor.

'Where did you wash it?' Cuthbert asked.

'Some place in the city, coin-operated, do-it-yourself,' I said, because such places didn't give receipts that could be traced. 'I spotted it, driving by. I probably couldn't find that place again in a million years.'

'Herbert Sunheim,' Raines said. 'What's your interest in him?'

'Do you know Detectives Kopek and Jacks?'

'Heard of them,' Raines said.

'You're working the same case. I've discussed all this with them.'

'Discuss Sunheim with me,' he said.

'As you must know, Herbie was the realtor who brokered the sale of Central Works. As you must know, Rickey Means, the man found on the boxcar, was the lawyer on that sale. Herbie hired me to take photos of the building and the railcar the day after Means was found. You remember that, right, Raines? I even took one of you, frowning. I sent the photos to Herbie, and heard nothing afterward. He'd quit answering his phone. I got worried and called the police, to see if Herbie had been found somewhere.'

'Found how?' Cuthbert asked.

'Found dead. Until just a few moments ago, I assumed Kopek and Jacks were the lead detectives on the Means investigation, because they were the ones who responded to my missing person call. But now you've arrived. I'm struggling to see how you fit.'

'It's a complex case,' Raines said. 'We're working different angles.'

'Including following Violet Krumfeld? That's how you found me, right?'

They were wild shots, fired across their bows. There was no way of knowing whether it had been them in that dark car, or Kopek and Jacks, or other cops, or just some innocent passing Impala happening to pull up behind Violet as she left to go back to the city. But my wild shot seemed to nudge Raines just a bit, and he shot Cuthbert a quick glance before he fixed his eyes more resolutely on me.

'Sunheim's assistant?' he asked. 'She was here?''

'Kopek and Jacks will tell you she delivered a message from the rail carrier that routed the boxcar to Central Works.'

'Why the hell did she have to drive out to tell you that?' Cuthbert asked.

'Kopek and Jacks will tell you I misplaced my phone.'

'You have no idea where Sunheim is?' Raines asked.

'Why tail Miss Krumfeld?' I asked.

They both shrugged, good shoulders in good suits.

Raines gave me a card, Cuthbert gave me a scowl, and they left without asking me anything more about Violet Krumfeld, or Herbie's wife, or Walter Dace, or even baseboards.

I slumped into my electric-blue LaZBoy at five o'clock and picked up my ancient four-inch television to get dosed by the evening news.

Breaking News! the screen offered up, as it had been doing relentlessly when introducing each new story, urgent or not. This one, though, cut straight into me.

The reporter, a twenty-something cutie with nary a line on her face reflecting previous thought, stood in front of the downtown building I'd slunk away from so recently.

'Two victims of an office invasion were discovered this after-noon,' she began. 'Chicago police have not released their names, but the victims are believed to be a middle-aged man and his assistant, a young woman in her mid-twenties. They were discovered by a messenger from a parcel delivery service. Police are on the scene, investigating.'

Walter Dace and his impeccably finger-nailed receptionist had been found.

I got up and paced and, a few miles later, I got inspired.

I called Leo. 'Are you in Rivertown?'

'This business of running a gourmet restaurant is time-consuming. Endora's working late at the Newberry on a collection that's set to display next weekend, so I'm using the night to catch up on my regular stuff.'

'I thought Ma and her friends were going to help.'

'That's for later.'

'With bells on sticks?'

'And goats, don't forget. And ice cream, should you be so willing to free up my freezer. We're going to have it all.'

'How about a distraction tonight?'

'What sort?' he asked.

'A drive-by in your white van, not your noticeable Porsche, to test some new thinking I just came upon.'

'I'll pick you up?'

'I might be under surveillance by cops in the spit of land.'

'No way of seeing anyone hiding in there,' he said, of the mess between my street and Thompson Avenue. The lizards that ran Rivertown called it a park, simply because it had trees, but no one ever went in there because half of those trees had fallen, leaving the would-be park a tangle of fallen limbs and branches, all mounded over by years of rotting leaves. It was an excellent place for any cop to hide.

'I'll meet you in the first block on the other side of Thompson Avenue,' I said.

'M-E-A-T?' he asked, ever the wit, spelling it out as another gentle nudge to rid his freezer of my contents.

'No,' I said. There was nothing funny in his soft prompt. If he knew what I'd parked in his ice cream freezer, he'd see nothing funny in it, either.

I went out the door in my shirtsleeves, carrying my peacoat and watch cap in a paper bag as though I was taking trash to the garbage can behind the turret. Blocked now by the turret, I slipped on the coat, tugged on the watch cap and ran down the crumbles of the river walk to the broad lawn that fronted city hall. Staying low, I ran back across my street and up through the darkness alongside the spit of land to Thompson Avenue.

Leo was waiting on the first street past the neon. 'I need to drive,' I said, climbing into the passenger's side. He slipped back between the front seats so we could switch places.

'So, what's the madness for tonight?' he said, after I got behind the wheel.

'I need you to tell me what's going on.'

THIRTY

I drove first to the flattened ground that had once been the Central Works.

'Nothing here now except that railcar,' Leo said of the box shape faint in the moonlight.

'That railcar was full of fixtures.'

'Fixtures?'

'Restaurant stuff, the railroad's insurance man said. Probably sinks, counters, cabinets, maybe even some plumbing and electrical.'

'All lost when the building blew up,' he said.

'No. I was in that building beforehand, remember? I saw no

fixtures. But I might have seen them being unloaded at another building.'

'That was lucky, getting the stuff out in time,' he said, and paused. 'Or are we talking arson that was owner-inflicted here?'

'Perhaps,' I said.

'*Perhaps?*' He turned to me. 'Are the owners filing an insurance claim or not?'

'Just the opposite. The property manager told a fire chief they never insured the building because it was slated for demolition.'

'Then why ship in—?'

'Fixtures for an uninsured building they were going to demolish? More importantly, why didn't they push it over with the others they bulldozed right after they acquired the property?'

'And the obvious answer is?' he asked, right on cue.

'They'd originally intended to keep that one building, but didn't insure it because they didn't want insurance inspectors dropping by,' I said.

'But when the building attracted too much attention, following discovery of the corpse, they had it torched?'

'They like their privacy,' I said.

He laughed, thinking it was a joke.

I headed south, intending to give Leo a fast look at the Vanderbilt Supply building and myself a fresh one as well. Abducting Herbie had been lunacy, a cranial short-circuit, and I was going to put him back and then tip the cops anonymously so they could make of him what they could.

When we got to within a block, I spotted a group of six gangly black teenagers loitering at the edge of the cleared ground, checking out the building like they were contemplating trouble. I switched off the headlamps and pulled to the curb.

'Why are we stopping?' Leo asked, nervous in the ruined neighborhood.

'I want to see what's interesting those kids.'

Leo squinted into the distance. 'Just kids, hanging in no man's land.'

The boys left the tilt of the broken sidewalk and began running toward the black shape of the building. They disappeared into the darkness.

A muzzle flashed from the darkest part of the grounds; a gun had fired from close to the building. In an instant, the kids came racing out of the gloom and tore down the sidewalk, running like they were fleeing the hounds of hell. I counted all six. None moved as if he were wounded.

I wheeled us around and sped off in the opposite direction.

'What did we just see?' Leo shouted, looking behind us as we raced away.

'Confirmation,' I said as we shot through the next intersection.

'Confirmation of what?'

'Confirmation that there is now a guard.'

'A guard at an empty, derelict building?'

'A guard at a building slated for bigger things. The gunfire was meant to scare those kids away, not kill them.'

'So, no big deal?'

'With me at the Central Works, they used a big-tired off-roader. In Austin, they used gunshots, like we just saw.' I told him what I'd run into, with Weasel.

'But still, only to scare you off and not to kill?'

'I hope so.'

'That bastard, Weasel, set you up for that?'

'Using the kid's disappearance as bait. I want to squeeze the truth out of him, to be sure the kid's OK, but Weasel's hiding.'

'You're crazy. Crazy damn crazy.' He slumped back in the seat and we drove the rest of the way to the Bureski building in silence.

'Notice how it sits isolated in the middle of what had been a multi-building complex,' I said as we drove by.

'Bulldozed ground, just like Central Works and the Vanderbilt building. You think there's a guy nearby with a gun, like at the Vanderbilt Supply building?'

'I think the guys behind Triple Time are being extra-vigilant with their remaining properties.'

We got to the fourth and last of Triple Time's buildings twenty minutes later. I'd intended to pass by slowly to show Leo where I'd seen all the truck activity, but headlamps were approaching along the side street, so I sped on by. The headlamps stopped in the intersection we'd just driven through, as though the driver wanted to get a solid look at us.

I turned at the next street, and headed us back toward Rivertown.

'Googling all four of their locations shows satellite photos, likely taken last summer,' I said, eyeballing the rearview mirror and trying for a steady voice. 'Lots of surrounding buildings, lots of trees.'

'OK, so that last building sits alone in the middle of a sizable plot of land, just like the others. And if those Internet photos were taken just last summer, then Triple Time bulldozed all their sites after acquiring them. Doesn't that simply mean they're readying their properties for development?'

'Absolutely. In fact, I saw trucks unloading at that last property. The fixtures, I think, that were never unloaded at the Central Works.'

'Fixtures, like sinks and counters, you said. Probably removed from the railcar before the body could be discovered.'

'Fixtures not destined for a restaurant,' I said, prompting.

'A drug lab,' he said.

'Their first,' I said. 'Four were intended, now down to three with Central Works gone. Lots of guards, lots of equipment, state-of-the-art labs for synthesizing whatever is currently stylish, set in the middle of broad, cleared ground.'

'Like the moats medieval barons used to protect their castles,' he said, nodding, understanding.

'Easy to spot people coming up, like those kids we just saw getting scared off. Plus, I think each building has been wired to blow, should marauders arrive that can't be rebuffed. The fire captain at the Central Works said it was no simple arson there. That building was blown to smithereens.'

'To destroy evidence, should things go awry,' he said.

'And to kill their enemies, of which they would have plenty. And not just cops, but stupid small-gang types from here in Chicago, and smarter, bigger outfits from out of state.'

'Who are these guys?'

'I don't know, but my guess is they hired Walter Dace, a two-bit property manager, to hire Herbie Sunheim, a two-bit commercial realtor, and Rickey Means, a two-bit lawyer, precisely because they were two-bit players and could be easily controlled.'

'To do what?'

'To acquire real estate parcels without asking questions. Herbie located and contracted the abandoned sites for them. Rickey Means, the lawyer, did the legal stuff to buy the parcels. Dace, the property manager, arranged for the bulldozing and redevelopment.'

'So Means and Herbie got greedy, and thought to snag bigger slices for themselves? That's why Means got tossed and Herbie's disappeared?'

'That was my first guess, but now I'm not so sure. Rickey Means bought himself some expensive duds and Herbie leased his troubled wife a Cadillac Escalade, but that might have been the extent of it. They might have been happy with what they were getting.'

'Then why did Herbie hire you to take pictures at the Central Works?'

'Maybe so I'd be *seen* taking pictures, the day after Means was discovered on top of the railcar.'

'To announce an ace investigator was on the job and had his back?' He forced a laugh that was all nervousness and no mirth. 'I don't know how that helped him. Herbie Sunheim has disappeared.'

'He didn't run off.' I told him then what I'd found behind the baseboard in Herbie's rented room.

'How'd he score that?'

'I don't think he did score it. I think it was Triple Time cash, to be used for acquiring more properties. Herbie never intended to take off.'

'So where is he?'

'Dead, most likely,' I said, without adding that, by now, Herbie was likely frozen solid in Leo's own freezer.

'That leaves the property manager, that guy Dace?'

'Two more have been reported dead.'

He turned on the seat. 'Who?'

'Did you catch tonight's news?'

'Not . . . those two killed downtown?'

'Walter Dace and his receptionist. I found them before the cops did.'

'Crazy damn crazy,' he said again.

'Dace's computers were taken, no doubt along with his files.'

'Triple Time people, covering their tracks?'

'I'm not sure about that, either.'

'Were you seen there?'

'I don't know. Two sets of detectives have come by but, so far, nobody's pressed me about Dace and his receptionist. The cops are keeping a lid on their identities, like Rickey Means.'

'Someone's cleaning up loose ends, Dek. You've got to go to the cops.'

'Remember that car we just saw, approaching along the side street?'

'Yep,' he managed, his voice rising.

'It was a black Impala, a detective's car.'

THIRTY-ONE

Leo dropped me at the same place he'd picked me up, and I hoofed back across Thompson Avenue and the far edge of the spit of land to the river walk. Only when I got close to the turret did I notice the figure sitting on the bench by the water.

'Elstrom,' he said, straightening up.

'Detective Jacks.'

He stood and motioned for us to head up the rise to the street. No surprise, a black Impala was parked at the curb, with Detective Kopek parked inside. Jacks tapped on the window and Kopek got out.

'Fine night for a walk,' Kopek said.

'Cold, but all nights are fine nights for walks,' I said.

'Fine night for long walks and short walks,' he said, making me wonder whether he'd been waiting a long time or whether he'd just arrived, perhaps driving in from a mostly deserted factory district in Chicago.

'All are good,' I said, waiting now myself.

'Mrs Marge Sunheim,' he said. 'Ever wonder if she was involved in her husband's nefarious activities?'

'Nefarious?' It was not a word a *kolachky*-cognizant cop would ordinarily use.

'You know, up to no good?' he nudged.

'I don't think she likes being involved with Herbie in anything. She threw him out to go live in a room with a loose baseboard.'

'Got any thoughts about why her house got trashed, or what someone might have been looking for?'

'Her house got trashed?'

'Maybe not trashed, exactly, but it was searched, and not too unobtrusively.'

'Marge Sunheim told Herbie Sunheim's assistant that you and Jacks stopped by, wanting a look around inside her house. She told you to get a warrant.'

'Someone else stopped by after us, when she wasn't home. Her house got searched right after you supposedly found nothing in Sunheim's rented room,' he said.

'Did she have a funny baseboard, too?'

'Don't crack wise, Elstrom.'

'Then don't accuse me of things I know nothing about.'

'Walter Dace,' he said.

I played it dumb. 'Him I know something about, as I already told you. He's the property manager for the buyers of the Central Works property.'

'You told us you went to see him,' Jacks said, then stopped so I could incriminate myself by knowing more than what had been reported in the news.

'I gave him the same report I dummied up to leave at Rickey Means' answering service. I was trying to maintain the charade that Herbie Sunheim was directing my activities.'

'Walter Dace was found shot to death along with his receptionist,' Kopek said.

I presented what I hoped was appropriate shock. 'Who did it?'

'Odd, you showing up where people are later found dead, Elstrom.'

'I didn't kill Dace, Detective Kopek. I went to see him twice, and only for a couple of minutes each time. He blew me off, protecting the privacy of his building owner.'

'There's more.'

'Damn right there's more,' I said. 'I'm looking for Herbie Sunheim and I'm looking alone. Like Rickey Means, he's linked to the four properties that Dace managed, though what there is to manage is doubtful. Three of the four buildings look vacant and the fourth looks blown up.'

'How do you know about those other properties?'

'Clever investigative work. I went to the county recorder's office and asked what properties Triple Time Partners owns.' And then, thinking about the black Impala Leo and I had seen just a short time before, I said, 'I drove by each one.'

'You know more than that.'

I met his glare. 'Hard to keep track of what everybody thinks I know,' I said.

'What's that mean?'

'Raines and Cuthbert,' I said.

'Who?' he asked, but there was no confusion on his face.

'Your fellow detectives. They've taken to stopping by to question me instead of working more closely with you.'

'Different department,' Kopek mumbled.

'They did say they were working a different angle,' I allowed.

'I don't know what damn angle they got,' he said. He motioned abruptly to Jacks. They got in their Impala without another word, and drove away.

I went inside knowing even less than I had just a few hours before.

I'd cracked one of the slit windows open for fresh air before going to bed. That was enough to wake me when the familiar clattering of a poorly tuned automobile turned onto my street. The car stopped. Two doors opened and closed, as before. It was just past three in the morning.

I hurried up the stairs and the ladder to the roof, taking care to ease the hatch open quietly as I climbed up and out, into the night.

Rustling came from down below; footsteps on old leaves at the back of the turret. A moment later, the tapping started. The thing was moving its way up the limestone blocks, its whirring growing louder in the still night.

I grabbed the large pole net, moved low to the center of the circular roof and crouched down. Standing, I'd be invisible behind the balustrade to anyone looking up from the ground, but there was no way of telling whether the camera attached to the light that was making its way up the turret was recording internally or broadcasting to someone watching on a monitor nearby.

The tapping and whirring grew louder against the limestone, and at last the light rose up above the balustrade and hovered, not moving. I stayed low, crouched at the center of the roof, my right hand tight around the handle of the pole net.

A moment passed, and then another, and then the light began moving slowly toward the center of the roof, whirring just five feet above me in the night sky, a thing almost of science fiction. Searching, though not for me.

I moved my left hand onto the pole, now gripping it with both hands. I'd get one chance at a fast swing.

The light was directly overhead. I jumped up and swung. I didn't get it all, but I got enough, snaring at least two of its rotors.

I swung the thing trapped in the net down hard onto the roof, stomping my foot onto the pole handle as if to pin some vicious, flailing evil. I tore off my peacoat, threw it over the net to blind its lens, and left it there, imprisoned in the net beneath my thick wool coat. I padded over to the roof hatch and eased the door open, careful to lower it silently behind me as I climbed down the first rungs of the ladder. There'd be a ruckus outside now, down on the ground, when the thing did not appear in the sky.

I went down to the second floor and looked out of one of the windows facing the river. Two beams of light had begun dancing upward from down below, touching, parting, searching. They'd brought flashlights.

The beams split up, one to each side of the turret. I crossed the floor to a front window and watched as they moved toward the street, casting wide bright arcs down into the bramble in the spit of land. The decades of blown-down branches and fallen tree limbs would make the search hellish for hours to come. Wonderfully, it would be for nothing. The thing they wanted was trapped on my roof.

I watched the flashlights dance their merry tango for another fifteen minutes, until at last I got tired enough to go back to sleep.

THIRTY-TWO

Kopek and Jacks found me on the bench by the Willahock the next morning, drinking coffee and watching plastic containers recycling their way downriver.

'Don't the police ever sleep?' I asked.

'What are those two round young people doing in that mess of dead trees across the street?' Kopek said, sitting down next to me. Jacks stayed standing, probably because he was younger. And because the bench is small.

'That's not a mess of trees,' I said. 'That's a park.'

'Whatever. What are they doing?' He took a smashed two-pack of white Hostess Sno-Balls out of his pocket, tore open the cellophane, took one of the coconut encrusted pucks and offered me the other.

'Looking for something they will not find,' I said, taking a bite.

'Like looking for Herbie Sunheim?' he said.

'You don't think he'll ever be found?'

'I'm wondering if he absconded with a large amount of money.'

'Because his house was searched?'

He shifted to look me in the eyes. 'His rented room was searched, too.'

'Ah, that jiggered baseboard again,' I said. 'Is that why you've come back to see me so soon?' I quite reasonably asked, through the Devil's food cake and coconut.

'He's like one of those Russian nesting figure dolls, a man within a man within a man.'

'I thought Herbie was fairly straight-up,' I said, taking another bite. 'A bit of a grub, actually.'

'Remember Walter Dace?'

'How could I forget? Seems to me you waited awfully late for me to get home last night, just to tell me Dace and his assistant were shot to death.'

'I forgot to ask you where you were last night,' he said.

'We talked about long walks and short walks.'

He shifted on the bench to look at me. 'Dace got one of your dummied-up reports?' he said. A speck of white coconut clung to his lower lip.

'That's another thing we've already discussed.'

'You also told me Means' answering service got another, and of course he's dead, too.' He felt the speck of coconut and brushed it off.

'Means' got delivered after his death.'

'Herbie Sunheim's assistant got another.' His eyes were unblinking on me.

'No. She got an invoice for my time.' Something oily began working up the back of my throat, a sign my gut knew something my brain had not yet absorbed. 'What did you come here to tell me?'

'There are too many dead for it to be a coincidence,' Kopek said.

'Who's dead, damn it?' I straightened up on the bench but didn't stand.

'Sunheim's assistant.'

The air went out of the world, then. Quiet Violet Krumfeld, a mouse of a thing who'd kept on loyally working for Herbie long after he'd quit showing up for work, the mouse I'd told to flee, was dead.

'Dead?' I asked anyway, whispering like her now. The cake in my throat had turned to paste.

'Found bludgeoned yesterday afternoon on a forest preserve running trail in Belle Plaine,' he said, naming another suburb at the city's edge, like Rivertown.

'There was nothing on the news last night,' I said inanely, as if that prevented it from being real.

'I told you we were having trouble tracking her down. Whoever's got jurisdiction on her must be having the same problem, and is withholding her name until they find her next of kin. We got notified only because her name is on our potential witness list.'

'I told her to get the hell away from that office,' I said. 'I said she'd never get paid, that Herbie was never coming back, that—'

'So you said before. You told her Sunheim would never return, but how did you know that?'

I told myself to think before I got stupid. 'Herbie's been gone too long,' I said after a moment.

He studied my eyes for a moment, and then relaxed. 'I suppose that makes sense,' he said.

'She was assaulted? Raped, mugged, what?'

'Blunt force trauma to the head is all I know. An off-duty cop, a runner like her, found her. He called an ambulance but she died en route to the hospital.'

'Leads?'

'Apparently they don't know a damned thing. We're hoping you know something – anything – about her, like whether she was married or single, what she drove, whatever. They're assuming she lived near Belle Plaine, because that's where she was found, but even that's a guess. You must know something that might help.'

'She's got a sister who took an art class when they were kids,' I said, like that mattered.

'How would you know that?'

'Violet was proud of a ring. She designed it and her sister made it when they were children. It's an ugly thing, clumped with too much solder. Got a little flower in the middle of it, a purple one.'

'A violet,' he said.

I nodded. 'And she drives a green Chevy Volt. Quiet thing, makes no noise, sort of like her, I guess.'

'That doesn't figure,' he said.

'What doesn't?'

'Besides trying to locate a phone number for her, we also tried a trace by driver's license and vehicle tag. We struck out.'

'Why aren't you and Jacks in charge of investigating her death?'

'We could be part of it, I suppose, if we can show there's potential she was killed because of the Central Works thing. How much did she know, Elstrom?'

'You talked to her. You brought her strudel, she said. With raisins. She was charmed.'

'She was a sweet thing – fragile and trusting,' he said. 'And innocent, I thought, of anything to do with the case. But I need to be sure. Can you remember anything at all she might have mentioned that would tie back to Central Works?'

'She insisted she knew nothing about any of the Triple Time acquisitions. She found no office records of sales or commissions involving them, which she said meant Herbie worked those four deals out of his car. That's what she called it, working out of his car. Check with his wife – maybe he left documents at his house. You saw his rented room, Detective. He left nothing there.'

'That funny baseboard,' he said.

I thought to nod in agreement. 'Maybe that's what was hidden in the wall. Records relating to those four properties, though why they'd need to be hidden is beyond me.'

He stood up.

'Who's investigating her murder?' I asked.

'It's outside of Chicago PD, I was told. Actually, I wasn't told anything directly. A message was left in our office about her death. County, maybe, or state police, probably. I doubt it would be the Belle Plaine coppers. It's a tiny suburb. They've got no expertise.'

'It was nice, you bringing her that strudel,' I said.

He looked at me, surprised.

'Meaning maybe not a lot of people were nice to her,' I said.

'Sure as hell, not yesterday,' he said, and they left me alone to stare at the flotsam floating along in the Willahock.

I hadn't moved from the bench when Cuthbert and Raines came an hour later. I'd been barely able to breathe.

Violet Krumfeld, murdered.

'We're here about Walter Dace,' Cuthbert said.

'He and his assistant were murdered.'

'How did you hear that?' Raines asked.

'Your pals, Detectives Kopek and Jacks, told me so last night, though they didn't have much to say about that this morning.'

'What are you talking about?' Raines said.

'They were just here. And they were here last night.'

'So what did you tell them?'

'What I always say: Dace was the property manager for Triple Time Partners. Herbie Sunheim was the realtor on the deals and Rickey Means, the man on the boxcar, did the legal work for the acquisitions.'

'That's it?'

'I also said I dropped off a dummied-up time report for Dace.'

'Why?'

'To see if that would prompt him to spill anything about the Central Works, which I think is related to Herbie's disappearance. It didn't work; Dace said nothing. And that, gentlemen, is what I know. Best you check with Kopek or Jacks if you have any more questions. You could even carpool out here together next time, save my time and your time and your gas. Now, tell me about Violet Krumfeld.'

'Sunheim's assistant?'

'Of course Sunheim's assistant. I heard about her the same way I heard about Dace, from Kopek and Jacks. You know, those other two detectives who are working the Central Works case?'

Raines shrugged. 'We've got brass that likes independence of thought. We're working our own angles, is all.'

'Violet Krumfeld,' I said.

'She was assaulted, bludgeoned on a jogging path in Belle Plaine. We got notified because she's tangential to Sunheim, who, like Rickey Means, relates to Walter Dace. We don't think her death is related to her boss's disappearance.'

'So, you're not here to find out what I know about Violet Krumfeld?'

'Her murder is not our case,' Raines said.

'Whose, then? The cop who found her?'

'Listen, Elstrom. We're trying to stay focused, and that means finding out what you know about Walter Dace.'

We went over what little I knew about Dace and his relationship to Means, Sunheim and Triple Time.

'We're done,' Raines said.

'You guys could save the department big payroll if you worked together with Kopek and Jacks.'

'Don't be an ass,' Cuthbert said. 'This is a complicated case.'

'Many tentacles,' Raines added.

'Well, speaking as a tentacle, it seems you guys are deliberately not sharing notes with each other.'

They headed up the rise to the street without saying anything more.

I stayed put, staring at the river until I had the stomach to pull out my phone and search the Internet. None of the news sites offered anything beyond short reports of an as-yet unidentified woman who was found bludgeoned on a jogging trail in Belle Plaine.

Violet Krumfeld had made little noise and attracted little notice in life, and now she appeared to have attracted even less in death.

THIRTY-THREE

Belle Plaine, the upscale, lush suburb where Violet had been murdered, was ten miles and thousands of per-capita income dollars north of Rivertown. All the way there, I told myself I'd warned her in the strongest terms to leave Herbie's office and never return. All the way there, myself didn't believe.

Belle Plaine's white brick municipal building was at the end of a curved street arched with ancient trees and lined with what would become professionally maintained flower beds once the last of the muck of March melted away. The police station was across the corridor from the town's municipal offices that a propped cardboard sign said were still closed for lunch.

The door to the police department opened into a tiled reception area with four blue plastic chairs and a low, wood-grained table that held brochures describing the town's substance abuse hotline and counseling programs. An open glass window was set in the back wall. Behind that, a sergeant sat at a desk, eating a foot-long meatball sandwich. I'd eaten nothing since one of Kopek's coconut Sno-Balls all day, and that was before I learned Violet was dead. I doubted I'd be hungry for some time.

The desk sergeant put down the foot-long and got up to come to the window when I mentioned Violet's name. Studying my insurance investigator's business card, he said, 'You guys amaze me. When a problem is first reported, you're all johnnies-on-the-spot, anxious to assess your risk. But when it comes time to actually pay on a claim, you move slower than frozen molasses.'

'You have marinara at the corner of your mouth,' I said.

He wiped at it with the back of his hand, glaring at me. 'Am I right, or am I right?'

'I don't process claims. I merely do preliminary reports.'

'Whatever, you're wasting your time with me, pal. We're not handling the case because the malfeasance occurred in a forest preserve. The county sheriff has jurisdiction.'

'You must have responded to a call about the, uh, malfeasance,' I said, mimicking the meatball's use of the word 'malfeasance.' I wanted to yell that nobody used such an unnecessarily long word, except maybe lawyers billing by the hour. And I wanted to scream that the residue from his sandwich still remained stuck to the edge of his mouth. But I took a breath, suspecting that my rage at Violet's death was likely being misdirected onto his pomposity.

He looked at me funny for a moment, decided I was harmless, and said, 'The runner who found her was an off-duty cop. He knew what to do. He called an ambulance, and rode with her to the hospital. She was pronounced dead in their emergency room. He notified the sheriff's from there, and then called to inform us as a courtesy.'

'That was the first you heard of it?'

He nodded.

'What hospital?'

'Our rookie took the call.'

'Meaning he didn't think to ask.'

'Really, there was no need,' he said, having gone defensive.

'What ambulance service?'

'Why would that matter?'

'Because I heard she died in the ambulance.'

'Don't matter. She was pronounced at the hospital. Anything more, check the report.'

'At the sheriff's office?'

'Sure.'

'Witnesses?'

'Look, Mac, it was just that off-duty cop. There aren't many runners along the trail early afternoon. We sent a man out there anyway, once we found out that the malfeasance had occurred, but that part of the trail runs through woods, invisible from the park. No one saw a thing. We figure the killer was a runner, came up on her, struck her, hauled her into the trees and ran on. Slick and fast, a crime of sudden opportunity.'

'A mugging gone bad, for money?'

He shrugged.

'Who processed the crime scene?'

'County, probably. We have no personnel for that sort of thing, though our man did walk the trail and go into the trees. He found nothing that indicates where she was killed. The perpetrator could have dragged her along the trail – it's paved – for several hundred yards without leaving a mark.'

I asked him for directions and he sketched a one-minute map on a blank sheet of paper that was nothing more than a dozen curvy lines, expecting me to remember what they were for. He said I'd know the trail because the patrol officer he'd sent out initially was still there, questioning passers-by if they'd seen anything, but we both knew that was a Hail Mary shot, because any well-meaning witness would have already come forward.

'Why keep a man out there, if it's not your case?' I asked.

'SOP,' he said.

'Standard Operating Procedure for murder malfeasances?' I asked, because I'd most certainly not yet become benign.

'Chief said that part of the trail was within village limits, and since nobody from county did us the courtesy of bringing us into the loop, we were entitled to do a little investigating of our own.' Entitled to act like cops was what his chief meant, to cover their butts in case someone like me came along to inquire why they'd done nothing about a murder on their turf.

'I'll need the name of the cop who rode with her to the hospital,' I said.

'He forgot to leave it.' He held up his hand. 'I know, I know, we should have demanded, but like I said, it was a rookie working the phones.'

I didn't need the map he'd scribbled, because the park was big and the town was small, and I began walking the running trail fifteen minutes later. I spotted the Belle Plain patrolman almost immediately, pacing back and forth, looking at the ground alongside the path like he was hunting a lost contact lens. He was in his early twenties, young enough to have been the rookie who'd misfired, working the phones.

I gave him a card. 'Are you the officer that took the call?'

'That was Jake. He's younger,' he said.

'Find anything interesting?' I asked, gesturing toward the ground he'd been scrutinizing.

'No signs of struggle, which means nothing if she was clubbed on the pavement. For sure, there is no blood evidence.'

'It could have been scooped up by the county's forensics team.'

'Sure enough, except . . .'

'Except what?'

'Except I can't find any trace of their work, either.'

'They can be especially tidy,' I said, because it was true. I'd been at a hundred crime scenes. Some technicians were slobs but most were fanatical neatniks.

'I've asked everyone running by if they saw or heard anything yesterday,' the cop said. 'They asked what time, I said early to mid-afternoon. They asked what happened, I said assault. They asked if the victim is OK, I said no. They said they didn't see anything.'

I probed the scrub alongside the path for fifteen minutes, not at all sure what I was looking for but owing diligence to Violet just the same. It was no use. Last autumn's fallen leaves were saturated from the winter's snow, and would have almost immediately plumped back up no matter how hard they'd been pressed down by a killer or a victim.

I thought, then, of the green Volt she'd driven out to the turret, a car the cops hadn't been able to trace to her, according to Kopek. I left the trail, walked the several blocks surrounding the park and then drove back to the police station. The same sergeant was sitting behind the front desk, but all that remained of the meatball sandwich were specks of red sauce on both sides of his mouth.

'What happened to her car?' I asked.

He didn't bother to get up and come to the window. 'Her car?'

'She drove an electric car, a green Chevy Volt. I walked the blocks surrounding the park and couldn't find it on any of the streets.'

'Don't know about her car,' he said.

'You have signs prohibiting overnight street parking, two a.m. to six a.m. Your patrol officers must have ticketed it.'

'I review the overnights myself before sending them to accounting. We ticketed no such car.'

'It had a decal in the back window, showing a round cartoon head with an index finger raised to its lips, whispering.'

He smiled, perhaps at knowing something I did not. 'That's a Responsible Rentals car. They rent to moonbeams, the environmentally conscious. They also rent lawnmowers, weed-whackers and such. Everything's electric with them, nice and quiet. Bunch of ex-hippies probably, maybe tree huggers. Dopers, no doubt. They're in the city someplace.'

'It makes no sense, not finding her car. You say Responsible Rentals is in the city?'

'You could look in the phone book,' he said.

I thanked him for the tip and said I'd be sure to do that, as soon as I found someone who owned a phone book.

THIRTY-FOUR

Responsible Rentals was on Chicago's trendy north side, in a neighborhood of health-food restaurants, basket and artificial flower shops, and, most appropriate of all, a folk music school for folks inclined to zither.

The narrow side lot was crammed with four Chevy Volts. All were green and had shushing cartoon heads on their rear windows. Any one of them could have been the car Violet drove out to my place.

I walked through multicolored jangly beads and into the sound of Joan Baez singing of the night someone drove old Dixie down, though, judging by her lyrics, it was likely not in an electric car.

The shop was small and contained three electric lawnmowers, three electric weed-whackers and one electric outdoor grill. All looked brand new, never used.

'Business good?' I asked the slender fellow behind the counter, handing him a business card.

'Insurance investigation?' he asked.

'A minor accident, yesterday. One of your Volts is still out for rental?'

'Sadly, they're all here and accounted for. That part of our business is killing us, what with the car payments and all.'

I resisted the urge to eyeball the unused mowers and whackers, thinking the guy must have been selling weed out of his back room to get by.

'You're sure? One of our insureds reported she had a, uh, malfeasance in one of your rental cars.'

'A woman, you say? No, not today, not yesterday, not for a long while. It's been two months since a woman rented one of our cars, and she's a holistic healer in her sixties. Our cars are all here, undamaged and mostly unused.'

'A slender woman, curly brown hair, thick glasses, about thirty years old. Talks in a whisper?'

'Like our logo?' he asked, smiling as he pointed to a larger rendering of the shushing cartoon head above the cash register. 'No. The last Volt we rented was to a man in his early thirties.'

'When?'

'Real recent. I don't like to give out customer information.'

I supposed it could have been the day Violet drove out to the turret. 'Maybe he rented it for his wife to use,' I said.

'That I couldn't say.'

'How long was that car out on rental?'

'Just for a day. What's the name of your insured person?'

'Violet Krumfeld.'

'Rings no bells.'

'Can you tell me the name of the man who rented that Volt?'

'No can do,' he said, pressing his forefinger to his lips to mimic his cartoon logo. 'Like I said, we respect all confidences.'

He wanted to walk out to his side lot, then, to make sure his cars were undamaged. I had to pretend interest in doing that as well, and we spent the next fifteen minutes looking for damage that was never there.

'You're sure I can't have the name of the man who rented your car?' I asked.

He put his finger to his lips, and so I left him and his confidences, not at all confident about what I'd just learned. Violet had driven out to Rivertown in a car someone else had rented. Conceivably, that could have been because her own car was being repaired, though that was a long shot because the cops had been unable to link her to any vehicle. More likely, she didn't own a car and simply borrowed the rental – a car that had only been rented for a day and perhaps only to be used to drive out to the turret, though that seemed too far-fetched to be believed.

I called the Belle Plaine police department when I got outside, and got the desk man I'd spoken with earlier.

'This is Elstrom,' I said. 'What sorts of cars were ticketed recently for overnight violations after the woman was found dead?'

'None. Not one for a week,' the desk sergeant said.

'You're sure?'

'Nothing for a whole week. But since you're so eager, let's find out what she does drive, shall we?' He set the phone down and I could hear him tapping at a keyboard. Embarrassment over his rookie's lack of curiosity must have energized him.

After a moment, he picked up the phone and asked, 'We are talking Violet Krumfeld, right?' He spelled out both first and last names.

'Violet Krumfeld, yes,' I said.

More tapping came, and then he put me on hold.

Fifteen long minutes later, he came back on the line. 'Something's wrong, Elstrom. The Illinois Secretary of State has no record of issuing either a driver's license or a vehicle license plate to a Violet Krumfeld. The Illinois Department of Revenue shows no one by that name as ever paying sales tax on an automobile purchase. In other words—'

'In other words,' I interrupted, 'she's now using a different last name.' It was no surprise; Kopek's people would have gone through the same exercise.

'Happens all the time,' he said. 'Women get married or divorced. Plus, she could have been given a ride out here to run, or taken a bus or a train.'

'Want to know what my next questions are?' I asked.

He sighed. 'What hospital was she taken to, what ambulance took her and what cops are now investigating her murder?'

'You can get answers faster than I can.'

He called me an hour later, just I was stepping into the gloom of Herbie's half-lit office hallway.

'Nothing,' the desk sergeant said.

'No Violets with any last name were pronounced dead anywhere?'

'No Violets, no Krumfelds, no blunt force traumas anywhere that fit her description,' he said. 'And believe me, I checked it right.'

It made no sense and yet it so strangely mirrored what Kopek seemed to suggest when he came to tell me of her death and to ask what I knew of her life. Violet Krumfeld was unknowable, a mist, a vapor, a chunk of the big Herbie Sunheim jigsaw puzzle that butted against the others, refusing to fit.

'I sent an email blast to every hospital within fifty miles,' the sergeant went on. 'Not that any sane person would transport a dying or dead woman that far. They'd head for the closest place to get her pronounced dead. I got replies from every one. No woman in her early thirties suffering blunt force trauma was brought in, dead or alive, from Belle Plaine that afternoon.'

'And the ambulance companies themselves?' I asked.

'There are four, though one has the lion's share of the business. No pick-ups in Belle Plaine that afternoon. Zero, nothing, *nada*.'

'How about a very private ambulance?'

'You mean one of those one-vehicle operations that very rich people use for privacy? Possible,' he said, 'but I wouldn't know how to get through to those.'

'Neither would the cop running along the trail who found her, most likely,' I said. 'Speaking of the name of that cop . . .?'

'No dice on that, yet. I emailed Chicago PD, Cook County Sheriff's, Cook County Forest Preserve, Illinois State Police and every surrounding local within twenty miles. He could have come from any of them. I'll let you know when they respond.'

A credit card popped the flimsy lock to Herbie's office. Inside, it stunk of a serious dousing with disinfectant. And that made it stink of too much orderliness.

I'd seen previously that Violet had removed the mess of files from Herbie's desk, thinking she'd gone through them for Triple Time documents and then refiled them. All that remained on his desk now was an empty Campbell's Tomato Soup can full of pens liberated from the closest of Chicago's downtown hotels and a stack of the small notepads hoteliers set out next to their room phones. It wasn't hard to envision Herbie cruising the upper floors of the Palmer House and the Chicago Hilton, looking to replenish his office supplies from untended maids' carts.

Herbie's desk drawers were completely empty and smelled strongly of the disinfectant that permeated the whole office. There were no backup office supplies, no surplus hotel pens or scratch pads or notes or files or stray anything in any of them. Not even a loose paperclip stuck in a corner. I was beginning to understand the strong disinfectant. Drawers didn't get that clean unless they were dumped and then scrubbed.

The drawers in the file cabinets along the wall had been completely emptied of papers and folders, and they, too, smelled strongly of disinfectant. Even the company checkbook so desperately wanted by Herbie's wife was gone. Everything had been taken away.

Violet's desk was as bare as Herbie's, the top clear except for her desk phone, headset, ancient IBM typewriter and one scratch pad from the Drake Hotel. The thought flitted through my mind that Herbie probably handed out his stolen hotel pads one at a time, to promote frugality.

Then again, the man had died with three hundred thousand dollars stashed behind his baseboard. I wondered who else knew about that money, and who had burgled Mrs Sunheim's house looking for it. And I wondered if Kopek and Jacks knew about that money, and if that was why they'd asked to search her house.

Lots of people knew lots of things that I didn't know.

Violet's desk drawers were also empty and smelled of the same disinfectant. On a hunch, I leaned down to sniff the typewriter. It, too, stunk of the disinfectant. The office hadn't been cleaned; it had been scrubbed down to remove fingerprints.

I picked up her notepad from the Drake. There were only three sheets left. The top two were marked by indentations from hard doodling on a higher sheet. Violet had sketched violets.

It was possible she truly loved the little flowers.

Or, it was possible she needed to be reminded of the name she was using.

For sure, Violet Krumfeld had skipped lightly, whispering, leaving nothing but the faintest indentations of herself behind.

THIRTY-FIVE

D riving back to Rivertown, I called the cell number printed on Kopek's card. 'How did you learn about Violet Krumfeld's death?' I heard voices in his background; he was at his precinct.

'A phone message, left on my desk.'

'From whom?'

'Why is this important?'

'Remember you told me your people were having trouble getting a fix on Violet's life, like where she lived and all?'

'We're still having trouble. The woman didn't have a phone, a car, credit cards, nothing in the name of Violet Krumfeld. Have you learned something?'

'I learned you're right. The Belle Plaine police tried to trace her through the ambulance that took her away and nearby hospitals. They found nothing, too.'

'Obviously, she was working under an assumed name. Unfortunately, we can't get at Sunheim's federal or state payroll reports. The woman was afraid, probably of whoever caught up to her on that jogging trail, or she was up to no good in that office. Hold on.'

He yelled to someone in his background. 'Shirley, you're sure the guy who phoned about Violet Krumfeld didn't leave a name?'

'I told you, he hung up before I could get it,' a woman's voice came back.

Kopek sighed into the phone. 'And there you have it, Elstrom. Police efficiency. I don't know who called. More important, I had Shirley call around to the other agencies, to see if we could chase down more on Miss Krumfeld. Nobody has a damned thing on her, which might mean a lot, or might mean only that somebody screwed up, mislabeling a file.'

I called Cuthbert next, and asked his voicemail who'd notified him of Violet's death. I asked Raines' voicemail the same thing.

Back at the turret, I frittered myself into the evening, sitting and standing and prowling the turret, knowing what I had to do next but not knowing what to do after that. Herbie Sunheim had to be put back. And Violet Krumfeld, whoever she was, had to be known.

The men behind Triple Time – the faceless, shapeless creatures who'd likely set off all the killing – had to be found, too, but finding them would be next to impossible. Men like them believed in multiple layers of insulation. Whoever was killing on their behalf reported to people who reported to people who reported to people who could never be identified. People on high.

People on high.

It was the nubbin of a thought.

I grabbed a gray plastic shopping bag and went up the stairs to the ladder to the fifth floor, the floor to which my grandfather, contorted thinker that he was, had never extended stairs, probably because he, like me, had no idea what to do with a fifth floor. I'd brought the drone down from the roof and left it there with its belly camera facing the dark of the stone wall, because I didn't know what to do with it after I snagged it.

Until now, perhaps.

The camera and light were attached with Velcro to the belly of the drone. A strong tug broke them loose. I put them in the gray bag and placed it back into the shadows with the lens facing the wall.

I sat on the rough plank floor with the drone in my lap. It was a sizable thing, about two feet square, but surprisingly light, with a helicopter rotor at each of its four corners. Big enough to carry a camera and a light, it might well be big enough to carry something else.

I mulled that for a few minutes more, then went downstairs, slipped on my coat and went out into the night. I went on foot, having decided it would be safest for Booster Gibbs if I were not noticed arriving in my noticeable Jeep to seek his counsel, should what I'd been mulling go awry.

'Don't tell me you lost your Jeep again, Dek,' Booster said, pulling his surgical mask down to free the huge smile in the middle of his beard.

'Something more sinister, I'm afraid. I need a referral to someone who can make a device for a burn.'

Booster turned his head slightly away, but not enough so I couldn't see his grin being replaced by shock. 'Not a kill, Dek.'

Rivertown, for all its corruption, its kickbacks and hookers and illicit gambling machines, was a moral place. Modern viciousness – modern murders and modern drugs – were not allowed. Most certainly, the lizards that ran the town, mostly members of one extended family in tight control, did not allow killing.

'No kill, absolutely not,' I said. 'I need expertise to burn a drug lab.'

'Surely there's not one here?' he asked, clearly alarmed.

'Not in Rivertown. It's in Chicago, and it's destined to be no trailer operation. This thing looks to become a high output manufacturer, perhaps the first of several.'

'A righteous burn,' he said, looking relieved.

'So far, minor league bad people have died – the lawyer, the realtor and the property manager who set up the sites. But three innocents – a kid who tipped me to some of the goings-on, the property manager's receptionist and, just yesterday, the realtor's secretary, have gotten caught up in the mess, too. More innocent victims will follow when the lab gets into gear.'

'Weasel's dirty in this?'

'Hard to tell where Weasel comes down. Some of his clothes were grabbed out of his house. He might have escaped.'

'A drug lab, you're sure?'

'One big-time facility is being set up now. Two more buildings are being kept, and guarded, for later.'

'You're messing with cartel,' he said.

'Someone big, for sure.'

He looked down the street, thinking. 'There's a guy I've done work for. He's something like you, Dek. He loves a challenge and comes across as righteous.'

'All I want from him is a device and expertise.'

'He'll have to check things out, make sure you're on the level and that the target isn't.'

'How do I contact him?'

'You don't; I do. If he's interested, he'll contact you. He'll want details, and then he'll verify them. He works only with burner phones. You'll never see him, you'll never meet – at least not face-to-face.'

'It's important.'

'I'll make contact,' he said, and went back inside.

THIRTY-SIX

They returned to search the bank of the Willahock at nine the next morning. I walked down, for I'd been up half the night, working out details. They were two of those details. I was fully inspired.

I knew the squat, unshaven fellow in the army surplus camouflage jacket and backward Oakland Raiders ball cap, of course. He was Benny Fittle, the town's parking enforcement officer, the fellow I'd awakened after he'd fallen asleep in the process of parking his orange Maverick.

I did not know the girl in the slightly smaller army camouflage jacket, though I'd seen her with him often, the past few months. She was dumpy like him and also wore rock band T-shirts in warmer weather. I'd never seen her up close, but as I approached them, I saw that her face had the familiar pinched features and small eyes of the clan that ran Rivertown.

'Oh . . . hey, Mr E,' Benny said, as startled as when he'd jerked awake in his half-parked car. There was no longer any mystery about what had tired him so powerfully that day; he'd been spending most of his nights fully awake, helping his squeeze bang a drone up the side of my turret.

He turned his back to the muck along the riverbank, as though frightened that what they were searching for might suddenly burst up from the water like a joyous, whiskered carp and reveal itself, and its mission, to me.

'Looking for something, Benny?'

'Sorta.'

'And you are?' I asked, turning to the girl staring at her muddy, high-topped green sneakers.

'Edwina,' she said, still looking down. A flush had risen on her pale, acned neck.

'Edwina who?' I asked, like I couldn't guess.

'Edwina Derbil,' Benny said, ever the helpful gentleman.

'Elvis's . . .?'

'Niece,' she said, looking up at last. She fished in her muddy jeans pocket, and came out with a crumpled business card. Below the City of Rivertown seal, emblazoned with a rendering of my turret at its center, it read, 'Edwina Derbil, Aviation Department.'

It so figured – an aviation department created to oversee the operation of one drone, a drone that had now gone missing – as a brain spasm of her uncle. Elvis Derbil, Rivertown's zoning commissioner, had been my nemesis since the day I'd materialized unexpectedly in his office, flat broke, unshaven and likely stinking of whiskey, to request an occupancy permit to move into the five-story limestone turret that I'd inherited.

It had been decades since Rivertown's ruling lizards, invoking eminent domain, seized most of my grandfather's acreage and all of his great pile of unused limestone blocks to build a magnificent city hall of tiny public rooms and expansive private offices along the Willahock River. They'd not wanted the turret – the only part of a castle my grandfather managed to get built – and so it had languished in my family's hands, who'd not wanted it either. For years, it accrued unpaid taxes and pigeon streaks, until the lizards sought to lure new developers to their greasy, rusting old factory town. They termed this potential rebirth the Rivertown Renaissance, and adopted the turret as its symbol, it being the only medieval-looking structure around. To make sure their new symbol would remain unchanged by any future owners, they offered my aunt, the last known survivor of my grandfather's children, a deal. They would wipe away all the years of unpaid taxes in exchange for being allowed to rezone the turret as a municipal structure, thereby ensuring that the exterior of their new icon could not be changed without lizard approval. Such a zoning change, reclassifying a privately owned building into a municipal structure, was something that could only have been conceived in a slick grease pot like Rivertown.

My aunt, no dummy, seized the deal to free herself and her children from any liability for those back taxes. But to make doubly sure she and her heirs would be free of them forever, she willed the turret to me.

As a municipal structure, it accrued no new taxes and so, for years, I ignored it, too. But then I'd gotten falsely accused of faking evidence in a notorious criminal trial. I was exonerated, but my notoriety cost me clients and I'd spiraled drunkenly out of control, and out of my marriage. Wisely, Amanda had thrown me out of her home. I had no place to go except to the turret, which, in one of my foggiest inspirations, I began to see as something I could restore into a saleable residence, while maybe, just maybe, restoring myself.

Elvis Derbil had to give me an occupancy permit because I owned the turret, but he'd warned me of the codicil. The city of Rivertown, protecting its icon, forbade any modification to the turret's exterior. For a recovering drunk in dire need of shelter, I accepted the restriction as something I could fight later on, when the turret, and I, dried out.

Now Elvis had sensed an illegal modification. He, or one of his grubs, must have spotted the delivery of my furnace some months before and figured that where there's fire, there must be smoke, and therefore an unallowable chimney vent cut somewhere into the turret's exterior. And so he'd created a department of aviation – in a suburb that had no runways, no hangars and no planes – and outfitted his niece, Edwina, and her tag-along boyfriend with a camera fitted to a drone to find proof of the illegal exterior modification. It was but the latest round in a series of bouts between Elvis and me.

'You've spent quite a bit of time lately looking for something,' I said now to Edwina, the aviation czarina.

She nodded, and so, therefore, did Benny.

'Using something you've been banging up the side of my turret, ruining my sleep.'

Only Edwina nodded this time. Benny simply yawned.

'A drone to surreptitiously photograph the exterior of my turret,' I said.

Edwina Derbil looked away, likely from embarrassment. Benny said, 'Huh?'

'"Surreptitiously" means "sneakily,"' I said to him.

He smiled and nodded in agreement.

'And now your drone, Rivertown's sole aircraft, has gone missing?'

'My uncle will kill me,' Edwina said. 'He spent six hundred dollars on it.'

'Including the camera?'

Tears began streaming down her face. 'That was extra.'

'I'll help you look for your drone, but if I find it, you have to spend a couple of hours teaching me how to operate it,' I said.

Edwina nodded quickly. Benny yawned.

'Until then, don't waste your time searching,' I said, 'and, for sure, don't waste your time searching for changes to the turret.' There'd been no changes. I'd snaked the heatproof vent piping up through one of the fireplace chimneys so it wouldn't be spotted.

Edwina smiled, full of hope for the drone. Benny smiled, too, full of hope for sleep. Watching them both leave, I had the thought I'd like some hope, too.

Five minutes later, my phone rang.

THIRTY-SEVEN

'**M**r Elstrom?' The call was coming from a blocked number. 'Yes?'

'You've been referred to me.' The voice, tinny and mechanical, was coming through some sort of voice synthesizer.

'Yes.'

'We'll meet.'

'I thought it was only by phone.'

'It's both.' He named a Wal-Mart five miles away, in the city. 'Be in the parking lot in twenty minutes.'

'Where shall I park?'

'Wherever you'd like.' He clicked off.

The man was careful, not only in using a synthesizer and a burner phone, but in setting up a meet on the spur of the moment, too quickly for anyone to mobilize something against him. I figured he was already in that Wal-Mart parking lot, watching now to see who arrived. I hurried down to the Jeep.

The parking lot was two-thirds full. I took a slow turn around the perimeter, sure that Booster had told the man what I'd be driving, and then parked in the middle so he'd know I wasn't interested in isolating him to be seen.

My phone rang a moment later, from a different blocked number. 'Now, exit your vehicle,' the synthesized voice said. 'Remove your outerwear and stand by your front bumper.'

I got out, tossed my peacoat back into the Jeep and went to the front bumper.

'Thank you,' he went on. 'Tell me what you wish, and why.'

I didn't look around. It wouldn't have done me any good. The man was too careful, too cautious. He was sitting in one of the cars or trucks parked close enough to have a clear view of me, likely behind dark tinted glass.

I began by telling him of the corpse found dead on the railcar, and the subsequent explosion of the Central Works building.

'I read it was arson,' he said.

'Fire plus explosion. The building – an abandoned, uninsured building – was wired to explode in case uninvited competitors or cops stopped by.'

'Professional rigging, professional explosion.'

'The purchasers of the Central Works bought three other buildings, so the loss of one wouldn't slow their mission. All might be wired to explode in the same way.'

'Police?'

'I'm worried some higher-ups are corrupted. Two teams of detectives are working the Central Works victim and the deaths that followed. The lawyer who handled the real estate purchases, the realtor who found the properties, the property manager and his receptionist who fronted for the real buyers have all been killed, their links to the property buyers eradicated. The cops are fumbling with it all, perhaps being deliberately directed to not collaborate.'

'That's why you're taking back? Because the cops won't?'

There it was again, that phrase, 'Taking back.' It wasn't just Amanda's; it wasn't just what was crudely lettered on the Rules of the Block boards in Austin. 'Taking back' might have become the budding mantra for those in Chicago furious enough to begin taking matters into their own hands. And, I supposed, I'd become part of that movement, and it was why I'd come to that Wal-Mart parking lot.

'Innocents are dying,' I said. 'Innocents like the realtor's assistant, who got murdered a couple of days ago. Innocents like all the hapless kids that are going to overdose on the drugs made in those drug labs.'

I told him of the Vanderbilt Supply and the Bureski buildings, boarded up and empty except for armed guards and, likely, explosives. And I told him of the fourth building, where I supposed the fixtures and equipment originally destined for the Central Works site had been rerouted.

'You're sure it's being outfitted as a drug lab?'

'Sure enough to set a fire, at least. My evidence is circumstantial, but if that building, or either of the two others, was intended for a good purpose, the projects would have been hyped by aldermen, and even the mayor. I've searched the Internet, where everything seems to get reported. I found nothing. Everything's being kept under the radar.'

'How about building inspectors? Bought off?'

'It's been known to happen, especially in Chicago.'

He paused, thinking, and then asked, 'You want to level that building to the ground?'

'I want it to be noticed. I want it to be swarmed by firefighters, cops and news people. I don't need to destroy that building and risk killing any innocent people working inside. I do want to kill what's being planned by shining a harsh light on it, and that means a fire on the roof hot enough to spread down a floor or two. I want an investigation to follow that no one can kill.'

'But if it's wired to explode . . .?'

'Then that's an answer in itself.'

'What are you envisioning, exactly?'

'As I said, a burn from the top down. I want to land a drone on the roof to set the fire.'

'Visible for miles around? Intriguing, but why not simply approach on the ground?'

'The building sits by itself in the middle of a bulldozed clearing. It is heavily guarded. I'd never get close enough.'

'Where is this building?'

I gave him the location.

'I will assess this. Do you have experience with drones?'

'None.'

'I've prepared the sort of device you're seeking twice before.' He told me of a shop not far away that sold a specific model of hobbyist drone. 'Buy one, Mr Elstrom, and familiarize yourself with its operation. Become proficient quickly.'

'You require nothing more of me?'

'Our mutual friend assured me you're to be trusted for truth and confidentiality. Please drive off.'

'When will you get back to me?'

'No telling. Until then, you'll merely own an expensive toy.'

*　　*　　*

Six hundred and fifty dollars later – the price of the drone Booster's shadowy man had specified – I found Benny Fittle double-parked on his usual turf, one of the side streets immediately off Thompson Avenue. He was writing a ticket for a sedan whose meter still had eighteen minutes to run before expiring.

'We're set to go,' I said.

He put his stub of a pencil back to the top of his ear as comprehension descended on his face. 'You found it?' he asked.

I tried to beam like I'd actually searched.

'Wait till I tell Edwina,' he said, moving toward his car.

'We'll meet where?'

'Elvis Derbil, in a half-hour,' he said, untroubled by the fact that he was on duty.

I headed back to the turret, grabbed the City of Rivertown drone and drove to the park that Elvis Derbil, the city's zoning commissioner and uncle of Edwina, had named for himself. A manufacturer of harsh engine degreasing chemicals had operated there until its sewer drains began catching fire. The city bought the property – from a cousin of a previous mayor, which raised no eyebrows in Rivertown – and bulldozed the building. It was now a park in name only, a clearing bereft of playground equipment, baseball diamonds and goalposts, since grass wouldn't grow on ground that even years later oozed up noxious, dark liquids.

They were already there. Edwina spotted the city's drone on top of the box I was carrying and ran up, her arms outstretched.

'Oh, thank you, thank you, thank you,' she said.

'Some instruction will be thanks enough,' I said, unboxing my own drone.

'Yours is nicer,' Benny said.

Mine was black and significantly larger – three feet square. Though both drones had four rotors, Booster's mysterious acquaintance must have specified a larger one because it could carry a heavy object.

Edwina loaded the batteries into my drone and control unit, motioned for us to step back, and pressed a toggle-like stick at the center of the control. The drone rose slowly, straight up, sounding like bees.

She performed some simple maneuvers, back and forth, up and down, and piloted the drone back to a smooth landing. She seemed so proficient that I wondered why she'd kept banging her drone against the side of the turret, until I realized she'd been probing the limestone closely for the smallest of vent holes.

She handed me the control. 'It's simple.'

I pressed the button. The rotors whirred louder, and the drone lifted straight up. Manipulating the joystick, I aimed the drone in one direction after another.

She was right. It was alarmingly simple to operate and, five minutes later, I told them they could both go. I stayed around for another hour until the drone and control batteries wore down, and then I headed back to the turret to recharge them and my thinking.

THIRTY-EIGHT

B lue lights flashed in Kutz's clearing.

I'd planned on returning Herbie that night. I'd come to reconnoiter, to think, to plan out the simple steps I needed to drop him in that guarded clearing, after dark.

But cops were there now.

I shot my right foot to the brake pedal, to slam to a stop, to shift into reverse and be gone. But I'd be noticed. And maybe I'd be chased.

I eased my foot back to the accelerator and drove forward slowly.

The two Rivertown cruisers were nosed up to the trailer. One cop leaned against one of the cars, smoking a cigarette. The other cop wasn't visible, which might have meant he was around back. By the freezer.

I shut off the engine a good distance away, first thinking to sit in the Jeep, breathing deep, strategizing words to say and surprise to show. But such an obvious lack of curiosity about the presence of two cop cars would raise interest even in someone as sluggish as the leaning, smoking Rivertown patrol officer, for any normal citizen would jump out nosy, race up to the cop and demand to know what was going on. So I did just that. I got out, a normal nose, and walked up to him on legs that didn't feel normal at all.

'Hey, Elstrom,' he said. He knew me. All the cops knew me.

Some, the veterans, remembered when I'd been a murder suspect in high school. Others, younger, knew me as the oddball that lived in the stone cylinder they passed several times a day on their way to and from the police station hidden discreetly at the back of city hall. He was one of the younger ones.

'Trouble?' I asked.

'You could say that, yeah.' He flicked his cigarette butt into the nearby woods, where it could have ignited the trees if the ground wasn't still so damp from snowmelt.

'Where's the restaurateur?'

Confusion crossed his otherwise guileless features. 'The who?' Like most of the force, he was related to the lizards that ran Rivertown. The least crafty of them got to drive the patrol cars.

'Leo Brumsky,' I said. 'He leased this place from Kutz for a few hundred years.'

'Ah,' he said, nodding. 'He's around back with the other officer.'

'What's around the back?'

'The other officer,' he said, looking at me like I was crazy.

'And the back of the trailer,' I said, prolonging the foolishness because I really didn't want to go around to the back.

'Uh, that too.' He smiled, no doubt delighted that we were on the same page, geographically.

'I better wait in my Jeep, then,' I said, because my teeth had begun to chatter.

'Nah,' he said, lighting another cigarette. 'Everything's gone, anyway. Nothing to see now.'

His eyes, clear since it was not yet time for the free shots and beers along Thompson Avenue, had narrowed, going wary. For sure, I felt them on the back of my neck as I walked around to the rear of the trailer.

Leo and the other cop were staring down at the bank of the river. Both heard me and looked up.

'You saw, right?' Leo asked me.

The cop gave him a pat on the back and me a nod, and walked away.

'Saw what?' I asked.

Leo pointed vaguely at the ground between the side of the trailer and the woods.

I snuck a look at the freezer enclosure instead. Its wood lid rested down but the padlock was angled in such a way that I couldn't be sure it was snapped closed.

'Gone now,' he said.

'Forensics?' I asked, meaning crime-scene folks, summoned to work the freezer and the corpse found inside. Gone now, with Herbie.

'Forensics?' He laughed, but for only a second. 'That's a good one. That's what's needed: good forensics. But nah, nobody's going to take it seriously.'

'What?' I asked.

'No goats,' Leo said.

'No goats?' I repeated, totally confused. 'Why?'

'Why what?'

'Why are you babbling about your goats?' I shouted, snapping at the leisurely way he was unraveling what might be my own unraveling. Cops didn't come because of goats.

He looked at me like he was seeing someone he'd never met before. He pointed again at the space between the side of the trailer and the woods. 'You didn't see?' he demanded. 'You really can't see?'

I looked and saw. His coral was empty, his goats gone.

'It was Gregorio,' he said. 'I know it was Gregorio.'

'Gregorio?' I asked, sucking air deep in relief now that he wasn't going to mention Herbie.

'Gregorio found a way to lift the latch.'

'Gregorio . . .' I said, still not grasping.

'Gregorio, the brown-and-white, the master.'

'The big goat,' I said.

He nodded.

I remembered Gregorio. He did have an aura, I supposed. 'You think he nudged up the gate latch to let them all escape?' I asked, wanting to laugh long and loud at nothing at all.

'Now the cops are ticketing me for letting them run free. I told them they should ticket Gregorio.'

'The damned cops!' I said with gusto, because Leo was my friend. 'Still, it's tough getting goats to pay fines, I imagine.'

He frowned. Clearly it was not the time to offer humor.

The sounds of cars pulling away came from the front of the trailer. '*Rivertown* cops!' I said. 'Never any good when you need them.'

'They managed to go through the motions, waltz through the woods, but they're too slow to catch up with my goats.' He made a dismissive motion with his hand.

A head peeked around the corner of the trailer. It was a familiar head, sort of, and then I recognized it as belonging to the man I'd seen earlier, patting the dancing goats. The veterinarian.

'Mr Brumsky,' he said.

'You saw?' Leo asked him.

The man nodded slowly, properly mournful. 'Best you wait them out. They might come back on their own.'

'Want me to go into the woods?' I asked Leo.

'You might scare them,' the vet said.

'But we've been waiting since we discovered them gone at noon,' Leo said, walking over to the vet. They stepped around the corner.

It was the break I needed. I gave the padlock on the freezer enclosure a tug. It was securely closed. I bent down and pulled the freezer plug out of the trailer's electrical receptacle.

Herbie needed to thaw to become pliable enough for easy removal.

'We're going into the woods,' Leo said, coming back to me.

I killed the hours until dark walking through the woods with them, ostensibly helping to look for Leo's goats but, more important, I was hanging around to make sure Leo didn't notice the freezer was unplugged and plug it back in.

None of the four goats had wandered back by the time the sun began to set. The vet made to leave and I made to follow.

'Time to head home, Leo,' I said. 'They'll come back on their own.'

'I'm staying,' he said. 'I want to latch them in securely when they do return.'

And thus was Herbie assured of spending another night in the freezer.

THIRTY-NINE

Booster's mystery man called at three the next afternoon. I was back at Elvis Derbil Park, practicing aeronautics and reviewing the night's plan to return the hopefully thawed Herbie to the Vanderbilt Supply building. I'd just gotten off the phone with Leo, who reported that the goats had still not returned and that he was going home, to sleep.

'I've been observing your building,' the synthesized voice said. 'It's quite heavily guarded.'

'Too much for it to be a legitimate enterprise.'

'One would think,' he said. 'Nonetheless, I contacted an acquaintance at city hall. A building permit was issued to renovate the structure into a cabinet-making workshop.'

'Cabinet makers don't need armed guards.'

'I counted four – one at each corner.'

'And yet the place is still not in operation,' I said.

'You've become proficient with the drone.' He'd been watching me, too, not just my target.

'I believe I can land it on an isolated roof in a clearing.' I'd been practicing simulated landings in the park.

'I believe so, too. You're navigating above the trees quite nicely.'

I looked at the edges of the park. There was a Shell gas station and a strip mall that held a dry cleaner, a bankrupt movie rental store and an investment counselor who was related to the tribe that ruled Rivertown. Booster's man could have been anywhere, watching me, being careful, double-checking.

His synthesized voice laughed, shrill and tinny. 'You won't see me, Mr Elstrom. You won't spot the glint of binoculars or the odd man, standing behind a tree.'

'Of course,' I said.

'You have a small woodpile at the river's side of your, ah . . .' He paused.

'Turret.'

'Perfect! Yes, turret. Inside the stack, you will find a small box. Inside is another small box with both sides of a Velcro strip attached to its top. Press it firmly onto the underbelly of your drone. You will see I have also left you a remote transmitting device. Be very careful to not press its button until you have landed onto your target. Activation will trigger nothing that is immediately visible. Three slow-burning flashes will commence in precisely ten minutes – more than enough time for you to drive safely away. Call the fire department from an untraceable phone. Best of luck.' He hung up.

I spent another twenty minutes practicing landings, trying not to think of the corpse that had to be dropped out of sight of the Vanderbilt guard, the fire that had to be set to the drug lab, and the darkness of a night that would make doing them doubly dangerous. When the batteries gave out, I drove back to the turret.

The cardboard box in my woodpile was green. The one inside of it, glued securely shut with Velcro on top, was black. The remote signaling device next to it was also black.

I took them inside to get ready for the darkness.

Eleven o'clock. A night full of clouds. A night dark enough, I hoped, to obscure.

I cut the headlamps and crept the Jeep down the river road in the darkness. Kutz's trailer was faintly white in the clearing, barely visible against the few silvery ripples of the Willahock. I backed up between the paddock and the trailer, got out, unzipped the rear plastic curtain, reached down and opened the half door.

Around the back, I aimed the narrow beam penlight directly at the combination lock on the wood enclosure, dialed the numbers and tugged. It didn't pull open. I spun the dial, found the numbers again. The lock stayed shut. It made no sense. The lock was a standard chrome Master with a black dial, the kind that sells in the millions because they never fail. I dialed the combination for a third time. The padlock would not open.

I hurried back to the Jeep for the small bag of tools I keep for when random parts fail. It only took three strikes with the hammer and steel chisel to splinter the wood surrounding the lock and hasp. I lifted the broken wood top, reached in and opened the freezer, ready now to touch the cold plastic shrouding the thawed corpse of Herbie Sunheim.

Nothing.

I plunged my hand all the way in and jammed my fingers on the bottom. Herbie was gone.

I would not think, not yet. I had to focus on the simple next things. I went back to the Jeep, leaned in the open rear door, put the bag behind the front passenger seat.

He hit me hard at the back of my knees as I straightened up. Falling, I banged my head on the Jeep's rear bumper as I dropped to the ground. I rolled onto my knees and looked up. I had to stand, to fight, to run.

Yellow eyes looked down at me from just inches away, its breath hot and foul on my face. He pawed at the ground, watching, waiting.

Leo's goat – one of them.

I scrambled up and lurched the few feet to unlatch the paddock gate. It pleased the goat. He ambled into the enclosure. I reached to close the gate and stopped. More yellow eyes had appeared in the darkness. Four of them.

I held the gate open, as would any doorman wise to the ways of goats, and the two followed the first goat into the fenced enclosure. I eased the gate closed but did not latch it, instead standing stock-still to listen. There was one more goat out in that night, somewhere. But the only sound I heard was my own blood thudding in my ears. I let another minute pass, and then I latched the gate.

There was no telling, in the darkness, if one of the three returned goats had been the crafty Gregorio, he of the deft touch with the latch. I reached into the Jeep, found a short piece of wire in the tool bag and looped it twice around the gate and the post, to be sure the goats stayed put.

The night had gone insane. I'd come for a corpse, found it gone, and stayed to usher goats into a paddock. I started up the engine and sped back up the river road. Only when I got to Thompson Avenue did I think to turn on my headlamps.

FORTY

D espite running the Jeep's heater full blast, I'd been shaking like I was fevered ever since I left Kutz's clearing. My gut had known that I'd been tailed the night I took Herbie, like my head knew now that it had been someone who'd snapped on an identical Master lock to replace what they'd cut off, to delay the discovery that Herbie had been snatched back. What neither my gut nor my head could figure now was why.

I parked three blocks short of the Triple Time lab and came up on foot, tightly clutching my parcel, wrapped in a black plastic garbage bag. The industrial and storage buildings that loomed above the sidewalk were dark. Some were vacant, some were not. The clouds that hung low over Rivertown had stretched to darken that south part of Chicago as well. I thought that was a mercy.

And then I was there. My target stood high and alone in the center of the clearing across the street, a shade darker than the night sky. There were no lights anywhere around, but there were guards there, professional men with guns, likely standing outside, straining to hear sounds in the darkness.

I knelt at the base of a burned-out street lamp, took the drone and its control out of the bag and set them on the ground.

Car lights flashed on in front of the drug lab, just a half-block away. Headlamps, coming fast toward me.

I left everything on the ground, scuttled back into deeper shadow, safe from the sweep of the car's lamps, and lay face down on cinders and stones and crushed glass. The lights had appeared too fast for happenstance. It was like they'd known I would come, like I'd been watched ever since I took Herbie.

The car slowed and then stopped at the intersection. It was a black Impala. A cop's car. A detective's car.

The wind picked up and rustled gently at the empty garbage bag I'd left by the lamppost, raising it up an inch then dropping it down, as if beckoning to be noticed in the lights of the stopped car.

The car's engine idled low. Just ahead, the drone's silver metal rotors glinted dully next to the rippling bag, not twenty feet from the Impala's windshield. Impossible to be unseen.

I pushed backward on my belly, desperate for more darkness.

The car eased forward and stopped again, right in the middle of the intersection. The drone was less than ten feet from the driver's door now.

Their high beams flashed on as if they'd seen something in the night, and the Impala revved up and shot through the intersection, passing the drone, passing me, speeding down the block, through the next intersection and into the block after that. I scrambled up to my feet to see.

Its tail lights brightened. The Impala had braked at the Jeep. Those in the car would know I was there, in the night. There were no other red Jeeps with green tops.

I stood, unsure. I should run like I had that night in Austin, run through that ruined district for a bus or a cab, come back for the Jeep sometime later when I could summon a lie that would hold. But then the bright red lights went off, disappearing entirely. The Impala had gone dark.

With luck, it was gone. With no luck, it was there, parked by the Jeep, waiting. Either way, I couldn't very well run around that neighborhood, carrying an armed drone. And what needed to be done would only take a few more minutes.

I ran out from the deep shadow, grabbed the drone and set it directly in line with the building. Thumbing the control sent the drone up into the sky.

I'd practiced dark maneuvering with the new weight snugged to the drone the night before at Elvis Derbil Park, and felt comfortable navigating by the little yellow light at its underbelly. But last night had been clear. This night was cloudy. The light was growing faint too soon as it angled toward the building across the street.

I had to follow the light. I stepped onto the street. If the black Impala came, I'd be lit up with nowhere to run.

Glass crunched beneath my shoes as I stepped over the opposite curb. I stopped. There were no other sounds in the darkness to mask mine.

The little yellow light had shrunk to a pinprick now. I'd have to guess, use dead reckoning from where I stood. Getting closer meant being heard; being heard meant being shot by men who'd have high-powered flashlights as well as guns.

I pulled back on the little joystick to send the speck of light higher. From so far away, it seemed to move only an inch at a time. I tried not to blink, for fear I'd lose the light in the darkness.

The roof, in the Internet satellite photos, was broad and flat. I told myself it was a big target, that I just had to come close.

I pulled back on the little joystick, leveled the little light's trajectory and descended it inch after maddening inch.

And then, high up, the light disappeared. I could only hope I'd crashed it onto the roof.

I aimed the detonator an inch below the spot in the sky where I'd last seen the light, pressed its red button and ran back across the street, down the block and the one after that. Booster's man had said nothing would happen for ten minutes.

I slowed to a walk as I approached the block where I'd left the Jeep, afraid that the Impala was waiting with its engine silenced and its lights switched off.

I crossed the last intersection. The Jeep stood in the darkness halfway down the block, alone at the curb. There were no cars parked along that deserted street, but that meant nothing. The Impala could have been left around the corner, out of sight.

I took a fast, last look behind me. The sky was black. I didn't know how many of my ten minutes were left, or whether the device had even gone off.

I pulled my ignition key out of my pocket, aimed it ludicrously like a sword and ran to the Jeep, expecting shouts at least, shots at the worst. But nothing came: no shots, no shouts. I jumped in behind the steering wheel, twisted the key into the ignition, and was away.

I drove in the dark for two blocks, afraid to turn on the head-lamps, then ducked up a side street and wheeled around. The sky glowed faintly orange.

I pulled out the burner phone I'd bought for cash at a Wal-Mart far from Rivertown and used it to make its one and only intended call, to 911. And then I turned on my headlamps and sped west, to Rivertown, uncertain of what I'd set off, but certain that I'd been seen doing it.

FORTY-ONE

My phone rang at two-fifteen the next afternoon, jerking me out of the deepest sleep I'd had since Herbie Sunheim first called.

'Huh?' I probably answered, fumbling the phone to a place at the side of my head.

'Your meat,' Leo's voice said quietly. 'And goats.'

I pushed myself up to sitting.

'Herbie Sunheim,' he went on, even more slowly.

I paused to remind myself that whoever liberated Herbie from behind the wienie wagon had liberated me as well from ever having to confess to using Leo's new ice cream freezer to store a corpse. So I asked, growing more confident, 'What about Herbie?'

'He was wearing one shoe . . .' He let the sentence trail away.

'What are you talking about?'

'I'm at the trailer,' he said, and clicked me away.

Somehow, he'd tumbled onto what I'd never wanted to tell him. I got dressed and beat it out the door without bothering to check the Internet for the news about Herbie. I'd get it all from Leo, like slaps to the head.

The streets were empty. Two-thirty in the afternoon is Rivertown's last sane lull of the day. In just a half-hour, the few factories that remained in neighboring towns would let out their daytime shifts, and the first of the day's johns would come, slow cruising to eye the winking early bird specials at the curbs.

But for now, the streets were clean and the lights were green, and both were conspiring to speed me to an accounting I didn't want to make. I got to Kutz's clearing too fast to think of words that might sound reasonable. I parked five feet to the right of Leo's white van.

'Dek!' he shouted next to me, followed instantly by the sound of his passenger door slamming. His narrow pale face, appeared at the all-too-clear plastic of my new side curtain. His eyes were unblinking, accusing.

I got out. 'Leo,' I managed.

'We got mysteries here, Dek.' He spoke in the same slow fashion he'd used on the phone, which he did when he was marshaling unpleasant facts. He'd figured me out, for sure.

'Have you heard about your client?' he asked.

'You woke me up,' I said, trying to sound aggrieved.

'They found your man Herbie Sunheim dead on the ground in front of a burning, abandoned factory, which you probably heard on the radio—'

'I didn't listen to the radio because the Jeep's got boosted years ago,' I said quite truthfully. And then I got stopped by realization. 'Wait. They found him in *front* of a burning, abandoned factory?' I couldn't imagine why they'd brought Herbie's corpse to the building they were outfitting as a drug lab.

'Want to know which one?'

'The lab, of course,' I said, because that was the one I'd set on fire.

'No. He was found in front of the Vanderbilt Supply.'

'The Vanderbilt Supply building was also torched?'

He took a step back so he could look up at my eyes. 'Where exactly have you been?'

'Asleep, until you called.'

'No, I meant last night.'

'First, tell me what happened.'

'Three supposedly empty factories went down last night, not just burned but exploded. The news didn't report exact addresses, but they did give intersections. I Googled them all. Want to know where they are?'

'Right where I showed you,' I said, hearing what he was saying but not comprehending, not yet.

'Did you go absolutely crazy last night, Dek?'

I struggled to make sense of it. Whoever had repossessed Herbie had brought him back to the Vanderbilt Supply and dumped him outside where he'd be seen, before torching that building, and the Bureski building, on the same night I'd dropped fire onto the drug lab. There could be no coincidence to any of it. The man, or men, in the Impala had seen the drone, recognized the Jeep and understood when the sky went orange. They'd then gone to torch the Vanderbilt and Bureski buildings.

Likely they'd recognized I could be blamed for it all.

'I've shocked you, haven't I?' Leo said, still looking up at me with those unblinking eyes.

'I torched only the one. The lab.'

'Once I caught the news about last night's fires, I assumed you'd need a mind of sterling quality to help you plan what you're going to say to the cops. Of course, that was before I saw what had happened here. Now that sterling mind wants to know what you're going to say to my sterling mind.' He led me, confused, around to the back of the trailer.

The top to the freezer enclosure lay back as I'd left it, splintered, the padlock and hasp still attached. He opened the freezer lid like he was readying a coffin for a viewing.

He pointed to the inside. 'What do you see?'

I gave it a glance. 'Damp spots of sudsy water.'

'The residue from an obsessive hour of power washing.' He pointed to the splintered wood. 'Someone broke the lock off the enclosure to get inside the freezer last night. That could have been any ordinary thief, wandering along the river. But then what did the thief do, after removing *your meat*?' He rolled his eyes. 'He took the time to escort three of my goats, who'd apparently returned home, back into the paddock. But here's the best part. The meat thief, who must have been carrying tools, then wired the gate latch shut, with the exact same type of wire I've seen before, holding a certain Jeep together. Now, what sort of *meat* thief would show such consideration for my goats?'

When I said nothing, he went on. 'Answer? No thief at all, but rather a friendly someone who came here thinking he knew the combination to the padlock and intended to be gone in just minutes, *with his meat.* Imagine what he must have thought when he realized the padlock had been switched, for there can be no other explanation why the poor fool had to break into the freezer, leaving such telltale damage behind. Yet, if it was only *meat* that was inside, surely the goat-escorter could have waited until he got the proper bolt-cutter, so as to not ruin the top of the enclosure.'

'Sounds like a puzzle, all right,' I allowed, only because I could think of nothing else.

'Most puzzling of all,' he went on, needing me to suffer, word by word, 'was what the non-thief left in the freezer.' He motioned me to follow him once more, this time around to the goat coral.

We stopped at the gate. The wire had been removed from the post. 'Look there, at the larger of the two brown goats,' he said.

The goat, intent on chewing something, paid us no mind.

'Do you see, Dek? Do you see what he's chewing?'

I looked harder. 'A shoe,' I said. 'A black shoe. A man's wingtip shoe, to be precise.'

'A wingtip that I found inside the freezer this morning. Without flaunting my sterling, Sherlockian powers of observation, suffice it to say that particular wingtip speaks much about its owner.'

'Like it was custom-made, and has its owner's name inside?'

'Almost as good, though certainly the opposite. That scuffed black wingtip, currently being enjoyed by its new owner – that brown goat – was worn by a most frugal man who'd had it cheaply resoled at least several times, judging by the tears where the leather meets the sole.'

'Very Sherlockian observation,' I said.

'That original owner also saved money by gluing on new heels himself, given the way the most recent one doesn't quite line up where it should.'

'A most frugal owner, indeed,' I said, trying to look approving while I waited for him to drop an anvil on my head.

'Now, as to your Mr Sunheim, did I say the news reported he was found wearing only one shoe?'

'You did mention a shoe when you called.'

He pointed to the goat, chewing contentedly. 'That shoe will be destroyed within an hour,' he said.

'I suppose you're wondering how a dead man's shoe got in your freezer?'

His slow self-control vanished. He started jumping on one foot and then another. He did that, sometimes, when he got particularly agitated. 'Herbie Sunheim was your meat? You put a corpse in my brand-new ice cream freezer? A dead, rotting man where I was going to keep mint chocolate chip, and moose tracks, and caramel swirl and maybe lime gelato?'

'I think he wasn't there but one night, and he was wrapped in plastic,' I offered, inanely.

'Ah, jeez, this is worse than last time.' He'd never forgotten when I'd borrowed his Porsche to pass as a rich guy in the piney woods of Wisconsin. That hadn't been one of my better inspirations, either.

'This is different,' I said.

'Worse,' he said. 'Last time, you only let a bear pee in my Porsche.'

'There was no bear,' I said, summoning as much outrage as I could muster, being severely on the defensive. 'Just lake muck from swimming for my life and being shot at. Besides, I cleaned up your Porsche.'

'You hung a virtual forest of tiny pine tree air fresheners to mask the smell of the bear. Or bears. Those disgusting fresheners smelled worse than the bear squirt.' He took a breath and settled at last onto both feet. 'What were you thinking, putting a corpse in my freezer?'

'I didn't want him discovered for a while. I had a vague thought that if I found someone who acted like he knew Herbie was dead, I'd know his killer.'

'Did it work? Do you know his killer?'

'No. Instead, I attracted someone who followed me here from the Vanderbilt Supply. They cut off my lock, replaced it with an identical one and took Herbie back.'

'To be found outside one of the buildings you didn't torch?'

'Apparently they had their own plans for him, but then they saw my drone, my Jeep and my fire last night, and modified those plans.'

'Any ideas who they were?'

'Men in a black Impala, a cop car. They've been watching me ever since I took Herbie.'

'Cops – you're sure? Or rival cartel trying to look like cops to chase away competition?'

'I don't know.'

'Why would they torch the two other Triple Time buildings once they realized what you were doing?'

I shook my head. I couldn't figure that either.

By evening, nobody in black Impalas – not Kopek and Jacks, not Cuthbert and Raines – had come by or called on the pretext of telling me what was already in the news . . . that Herbie Sunheim had been found and to demand to know what I knew about it.

So I called Keller. He always worked late fabricating half-lies for his sleazy column in the *Argus-Observer,* Chicago's premier gossip rag. And he was the only reporter I knew who didn't bother double-sourcing items for accuracy. He would print what I said, so long as it titillated.

'What the hell, Elstrom?' he asked, answering.

Most of the time, I called him to swear at him, to scream, to shout and to yell and to hang up. I've hated Keller ever since he ran vicious innuendo about my supposed involvement in a phony evidence scheme years ago. No matter that I was exonerated, his columns cost me my self-respect and sobriety, and those cost me my business and my marriage.

But that was back in the day, mostly. It had been a while since I'd called to vent.

'I've got a tip,' I said.

'Something baseless you want me to run for your own purposes?' he asked.

'Of course, but what I've got is true. It might even spoil your reputation for knowing nothing.'

'Fire away.'

'Remember that corpse found on the railcar by the old Central Works?'

'The body hasn't been identified, the killer hasn't been found, and the Central Works blew up or caught fire or something.'

'Tip number one: the victim was Rickey Means, the lawyer for the buyers of the Central Works and three other empty large buildings.'

'Big deal.'

'Tip number two: Walter Dace. Does that name ring any bells?'

'Dace . . . Dace . . . the guy who got killed a few days ago? His secretary got shot, too. She chose the wrong guy to screw.'

'You implied that in your column, but there's no proof they were involved. He was the property manager for the Central Works and those three other empty large buildings.'

'Not even lukewarm yet, Elstrom.'

'Tip three: the realtor for Central Works and the other three buildings was Herbie Sunheim.'

He paused, thinking, and then said slowly, 'He was in the news this morning, found dead in front of a burning building, wearing only one shoe.'

'An *exploded*, burning building,' I corrected.

'Exploded and burned, like Central Works?'

'Exactly like Central Works, and exactly like two other buildings that also got destroyed last night.'

'Four buildings, burned and exploded? Same realtor, same lawyer, same property manager?' There was never anything wrong with Keller's nose. He could smell something rotten, like a hyena.

'And the same owner,' I said. 'A trust front called Triple Time Partners.'

'This hasn't hit the other newspapers, or television.'

'Responsible journalists insist on double-sourcing, verifying before they print or broadcast.'

'Cut the crap. What's behind this?'

'Drugs, probably big-time manufacturing of synthetic chemicals. Central Works was supposed to be their first facility, but I'm thinking Triple Time blew it up when it got too newsworthy. They moved on to a second facility, the one that went up first last night. Sunheim was found at their third building, the Vanderbilt Supply. Their fourth site, and the last to blow up last night, according to the news, was the Bureski building.'

'Large-scale drug manufacturing, here in Chicago? Makes horrible sense. Saves the interception worries from having to ship stuff up here, for one thing.' He took a breath. 'So, who's blowing them up?'

'Could be them, destroying evidence, though I doubt they'd have left a corpse out front of one of them. More likely it was competitors. Two sets of cops are investigating this, seemingly independent of one another. There's a lid screwed down tight on this and I don't know why.'

'If you're messing with me—'

'To get revenge against you? Tantalizing, and definitely something I like to think about, but not this time. It's not just greedy bad people who are getting killed over this. Sunheim's assistant got murdered on a running trail the day before yesterday. Name of Violet Krumfeld. She's my price for giving you this. Put her in your column, make sure you write that she was an innocent, and ask for information about her. Anybody tips, you tell me first.'

I clicked him away. He had his own explosions to set off.

FORTY-TWO

I expected cops to come the next morning, furious about Keller's column, though I didn't know which pair to anticipate first. But it was Amanda who unlocked the timbered door and then had to knock because I'd put the inside bar in place. I'd gone to bed nervous about who Keller was going to infuriate.

She was dressed in worn jeans and the lightly frayed black cloth coat she'd been wearing the first time I'd first seen her, through an art gallery window on Michigan Avenue. She looked every bit as radiant as she'd been back then, certainly more than at any time since she'd shrugged into the weight of becoming a tycoon.

'You look every bit as radiant as when I first saw you, through that art gallery window on Michigan Avenue,' I said, appropriately.

'I'm lecturing at eleven o'clock!' she announced, stepping inside.

'Across the street from the Art Institute, at the school?'

'At the museum itself, to students from across the street. Just like old times.'

'Playing hooky from your tycoonship?'

'Only once a month for now, but I'm trying it out,' she said.

'Trying what out?'

'Trying out taking back,' she said, heading up the stairs.

'There's that "taking back" business again,' I said, ringing the wrought iron behind her.

'I guess I have been saying it a lot, but I'm trying to keep the idea of it fixed in my mind,' she said. 'I'm wondering if I've gotten too accepting of erosion in my life, too complacent or too busy or too whatever, and that's led me to cede things that I should have fought harder to keep close in my life.'

'I'm mad as hell, and I'm taking it back?' I said, bastardizing the old Peter Finch movie line.

'I'm mad as hell, and I'm taking you back,' she said, touching my cheek.

She took a pound of gourmet coffee out of her ratty Art Institute book bag because she knew I tossed my own grounds only when they grew fur. She filled the basket and added water.

'The lemon pants were not excited by your proposal to give kids jobs?'

'They're stuck on old ways, but that's not why I'm here.' She came to the table and pulled a newspaper out of her bag. 'The *Argus-Observer*, really?' she asked, dropping it to the plywood like a dead mackerel. As my wife, she'd suffered the sting of Keller's innuendo as much as I had, maybe more.

'Best place to find unsubstantiated news,' I said.

'"Details to follow,"' she added, quoting Keller's signature line. He always wrote that the details behind his outrageous allegations would appear in subsequent columns, but they never did. He skittered past serious legwork by simply moving on.

She went to the counter, poured coffee into Dubuque bank cups and brought them to the table. 'Once again, he's the talk of the town. He ties a series of building fires to names that recently have become familiar to me, including Herbie Sunheim.' She unfolded the paper to Keller's column.

'All of it,' she said. 'Tell me all of it.'

A thought struck me. I'd forgotten to look past her when she stepped inside. 'How did you get here?'

'Not in my lovely, rusting Toyota, if that's what you're asking. My escape, today, is not so complete.'

It was a relief, her being driven by her guards. Nasty people, such as those behind Triple Time, might have had ways of connecting Keller to me, and me to Amanda.

She took a sip of coffee, and asked again, 'All of it?'

I ran through it briefly, much of which she already knew.

She frowned when I was done. She'd sensed omissions.

She tapped the newspaper lying on the plywood. 'A cartel moving into Chicago, like it says here?'

'I'm guessing they're the only ones big enough to have acquired four sites at once.'

'Three buildings caught fire and exploded in the same night?' She arched her eyebrows. 'Three in one night?'

'I did light one.'

'I was afraid of that.'

'I only torched the one they were fitting out. Others did the Vanderbilt Supply, where Herbie was found, and the Bureski building.'

'Are you insane, Dek? Arson?'

'It was going to make chemicals to kill kids.'

She sighed. 'Do the people behind Triple Time know who torched what?'

'I don't think so.'

'That's great,' she said, the doubt thick in her voice. 'How about the police – do they know?'

'Something's wrong at headquarters. Two teams of detectives are investigating the Central Works victim—'

'Rickey Means.'

'Right, but they're still not releasing his name or any potential motive for his murder. And the two teams are not working together. More important, a lookalike for a detective's car passed slowly by me just before the drug lab went up. It stopped right next to the Jeep.'

'They knew you were there?'

'Absolutely.'

'Cops.'

'Don't know for sure.'

'So why go to Keller?'

'Nothing's being done about Herbie's assistant.'

She glanced down at the newspaper. '"Violet Krumfeld, killed while out jogging; send tips to Keller." She was your price?'

'She was a mousy thing. Sweet, well intentioned. Her life is a mystery. No one knows where she's from, where she lived.'

'She's involved more than you thought?'

I shrugged. 'I want her killer found.'

'And Herbie, your client?'

'I've discharged my obligation to him,' I said. 'He got greedy – went to the dark side.'

'And swiped that three hundred thousand?'

'I think that was cash for the next factory buy. For sure, Triple Time's looking for it – his wife's house got burgled. And one of the pairs of cops is looking for whatever was stashed behind his baseboard.'

'Was that smart, taking it?'

'I want to know who cares about it.'

'So, Triple Time didn't kill Rickey or Herbie for stealing?'

'I think Herbie remained a loyal soldier, so now I'm questioning whether it was Triple Time who killed him and Rickey Means and Dace and his assistant. I used to think the Triple Time people were covering their tracks, eradicating witnesses who could testify against them if things went wrong. But now there have been two fires that I didn't set, fires that draw even more attention to them, fires that have left me even more confused. I'm not sure what to think.'

'If not Triple Time, who could be doing the killing?'

I took a breath, and decided to tell it all, because I always ended up telling her everything.

'Whoever saw me bring Herbie to Rivertown,' I said

'You don't mean *after* . . .?'

'I found his body inside the Vanderbilt Supply building a few days ago,' I said, 'and I got inspired.'

She groaned. She knew about my inspirations.

'I thought if he wasn't found,' I went on, 'I might flush out his killer, so I sort of—'

Her eyes crinkled at the corners, the first tell of her succumbing to laughter. 'You took poor Mr Sunheim from—'

'It was meant to be a temporary relocation.'

'This is horrible, not funny.' She bit her lip, anxious to force away any hint of disrespect for the dead. 'Where on earth did you keep him?'

'Remember I told you Leo was planning on widening Kutz's traditional product offering?'

'To include ice cream. Sure, he bought a gigantic new freez—' Again she stopped, but this time she looked at me wild-eyed. 'You froze Mr Sunheim like fudge ripple?'

She howled, mumbling in short breaths between screeches of laughter, 'I'm so sorry, so sorry, so . . .'

'To no avail,' I said. 'My plan didn't work out.'

She leaned back, fought for air and, for a moment, simply admired the ceiling. Her breathing calmed, and her face turned serious. 'So you returned him? Surely you didn't leave him propped up in front of that Vanderbilt—?'

'No,' I interrupted. 'I intended to drop him in back, because the place was now guarded. But when I went to get him, he wasn't in the freezer. Whoever saw me take Herbie's body tailed me to Kutz's clearing, substituted a lock identical to the one I used to delay discovery and took Herbie back, probably within hours of when I first grabbed him.'

'To the Vanderbilt Supply building,' she said, to be sure.

'Not necessarily,' I said, 'just someplace where he wouldn't be discovered before they could use him. That time came the night before last, when they torched the place.'

'They wanted Herbie to be noticed,' she said.

'A message, perhaps to Triple Time.'

'Who knows who's sending the message?' she asked.

'I don't know that either, but I think I know who knew.'

I told her what I didn't know about Violet Krumfeld.

FORTY-THREE

After Amanda left, I drove again to Weasel's, as I'd done a dozen times since Austin.

I never had shaken off worrying about the kid, though it seemed almost certain that Weasel's story about his disappearance had been a ruse to get me shot at. Since I knew nothing about the boy other than he called himself Mr Shade, Weasel was the only one who could help me learn more.

But I supposed that what I really hadn't shaken off was my need to slap the truth out of Weasel about who wanted me to get shot at.

So far, I'd had no luck finding Weasel. Each time I stopped by, day or night, his house was dark. His back door was always open and the same mess lay on the kitchen counter. And his heap of a Taurus rested rusted and low on weak tires at the same exact spot in front of his house. That I was the surest of, because I'd chalked where the tires rested on the pavement, the first time I drove by after Austin.

It was that Taurus that nagged the most. Weasel was broke. He couldn't afford to hide out somewhere out of town without a car. So, if he was getting by without his car, he was getting by at home. And if he was getting by at home, he was stepping out now and again for milk to ease his ulcers. So I'd been driving by at various times, hoping to catch him loose inside his house or hoofing to a grocery.

Finally, it occurred to me that I was tipping him off each time to my arrival. Jeep sounds reverberated loudly in Weasel's otherwise deserted neighborhood, because there were no other sounds for them to compete with. The factories were long shuttered, and those houses that hadn't been burned were empty. Weasel might well have heard me driving up every time, and slipped into some secret place in his warren of cluttered rooms until the sound of my Jeep disappeared. Or, if he'd been outside, he'd have known to scuttle into some abandoned building until he heard me drive away.

So, that day I decided to play more cagily. I came up his alley on foot and marched right to his back door. The door was unlocked, as always, and just as he'd supposedly left it, fleeing in panic after he'd returned from Austin. I stepped inside, whistling loudly to announce my presence. If he were inside, tucked behind some mound, he'd know to stay hidden. That was fine. I wasn't looking to snag him in the first instant.

A half-gallon of milk rested in the same spot on the kitchen counter. I'd never actually touched the milk, figuring it sour and best avoided. This time was different. I felt the jug and found it cool. To be certain, I unscrewed the cap and sniffed. It was fresh. Crafty Weasel had left milk on the counter to confuse anyone stopping by, but he'd not thought of the way it should have smelled if it had gone bad from being left out for days.

Still whistling, I poured it into the sink and tossed the empty plastic container onto the floor beside the garbage spilling out of the overfilled trash basket. That overfilled basket might have been intended as another display of Weasel's cleverness, but I thought it more likely it had always been like that. Weasel was disgusting on many levels.

I looked inside his refrigerator. Another half-gallon of milk, fresh and unopened, lay on its side behind a wilted bag of lettuce that looked as if it might have been old when Weasel was but a small creature. I poured that half-gallon out in the sink, too, and tossed the empty container next to the other one on the floor.

And then I went outside and down the alley. The only close grocery was a struggling family operation that had been struggling for decades, five blocks away. I stepped between two leaning garages, figuring a Weasel out of milk would be a Weasel in a hurry.

Ten minutes later, footsteps came pounding along what gravel was left in the alley. When the pounding got really loud, I jumped out and punched Weasel in his anxious gut.

'What the hell!' he shouted, doubling over.

'That was for the running you set me up to do to get away from the gunfire,' I said, clenching both hands together and bringing them down on the back of his neck. 'And that's for the crouching I had to do, when your friends came up the alley, looking for me.' He fell satisfyingly to the gravel and began screaming. They were horrible, those sounds that came from my bullying, but the gunshots I'd run from in Austin rang louder.

I stepped on the back of his right hand and bent a little toward one ear. 'There's more, Weasel. I owe you for having to run all the way up to Chicago Avenue and having to hide in a burned-out storefront, waiting for a bus, and then there was the bus ride itself.'

'I was hoping you weren't supposed to die!' he yelled into the gravel.

'Nice that you weren't sure,' I said, conversationally enough considering I was stepping on his hand.

'Get off my hand!' he shouted, muffled a bit by the stones.

'Who ordered the set-up?'

'Some guy!'

I stepped down harder.

He shrieked. 'Some guy on the phone who said he'd put two bullets into my front door! He said he had four more he could put in me.'

I took my foot off his hand and stepped back. 'Who?' I said again.

He pushed himself up to his knees, his face smeared with dirt and gravel dust. 'I'm telling you, I don't know. I asked around plenty until I found a lawyer who knew a guy who knew about a kid named Mister Shade who worked sometimes for Rickey Means. Anyone could have found out I did that.'

He reached up with his good hand and I pulled him up to standing.

'Maybe I was supposed to die, but they took off too fast,' he said, rubbing his damaged hand.

'What about the kid disappearing?'

'I was just supposed to say that to get you into Austin.'

'How do I make sure he's OK?'

'You don't.' He rubbed his hand. 'Damn it, Dek. You didn't get hurt.'

I bunched the back of his greasy jacket in my hand and walked him out to the front and down to his house. The two bullet holes in his front door were fresh.

I told him I would always remember the gunshots in Austin, but that I wouldn't be back.

Cuthbert and Raines showed up just before noon.

Cuthbert carried a copy of the morning's *Argus-Observer.* 'Read this, Mr Elstrom?'

'Only when it's useful, and today it's useful.'

'Were you useful to Keller?'

'The radio said Herbie Sunheim was found dead outside a burning building. How was he killed?'

'Broken neck.'

'Was he tossed, like Rickey Means?'

'We're wondering what you know about it,' Raines said. 'Mr Sunheim was your client.'

'And he was the realtor for the building where he was found and for the two others that burned that same night.'

'Meaning?' Raines said.

'Meaning you already knew that, like you already knew that all three of those buildings, along with the Central Works, are owned by Triple Time. Surely that's of huge interest to sharpies like you.'

'Keller deals in innuendo, and that's unproductive,' Raines said. Then added, 'That's something you should know better than most.'

'Sometimes he's got a good nose.'

'This time he got his nose pointed by you, and that could be dangerous for you, and for him.'

'Keller reported that the fire department may have found lab

equipment in the first of the buildings that got lit that night, equipment that could be used to concoct nasty drugs.'

'The Chicago Fire Department has said no such thing.'

'What about his reporting that two pairs of detectives are
working this case, but are not communicating with each other?
Who's the lead?'

'That's unproductive,' Raines said.

'Yeah, but who's the lead?'

He shrugged. 'Kopek. He's a legend, lots of good busts in the
old days. He gets to work on what he wants.'

They turned to leave.

'What got Violet Krumfeld killed?'

They got to their car, two officious, arrogant pups. Cuthbert
paused to look across the roof. 'We're Chicago PD, not Belle
Plaine.'

'She was Herbie Sunheim's assistant, and she's just as dead as
Herbie, Rickey Means, and Dace and his receptionist.'

'She was found outside the city limits,' Cuthbert said.

'By whom?'

'Not our jurisdiction.'

'She was a Chicago resident, got a friend to rent her a car near
Lincoln Square,' I called back, but it was in desperation, grasping
at a last straw.

'A friend rented her a car in Chicago?' Raines laughed, getting
in the passenger's seat. 'That'll get us jurisdiction for sure.'

'What got Violet Krumfeld killed?' I said again.

It was Raines who answered. 'We want to know what's going
to get you killed.'

They sped away, having gotten nothing they didn't already know,
leaving nothing except their certainty that I'd been Keller's rat.
And maybe a warning as well.

I went upstairs to my computer and Googled the phone numbers
of every hospital within a ten-mile radius of Belle Plaine. I lied
the same lies to all, saying that I represented an insurance company
seeking to pay out on a death policy, that our insured had apparently led a complicated life, perhaps under an assumed name, and
that she might have been brought in by any one of a number of
private ambulance services, accompanied by a cop from any one
of a number of jurisdictions.

My lies got certainty and nothing else. No jogger, no unidentified woman – no one resembling Violet Krumfeld had been brought in on the date I mentioned.

I went outside, thinking to sit by the river and watch the debris pass by, but a visitor had arrived and was standing a few yards behind the Jeep. It was Gregorio, Leo's largest goat. He didn't bray, or bleat, or make whatever those crazed, high-pitched sounds I'd heard earlier at Kutz's clearing were called. He merely looked at me with baleful eyes, as though life on the run had been a lonely disappointment. I wanted to tell him I empathized, that life often presented unhappiness, but I did not want to have a conversation with a goat outside, where I might be observed.

I walked to the back of the Jeep. Gregorio watched patiently as I unzipped the plastic rear curtain, folded it back and opened the half door. I'd removed the back seat a couple of years before, to use as casual seating in the turret's third-floor master bedroom, so there looked to be enough room for Leo's largest goat.

Gregorio looked at me, looked at the open door, and then, with what might have been a faint nod, he ambled up. After some initial clumsiness, he managed to put his right front hoof up inside the Jeep. And then he paused, no doubt evaluating what move to make next.

A Rivertown police cruiser drove up, heading to the police station behind city hall. Both cops waved, but did not honk or hoot. Such was my reputation for eccentricity, I supposed, that the sight of me holding a door open for a brown-and-white goat to get in my Jeep sparked no real interest at all, and they passed right on by.

Gregorio put his other front hoof up into the Jeep and then, with a massive kick of both hind legs, he popped up into the Jeep as smoothly as Baryshnikov ever leaped in any ballet. He pivoted on his belly so he could ride with his head sticking out. I closed the rear door gently, and we were off.

Some motorists gave us friendly waves, and a couple honked their horns. We were in Rivertown, after all, and many unusual things could be seen in such a town. Gregorio seemed to enjoy the ride and the fresh air on his head, and might have even offered the other motorists a smile, though I couldn't be sure of that, being up front, driving.

Leo, though, did not offer up a smile when I backed the Jeep

up to the paddock. He opened the gate and then the Jeep's rear
door. Gregorio jumped out and entered the paddock with dignity.

Leo closed the gate, and then my Jeep's rear door.

'This doesn't square us with you letting a bear pee in my
Porsche,' he called forward through the open rear curtain.

'I must keep trying,' I said, of that and Violet Krumfeld, and
drove away.

A white plastic bakery bag was set against my door when I got
back to the turret. It contained six *kolachkys* – three cheese, three
apricot. No prune. And it contained a white, three-by-five lined
index card with 7:30 written on it in dark pencil.

Kopek had invited me to dinner.

FORTY-FOUR

K opek called precisely at seven thirty that evening. 'Enjoy
the *kolachkys*?'

'Just two, so far. One cheese, one apricot. Hard to tell
which is better, but I'll know more tomorrow.'

'Cheese versus apricot; the dilemma for any Bohemian, even a
half-breed like you,' he said. 'I'm at the eastern edge of your
marvelous little town, at a place called The Hamburger. They don't
have hamburgers on the menu. It's a fried fish place.'

'The place changes hands rapidly, but every new owner keeps
the sign to save costs. There's little enthusiasm for fine dining in
Rivertown.'

'Come by. I'll buy you a fish,' he said.

'Don't order until I get there.'

'Fish sounds good,' he said.

'There's concern they snag the slowest of them from the
Willahock.'

'How slow?'

'Some just floating on their sides.'

'Then I'll wait for you, but hurry.'

'You're really hungry?'

'No, I'm anxious and I've got something for you. You need to
keep your head down, really down, like you're crawling.'

'You didn't pop into Rivertown to enjoy our cuisine?'

'Nor to look at the lovelies working the curbs. You've angered people, Elstrom.'

'I suspected as much.'

'No, I mean you've *really* angered people.'

Kopek sounded scared.

'How angry, exactly?' I asked.

'Hurry over, and I'll tell you.'

I headed for the door.

The lizards that ran Rivertown liked to say that The Hamburger was built to be the first in a string of franchised locations to compete with McDonald's, but that it had gone bankrupt thirty years earlier because back then, especially, nobody really competed with McDonald's. That was baloney; there was no intent to franchise anything. The originator of the first The Hamburger, a second cousin to Rivertown's treasurer, was looking for a place to use the meat he caught falling off trucks. Supposedly, he planned on catching enough to fully stock at least five outlets of The Hamburger, all of which he would own himself. He got to build only one before someone tipped the feds, and the mayor's second cousin went to prison. The building changed owners and menus every couple of years, but the expensive rooftop sign naming the place The Hamburger hung on because it was too expensive to replace, and every new owner seemed resigned to failure, anyway. Driving over, I accepted that it would be an appropriate place to hear unsettling news.

Kopek sat by himself in a booth at the back corner. There were no other diners.

'So, no fish?' he asked when I walked up carrying two Cokes.

'Grilled cheese is coming,' I said. 'It's the most I can do, here, to thank you for the *kolachkys*.'

'The most?'

'The grilled cheese is safe. As I inferred, the least I could do would be to order the fish. You'd suffer. Where are Cuthbert and Raines?'

I'd startled him, but only for an instant.

'Who?' he said, like he didn't know.

'That other pair of detectives working the Central Works case. We've discussed them before.'

'Nosy bastards.'

'They don't report to you?'

'I don't know who the hell they report to.'

'Jacks?'

'He reports to me. He's safe at home,' he said.

'I've angered people?'

The counter clerk brought us our sandwiches. Kopek took a bite, nodded and said, 'You're not helping by talking to the press.'

'Your fellow constables, Cuthbert and Raines, accused me of the same thing, several hours ago.'

'And what did you say?'

'I told them to call the police.'

'Did they threaten you with arrest for withholding information material to a murder investigation?'

'They must have forgotten, but that's not why you wanted to meet.'

'What started as a simple matter of a fool lawyer getting pitched out of the Central Works has turned into a high-stakes mess.'

'Bottom line?'

He shrugged. 'Maybe drugs, like Keller said in the paper. Four buildings blown up, several deaths, perhaps no end in sight. You know anything about that?'

I shook my head.

'No matter. Everyone who knows anything seems to have been killed.' He took another bite of his sandwich, then a sip of Coke, and said, 'Except you, of course.'

I set down the sandwich I'd just picked up. 'You think I'm targeted?'

'I think that stupid piece in the paper has made you a walking dead man. You should have kept your damned mouth shut.'

'I wasn't attributed.'

'You've been asking around about the Central Works. We got an anonymous tip.'

'What kind of tip?'

'Someone wants you dead. You need to be careful until we figure out if the threat is real.'

'How close are you to that?'

'Not close.'

'How about identifying the people behind Triple Time?' I asked. 'It's got to be them.'

'No clues on them yet.' He reached down on the bench beside him and came up with a white cardboard bakery box.

'Goodies, after you tell me I'm marked?' At that moment, I couldn't have swallowed water.

He slid it the short distance across the table. 'Open it.'

I did. Inside was a .38 revolver.

'I don't know whether you have a weapon,' he said, 'but I want you to carry this. It's untraceable and already loaded. Just point, shoot, and throw the thing in the river so no one can accuse you of murder.'

'You really think this is necessary?'

'I don't know what's necessary. Do you have any idea who's behind Triple Time?'

'No.'

'That Krumfeld woman? She knew something,' he said. 'We still can't find her real identity.'

'She seemed to know nothing. Maybe she was just a hell of an actress.'

'And you, Elstrom?' he said, leaning across the fake woodgrain table top. 'Are you a good actor?'

The man's bulk was intimidating, his glare hot.

'What do you mean?'

'I mean somebody's set to kill you, and no gun I give you will protect you forever. What do they think you know? How can we use it to keep you safe?'

'Cuthbert and Raines implied the same thing.'

'Maybe it's obvious.'

'What's obvious is that something's wrong at the cops,' I said. 'You and Jacks are being shadowed by another pair of detectives. They say they're working different angles, but I don't believe them. I don't know that I even believe you.'

He leaned back. 'Maybe I wouldn't either. This case is such a mess. As far as those other two nosy bastards, they're not from homicide.'

'Where then?'

'Not sure.' He took the last bite of his sandwich. 'Put the gun in your coat, Elstrom, and don't go anywhere without it. And don't hesitate to fire.'

I put the revolver in the pocket of my peacoat. We stood up, and he took the box to the trash receptacle.

'So long,' he said, outside, reaching for his phone.

FORTY-FIVE

The bullet sparked off the limestone to the right of my head just as I raised my key to the door. Ducking, dropping the keys, I ran low around the turret's east side and down toward the river, more shots ricocheting off the limestone behind me. There'd been no car on the streets off Thompson Avenue when I drove up. The shooter was on foot, firing first from the bramble on the spit of land across the street, now charging after me around the turret.

He'd expect me to run west along the crumbling riverwalk, to the long lawn to city hall and the police station in back. It was too long, that broad lawn, and too brightly lit by moonlight reflecting off the Willahock. I'd be an easy target.

It took more guts than I wanted to gamble, but there was no choice. I turned and ran back up the rise to the other side of the turret, begging the night to make him think I'd kept running toward city hall. Past the turret, my footsteps pounded loud on the street as I crossed to the spit of land.

And then I froze, unsure where to go.

Thompson Avenue lay across the tangle, a tempting sanctuary of drunks thronging the sidewalks and slow-john cars clogging the streets. I could get safely lost among them, but first I'd have to high-step through fallen branches and limbs, backlit the whole way by the neon along Thompson. As soon as the shooter realized I'd not run toward the police station, he'd double back and see me contorting through the bramble like a jerk-stringed puppet. He'd have clear shots, masked by all the noise along Thompson.

A car turned onto my street. It came slowly, running without lights. Good people didn't run dark in the night. Killers came like that.

There was an old oak tree fifteen feet ahead. I half-jumped, half-stumbled into the bramble toward it, diving at its base. Rolling onto my belly, I crawled around behind it and pressed flat onto the blanket of branches and twigs and thorns. I lifted my head just enough to see.

The dark car coasted to a stop in front of the turret. Its engine went silent. A car door opened. The shadow-shape of a man got out. His hard-soled shoes moved quickly across the street toward the thicket, and then stopped.

I dropped my head, pressing hard against the ground. He'd seen me, this second man, as I ran across the street. He'd seen me hesitate, and then jump into the bramble. A quick glance across the spit of land had already shown that I wasn't working my way toward Thompson Avenue. He knew I was hiding somewhere close to the road.

He murmured, just feet away, barely audible above the ruckus that was Rivertown at night. He was talking into his phone, summoning the shooter who'd likely kept on running toward city hall.

I raised my head once more. The shadow-shape stood ten, fifteen feet directly in front of me, at the edge of the tangle. He was waiting. A minute passed, and then footfalls came running up the street. The shooter was back from the river walk. He stopped diagonally across the spit of land, a hundred feet farther down the street from the shadow-shape man.

I dropped back down and shifted to pull the revolver Kopek gave me out of my peacoat. Bless that pastry-loving cop for my one chance. Neither of us could have guessed how soon I'd need that gun.

Twigs cracked from the right, in front of me, and then from the left, farther away. They were working parallel, the shadow-shape and the shooter, stepping carefully into the bramble. They'd known I didn't make my way across the spit of land. The shadow-shape on the right sounded as if he was only a few feet away.

But I had a gun. I had surprise.

I rolled onto my left side, clutching the revolver with my right hand. A short, thick tree limb jabbed my ribs. I pushed my back against it and nudged it out of the way. Point and shoot, Kopek said. It's loaded; just point and shoot.

The tangle snapped loud, just ahead, branches and twigs breaking under the shadow-shape's weight, getting closer.

I did not know guns. I needed proximity. The nearest one, the shadow-shape, had to be close, so close I could not miss. Rise up, point, squeeze the trigger once, and again, and drop down fast.

Be invisible to the shooter, off to the left, who'd have to hold his fire for fear of hitting the shadow-shape.

Footfalls came down loud, only inches in front of my head. He was at my tree.

I pushed up onto my knees. He loomed huge above me.

Point and shoot; just point and shoot.

I pulled the trigger and pulled it again. The muzzle flashed bright in the night.

He did not fall; he did not fire back. He laughed. He took another step.

I dropped the revolver, then fumbled at the ground for something – anything – to swing. I found the short limb I'd nudged away. It was thicker than a baseball bat; I could not tell its length. Clutching it with both hands brought it free. I scrambled up to my feet.

The shadow-shaped man laughed.

I swung the short limb like I was swinging for bleachers and connected, hitting his head or his neck or his arm.

His gun fired, but it was up into the air.

I swung at the flash, and somewhere beyond the ringing in my ears, he gurgled in surprise. I'd caught his mouth or his throat. He crashed down, and his head hit my foot. I swung at it, crazed now, but hit only leaves. I raised the short limb and swung down again. I hit something a little higher than the ground. He exhaled hard. I'd gotten flesh, good, soft flesh, and maybe a good, hard bone. He lay silent.

Thrashing came from the darkness to the left; the shooter had seen the flashes and was hurrying to my side of the bramble. But he couldn't yet know who'd gone down.

Tires squealed as a car raced off Thompson Avenue, high-beam headlamps sweeping down the short street, and turned onto my own, lighting the ground and the sky all around. And lighting me.

The shooter off to the left raised his arm. I dropped to the ground as the shot rang out.

The new car screeched to a stop. Engine still running, high beams still on, car doors opened – one, two. Guns fired from the street. The shooter fired back. A man shouted by the car. Another man there yelled back.

I raised my head. The shooter had turned to scramble back to the street, likely to run for the river. I could only see his back. He was slender, medium-sized.

The bramble tripped him. He went down. There could be no running in the tangle of that park.

The men from the new car walked slowly down the street toward him, firing at where he'd gone down. I pressed my face to the ground. Thorns dug into my cheek. I pressed down harder, desperate for the gun I'd dropped. I did not know who would live or who would die.

Wild thrashing sounded from the left, the shooter desperate to escape the bramble that clutched him. More gunshots were fired at him from the street.

A huge wall of light rumbled off Thompson Avenue, up the short street and onto mine, lighting the whole of the spit of land brighter than ten midday suns. Pressed to the ground, I did not need to see. I knew that sound; I knew those lights. They'd found me once before and chased me across the flattened ground of the Central Works.

I pawed again at the ground, now harshest white and deepest black in the glare of the new lights. But there was no gun. There were only twigs and sticks and branches and, somewhere, the limb I'd swung to drop the shadow-shaped man who'd come for me.

The monstrous off-roader rumbled to a stop. The big engine went dead but the bright wall of lights stayed on.

Somewhere to the left, the shooter thrashed on in the night, a boar trapped in bramble, frantic to escape the lights and the men with the guns.

Two more shots came from the street. The thrashing stopped.

Footfalls entered the thicket, only one pair, only one man, dozens of yards away. A shot sounded, followed by another. But softer this time, and more muffled, like bullets fired right against flesh. The man who'd shot at me in my doorway was dead.

'Down, one,' a man said, off to the left.

Other footfalls came up toward me, slowly, carefully. Again, only one pair. I dared not look. I pressed my face hard into the bramble.

One step, two steps, three steps, footfalls slow and searching. They stopped, just feet from my head. Two more shots came, muffled by flesh like the ones a minute before, only closer. Kill shots for sure, if the man I'd clubbed wasn't already dead.

'Down, two,' the voice close to me called into the night. I couldn't recognize it above the fresh gun shots ringing in my ear. I focused on breathing slowly, quietly. They must not know a witness was there.

The second man came down the street from where he'd dropped the shooter. His footfalls entered the bramble, high-stepping toward the man close to me. They got close and stopped. A soft brushing began, accompanied by grunting and hard thuds but no words. The two men were dragging the shadow-shaped man away.

Five minutes later, a door on the street opened and then slammed. There were three vehicles stopped there. Two with smaller engines – the shadow-shape's sedan that had coasted up, running dark, and the high-beamed second car that had come just moments later, bringing the pair who'd stopped the men hunting me – and the off-roader that had lit everything in the night.

Footsteps moved down the street. A moment later, dragging sounds began, farther away and to my left. The shooter who'd chased me down to the river was being removed now. Insanely, I thought of Herbie – poor, stupid, greedy, dead Herbie. He might have been dragged like that, up to the Vanderbilt Supply, just before the building was torched.

The brightest lights on the off-roader went dark, leaving only its headlamps still on. Car doors opened and slammed. I did not dare to raise my head.

'Go,' a man on the street said. An engine started and new headlamps switched on. It was the car that had come up dark, the shadow-shape man's car, now driven by someone else. It swung around and headed for Thompson Avenue.

'Elstrom?' a man's voice called low, from my street, unrecognizable in the din coming from Thompson Avenue.

I stayed silent, pressed flat to the ground.

'Out of here,' the same voice said, and footsteps sounded fainter from the street. More car doors slammed.

I eased up to see. The engine of the second sedan, which had been left running by the men who'd jumped out to stop my would-be killers, was shifted into gear. It turned around, lowered its high-beams to normal and headed back to the short street that led to Thompson Avenue. The over-lit off-roader, still shining only its headlamps, rumbled its engine into life, turned around and followed. The spit of land faded into shadows as they pulled away.

The second sedan and the off-roader turned east onto Thompson Avenue, heading toward the city, and disappeared. The car leading the off-roader was a black Impala.

Behind me, the crazed carnival along Thompson Avenue sounded on – ladies laughing with shrill, practiced delight, drunks yelling at whatever they imagined to be in their mists, john cars idling slowly along the curb. Nobody had died along Thompson Avenue, not even me.

Still, I stayed down on my belly, counting to a hundred in time with the base beats pulsing from the jukeboxes across the spit of land, and then I counted to a hundred more. Finally, I stood and picked my way through the low tangle to the turret.

My keys lay on the stone threshold, where I'd dropped them in my panic. It took three tries for my shaking hands to pick them up. I unlocked the timbered door, stepped inside and closed it tight behind me, then moved quickly to insert the wood bar into the steel brackets so no one with guns could break the door down.

I went up the stairs to the second floor, heated the last of Amanda's fresh pot of coffee in the microwave and took it to the plywood table. I didn't want the coffee but I did want its warmth. I put my arms around the cup but I had to leave it on the table. My hands still trembled.

I sat there for a time, maybe an hour but probably more, trying to feel relief at the death I'd just cheated. But all I could see was the randomness of the things that had kept me alive: a missed first gunshot; a counter-intuitive run back up the other side of the turret; the bramble; the miraculous just-in-time arrival of saviors, whoever they were, who stopped those who wanted me dead, whoever they were.

I could make no sense of it. I was cold and adrift and afraid. I went upstairs, to the bottles of Liquid Bandage I'd learned to keep ever since I started cutting the turret's metal ductwork. I painted my face and my arms and my hands and my ankles, everywhere I'd been cut, scraped and punctured. And then I went to bed, not to sleep but to find warmth beneath my blankets. But the chill did not go away, no matter the blankets, no matter the coat I kept on. I trembled until the sun came to light the turret and, at last, to bring me sleep.

FORTY-SIX

'DRUG WARS: BAD COPS?' The *Chicago Tribune*'s bold-faced headline demanded, online. Below it ran a single black-and-white, close-up photo of the burned-out shell of an automobile.

The car was found in flames at two in the morning, thirty yards in front of the husk of the drug lab I'd torched with a drone.

Enough accelerant had been used to blister away the paint, melt the tires and char the two bodies inside beyond recognition. Nonetheless, the vehicle was easily identifiable. Its shape defined it as a Chevrolet Impala. The metal VIN plate at the base of the windshield defined it more, as an unmarked car owned by the Chicago police department.

The two victims had been killed before they were torched, their bodies punctured by multiple bullets. Additionally, one of the skulls showed evidence of blunt force trauma, perhaps by a wooden bat or large club. Or perhaps, I allowed, by a tree limb grasped in panic after a revolver had failed to take him down.

The *Tribune* said it was no stretch to call it a message. That two dead men, perhaps police officers, had been crisped in front of an alleged drug lab that had itself been torched just a couple of days before could only be seen as evidence of some sort of ongoing drug war, one that the police should meet head on with every available resource, the *Trib* said.

I clicked over to the *Argus-Observer*'s website to see what muck they'd summoned up. Unsurprisingly, their coverage was virtually the same as the *Trib*'s, as they often lifted whole paragraphs of copy from their competitors.

Their photographer, though, had taken a more distanced and editorialized view. He'd photographed the car from a hundred yards away that morning, in color, and centered it against the shell of the torched drug lab.

The building had been freshly tagged. An eight foot, bright yellow smiley face, with a happy, upturned black line for a mouth and round black eyes, had been sprayed onto the lab's brick wall.

There was no mistaking the tagger's delight in the destruction of the drug lab.

My head wanted to reason that Chicago was full of taggers. Any one of hundreds could have left the smiley face. But my gut wanted to wonder whether the artist who'd tagged Central Works had found his way to the building I'd torched.

To no one's surprise, the Chicago police turned turtle in those first hours, refusing to speculate about who'd been in the burned-out car. They said the medical examiner's office would work diligently to determine the identity of the corpses, but that the process would take days or even weeks.

The city's television, print, and radio reporters wouldn't sit back and swallow such poorly cut baloney. They'd pack police headquarters that day, demanding to know who hadn't shown up for work. Cop kills weren't unheard of in Chicago, but it was almost always the uniforms in marked cars that got blown away, dropped like ordinary gangbangers and kids and bystanders and motorists just happening along. Detectives – for it was almost always detectives who drove the unmarked Impalas – rarely got murdered and sent up in flames. The story would stay hot until the victims were identified.

I called the Chicago police department, and asked for Cuthbert or Raines. I was told both had been assigned out and would get back to me at their earliest convenience. I called Kopek. He wasn't in, either. Only as an afterthought did I call Jacks, his partner. I left a message on his machine.

I couldn't suppose I was no longer in danger. Whoever had come for me the night before had been killed, dumped and burned in the Impala, but they'd been underlings, minions like Means and Herbie and Dace, and maybe even the assistant with the well-tended fingernails. Maybe, too, like Violet Krumfeld.

Minions all, minions dead, while those that pulled the strings, the partners behind Triple Time, got to live on.

I leaned back in my chair. And remembered the revolver.

I'd tossed it aside in panic, desperate to be rid of it for something blunter, heavier, more sure. Incredibly, I'd not remembered it, but now the image of that gun lying on top of some mound of leaves, where some kid might find it, flashed hot in my mind. I ran downstairs in my shirtsleeves, unbarred the door and hurried across the street.

The bramble offered up signs of the killing that had been done there. Specks of blood lay on flattened spots on the ground by the tree where I'd hidden, and faint drag paths led from there to the street. I saw no brass casings, which meant everyone there had been firing revolvers, like me, and not semi-automatics.

The brush by the big tree where I'd hidden was still flattened. The revolver lay between two long branches, five feet away. I picked it up and put it in my pocket.

The chunk of tree limb I'd swung lay in plain sight, close to the base of the tree. In the daylight, it looked ordinary, just another three-foot section of tree limb, decayed by rot at one end. Except for the smear of blood that was embedded into that rot.

I picked it up and walked through the bramble. The patch where my first shooter had been dropped was easy to find. There were drag marks there and blood spatter, too. It would all be washed away by the next hard rain.

I left the spit of land, crossed the street and went down to the river. I threw the tree limb into the water and watched the Willahock carry it down toward the dam. It would bang about there for a time, bobbing and sinking and breaking up, until the dam tired of it and sent the smaller fragments, significant of nothing now, farther downriver.

I reached into my pocket, to throw the revolver in after it, but then I had a minor inspiration. That gun might have a story of its own. If so, it would not tell it to me. I went back up to the turret, wiped the revolver clean of my fingerprints, put it in a shoebox and wrapped that in a tan paper shopping bag. I typed a big label on my computer and addressed it to Chicago's main police head-quarters on South Michigan Avenue. I used *Anonymous* for the return address because Chicago cops would accept things marked that way.

And then I hesitated, unsure who to designate as the intended recipient on the lower left corner of the label. I'd first thought to type in all their names there – Kopek and Jacks, Cuthbert and Raines – because I didn't really know who, if any of them, was still alive to open the package. But labeling it that way would be sloppy, because it absolved me of the hard thinking I had yet to do about who'd tried to kill me and who'd come to save my life.

I made new coffee and went out to the bench by the river to force away bad guesses. After a couple of hours, I was left with one good guess. I went back to the computer, typed in the names, and printed out the label.

I drove to the cab stand on Thompson Avenue that the City of Rivertown provides for those late-night revelers too wobbly to drive. I found the cabbie that drove Rivertown's chief lizard, the mayor, to places where the man didn't dare to be seen driving himself, and handed him the package and fifty dollars. I told him I wanted a simple, fast drop-off.

And then, before heading into the city, I swung into The Hamburger for a grilled cheese and a Coke because I never had touched the ones I'd ordered the night before.

FORTY-SEVEN

'Tomorrow is Leo's grand opening,' I said to Amanda on the phone later that afternoon, as I was stuck in traffic on the expressway back to Rivertown.

'I knew you were safe because I sent someone around this morning. He saw you handing a package to a cabbie.'

She'd caught the news, seen the picture of the burned-out car. 'To see if I was still alive?' I forced a small laugh. 'Things are no longer dire,' I said, trying to sound sure.

'Why no call?'

'I thought we'd talk later. So, Leo's?'

'I'm looking forward to going . . .' Amanda said, and then stopped.

'Why the pause? There will be ice cream, at last.'

It elicited no laugh.

'And Ma Brumsky and her septuagenarian friends in short poodle skirts,' I said, seeking to entice further.

Still, she remained silent.

'Best of all will be the goat race,' I said, playing my trump card. Surely no one could resist watching goats race.

'Are you safe?'

'As I said, things are no longer dire.'

'Because two bodies were found burned beyond recognition in front of a building that, uh, some unknown person might have previously torched because it was being fitted out as a drug lab? They're saying it was cops in that burned-out car, but bad cops or good cops, nobody yet knows.'

'Bad guys, for sure.'

'You know this?'

'They came to the turret with guns.'

'My God!'

'I was saved by others.'

'You didn't—'

'No, it wasn't me. My rescuers lit that car.'

'What kind of rescuers—?'

'It's time to look forward to better things, like hot dogs, ice cream and, best of all, goat racing,' I cut in, to get us back to banter.

'What if there are others?' she asked, having none of my attempt at flippancy.

'There surely are,' I said. 'Bad ones and good ones, and some that are mixes of both.'

'What's that mean?'

'I don't know yet.'

'You're being cryptic, which is what you always do when you're dodging.'

'I'm not dodging so much as mulling. There's still much I need to think through.'

'At least tell me this: were the bodies in the car a message, as the news folks are saying?'

'Very strong, very pointed, just like the torching of those other two buildings the same night that anonymous fellow did the lab,' I said. 'Taking back; people taking things into their own hands. Maybe it's going on all over and I just haven't been aware of it. But for now, I need to concentrate on hot dogs done right, ice cream served up from a power-washed freezer, and goat races.'

'You did see the *Argus-Observer*'s website?'

'That smiley face? Might be the same tagger; might not.'

'Either way, it's happy art,' she said.

'Delighted for sure,' I said. 'About Leo's tomorrow?'

'Pick me up at work, eight tonight?'

'Even better.'

'I've got another address,' she said, giving me a number on a street in a rehab district a mile south of the expressway.

'I already know where it is.'

'Ah, my secretary? She adores you.'

'As well she should,' I said, without correction. 'Oh . . . your guards, they will be there tonight?'

'Sadly, yes,' she said, her voice gone wary. 'Why on earth would you ask that?'

'I never like to be wrong, is all,' I said, really meaning that until I was sure who'd gotten crisped in the cops' car, guards were good folks to have around.

Rivertown has only one bank – a veiny marble pile with the warmth of a mausoleum. Only two people work in the gloom inside. One is the bank president, who sits at the lone desk in the lobby. He is the mayor's brother-in-law, and a man who knows how to do as he's told.

The other is a batty ancient that perches behind the gilded teller window except for the hours she spends in the restroom, rinsing the seeds from the pomegranates she adores out of her teeth. She is the bank president's mother.

Rivertown's bank does not seek retail trade. It offers no teaser rates for new depositors, pays no interest on passbook savings and carries no mortgages for anyone not a member of the town's extended ruling family. It exists simply to channel the relentless river of crinkled green that oozes in each day from city hall and the tonks along Thompson Avenue. The bank's president knows how to get around the federal restrictions on accepting unexplained cash deposits.

'Ah, Elstrom,' he said, looking up from one of the ever-present, Just for Kids newspaper crossword puzzles he struggled with to stave off Alzheimer's.

A slight ping sounded from the teller cage across the vast marble floor. His mother had spit another seed into her metal wastebasket.

I'd brought in a medium-sized plastic garbage bag. He looked inside and shrugged. He'd seen such bags, and such contents, before.

I repeated the gist of my conversation with the downtown landlord and gave the banker the man's address. A check from an out-of-country bank managed by his nephew would be mailed at the first of every month.

On my way out, I checked the scratched plastic plate on the table against the wall. There used to be chocolate-chip cookies there, before the batty ancient switched to pomegranates. Now there was only one cookie, and it had a bite taken out of it. I remembered that cookie from months before, when I'd stopped by hoping to learn the true identity of a strange woman who gave me a cashier's check. The strange woman was now dead but the bitten cookie was set to live on, apparently, for forever.

I swung by Weasel's on my way back to the turret. I was still furious with him for setting me up but a small, annoying part of me was accepting how frightened he must have been, getting his front door – and potentially his head – shot at. Weasel wasn't much evolved from a cockroach, morality-wise, and I allowed he'd simply exercised the same instinct for self-preservation that had enabled cockroaches to survive for countless millennia.

His old Taurus was gone from the curb. More surprisingly, I saw faint smudging around the edges of the front windows. There'd been a fire, or rather several small ones, inside. I drove around and into his alley.

There were a dozen bicycles and tricycles back by his garage, seemingly left for the stealing. I got out, walked up to the kitchen door. It was unlocked, as he'd left it the last time. Then, it had been to fool. Now, I wondered if it had been left unlocked because Weasel, or someone else, no longer gave a damn.

The dampness that pervaded every cranny of the house – that mix of must and mildew – had gone acrid. A fire had been attempted at the back wall in the kitchen, next to the door that led down to the basement. The flames had not caught beyond smudging the vinyl wallpaper. Likely the wall was too damp to burn.

Two more fires had been attempted in the living room. The smallest of the cardboard shipping containers Weasel had hunted and gathered in various Chicago neighborhoods had been emptied and lay somewhat scorched in two piles, also too damp to burn.

It wasn't hard to imagine the scenario. Weasel had left the bikes and trikes he'd stolen out back for others to steal, and tossed whichever of the smaller stolen goods he could later sell into the trunk of his Taurus. He'd then tried to destroy all that damnable packaging, imprinted with other people's names and addresses, by torching his house – a valueless house in a burned-out neighborhood where nobody, except Weasel, had lived for years. It had been a last-gasp effort to shake off pursuers angry about Austin, more imagined than real, along with cops, more real than imagined, who were bound to come knocking eventually to inquire why his Taurus kept popping up in surveillance footages recorded in neighborhoods suffering rashes of package and bicycle thefts.

Yet, typical of the lack of fortune Weasel got from the world, his house refused to burn. Years of leaking shingles, un-caulked windows and wind-driven rains had dampened the house too much to ignite. Like Weasel himself, it had simply sputtered for a time, and then quit.

I sniffed at the thickening inch of milk in the half-gallon on the kitchen counter before I walked out.

It, too, had spoiled.

FORTY-EIGHT

Even if I hadn't been there that afternoon, trailed by Herbie Sunheim's spirit screaming in outrage, it would have been easy to spot the place in the yet-to-be rehabbed district, south of the expressway. A green Volvo station wagon, a black Chevy Suburban and two yellow cabs were parked in front of what, ordinarily, would have been a vacant storefront in a block full of empty storefronts. I pulled up behind the second cab and got out. I was fifteen minutes early, curious though fairly sure of what I was about to see.

Even though I believed the world had only one rusting red Jeep crowned with a green top, a large man in a black suit immediately stepped out from the passenger's side of the Suburban to eyeball me pulling up. He was one of Amanda's bodyguards. He recognized me and gave me a sort of half-wave.

I told him Amanda and I would be heading to Leo's grand opening the next morning, and to tell the day shift that there would be hot dogs and maybe even lime gelato in it for them if they dressed less like guards and more like guys simply showing up for hot dogs. No sense being noticeable, I said. He smiled and said he'd pass along the message.

I walked up to the store window and looked inside. The place was brightly lit. Two pairs of eight-foot-long folding tables ran down the center. Eight black teenagers – four girls and four boys – sat facing each other. Long strands of multicolored wires lay in the center of the tables. Small blue trays of red, gray and white plastic connectors, and clear plastic tubs of shiny, plated metal parts rested in front of each teen.

Amanda stood off to one side, behind a middle-aged man in a short-sleeved white shirt whose pocket was crammed with more pens and pencils than anyone normal could use in a year. Surely the owner of the green Volvo outside, and likely a manufacturing engineer, he was inserting multicolored wires into a red plastic connector, showing the kids how to assemble small wiring harnesses with the components that lay before them in the tubs and trays.

My mind drifted, as it so often did, to that first time I saw Amanda. It had been through a glass window very much like the one I was standing in front of now, only that window fronted a high-end art gallery on North Michigan Avenue, Chicago's most magnificently expensive mile. Being uneducated in art, then as now, I'd made a face at the painting on a wall that she was scrutinizing. She'd looked up, caught me, and made a face at the painting, too. I knew then that a moment like that was more than any man could wish for in a lifetime.

The manufacturing engineer set down his wiring assembly. Amanda clapped. The kids did, too, standing to grab coats and jackets piled on a table against the wall.

I stepped aside as the kids filed out, flushed, it seemed, with a strong sense of achievement. They were wearing jackets of another sort as well, those eight kids – jackets of promise. They split into two groups of four, crammed into the two cabs and were driven away.

I waited outside as Amanda finished talking to the man in the white shirt. He came out and, with a brief nod to me, headed down the block to the Volvo wagon.

She followed. Seeing me, she grinned. 'Slick, huh?' she asked. 'A fine beginning, for sure.'

She gave a thumbs up to her guards in the Suburban, linked her arm in mine, and we went to the Jeep. 'This is only a pilot project but already I have exciting news,' she said, strapping on her seat belt. 'At least one pair of lemon pants must be coming around. The landlord who owns this whole block of empty stores stopped by before we got started. The rent for our space plus the one next door has been prepaid for the next several years. Can you imagine?' she asked, flashing her huge grin at me. 'Several years? I'll have room for fifty, maybe even a hundred kids, by summer.'

'Magnificent,' I said, easing us east, toward Lake Shore Drive.

'Don't you want to know who stepped up to help?' she asked.

'Of course,' I said.

'Someone anonymous,' she said, laughing. 'Someone who doesn't want it known he's not quite solid behind the mayor.' Then, serious, she turned to me, 'Any news with you?'

'I called every law enforcement agency again,' I said. 'City, county, state, Belle Plaine, even the forest preserve cops. Nothing. Nobody's got anything on a Violet Krumfeld.'

'And that nags,' she said.

'More and more, and less and less.'

'There's that cryptic business again.'

'It's nothing I want to talk about, yet.'

'OK.' She knew my moods, my reluctance to put optimism into words for fear of jinxing a hope. 'How about the bodies in that burned-out car? Any identification?'

'Not in the news. I think the police are fervently hoping the press will back off,' I said.

'Kopek and Jacks, or Cuthbert and Raines?'

'Not one of them has returned my call,' I said. 'The brass knows who didn't show up for work. I think they're trying to keep the lid on while they investigate how far the corruption has spread.'

'The press will stalk the police superintendent every day.'

'Even Keller, with his grape-sized attention span, will probably follow up.'

'Understandable. It was his story, his and yours,' she said, turning to me. 'Speaking of Keller . . .?'

I shook my head. 'Nothing from him, either. I called him again today. He's not gotten one tip about Violet Krumfeld.'

'Mysterious lady,' she said.

'Maybe too mysterious,' I said. I'd been thinking that way since I made up my mind about who to send the gun to at police headquarters.

We passed Navy Pier and the enormous new Ferris wheel, lit up and ready for the riders who'd be coming in just days.

'You brought a change of clothes for Leo's?' she asked.

'Sometimes you've got to anticipate every possibility,' I said.

'Pajamas?' she asked, touching my shoulder.

'I anticipated that possibility, too.'

She kept her hand on my shoulder. 'And?'

'Nah,' I said.

She touched me even harder.

FORTY-NINE

Such was the reverence for Kutz's wienie wagon that fifty cars beat us to the clearing by the time we rolled down the river road, leading Amanda's guards, the next morning.

The three-dozen seniors roosting on Kutz's equally senior picnic tables had obviously arrived first. Ma Brumsky's age and older, they'd likely come at dawn, ready for lunch, as seniors often do. They sat, stood or leaned at various angles at the pigeon-strafed old tables, smiling, remembering. Many of them had been coming to that clearing since Kutz's old man ran the place, and plenty had carved their initials on the trailer's back wall, right above where Leo's new, multipurpose freezer now sat. No doubt more than a few had earned their first sexual splinters upon those very same wood tables, on mad, moonlit midnights long ago. It was barely the middle of March – the trees were bare, and the ground was still spotted with the last of the winter's snow – but for those at the tables, and just as probably for those standing along the Willahock, cradling hot dogs and fizzy sodas and cheese-slathered French fries, and those waiting in line to order, it was spring once again.

I couldn't see much of Leo behind the order window other than the flash of the red vinyl vest he wore to call at Ma's bingo nights or, more recently, when he'd chauffeured Ma, her lady friends, and me – crouched behind the driver's seat – to the home of an almost US Senator, where we'd gone to search for corpses.

I gestured to Amanda's two guards, invisible behind the dark

windows of their Suburban, that I'd get the hotdogs I promised
when the line shrunk a little, and Amanda and I went drifting,
enjoying the sounds and smells of the old place. The white flecks
curling off the forever peeling wood trailer, the bare dirt that would
never nurture grass or even weeds, the pigeon-splotched picnic
tables – all were as they'd been when I'd gone down to that clearing
after school to wait while my mother's sisters took turns bickering
over whose turn it was to take me in for a month. I'd never had
money, but the curmudgeonly Kutz never shooed me away, and
more than once the old crust slipped me a tepid hot dog and an
even warmer Coke. That clearing by the Willahock had been a
refuge, as had, later, Leo and his parents. It seemed a perfect
symmetry that he was in charge of it now.

Endora, Leo's girlfriend, came up, all grins and grease. A former
fashion model, truly a cover girl, she'd made enough to blow that
off to become an underpaid researcher at Chicago's Newberry
Library. She was a head taller than Leo but shared his stratospheric
intellect. And, judging by the yellow and red stains on her white
apron, she fully shared his latest dream, too.

'I'm in charge of the barbecue cheese fries!' she announced,
giving Amanda a hug and me a kiss on the cheek.

'Like everything, you wear it well,' Amanda said, laughing.

A great bell rang, the folks waiting in line to order froze, and
Leo stepped out from the trailer. He'd dyed his white chef's toque
into a swirl of orange, yellow and red that made him look like
an oversized wooden stick match, on legs, on fire. He carried an
enormous antique megaphone.

'Welcome, welcome all!' he announced through the horn, high-
stepping majestically to the gate in the fence surrounding his race
track. 'Welcome to the grand resurrection of Kutz's Wienie Wagon
and the introduction of thoroughbred racing to the banks of the
magnificent Willahock River!'

Everyone clapped as Leo, with great flourish, turned with
outstretched arms to the paddock. On cue, the veterinarian I'd seen
on earlier visits opened the gate and emerged, leading a small
parade. Up front were four goats, restrained on red leashes by Ma
Brumsky and three of her most ambulatory friends, all wearing
very short poodle skirts and pink down jackets. Each held a long
branch festooned with silver bells in her free hand. The goats were
surely large enough to drop each of the frail septuagenarians to

the ground with one strong tug, especially the beast Gregorio, who was being guided by Ma Brumsky, but all seemed well behaved and moved forward docilely.

Mrs Roshiska, Ma's oldest and portliest friend, brought up the rear, pushing her walker. She also wore a poodle skirt, though hers, because of her size, was decorated with substantially more poodles. Unlike the others, she wore no pink down jacket, but rather her customary pink sweatshirt and clearly, judging by the restless shifting of the fabric, nothing of restraint underneath. Mrs Roshiska, for all her advanced years, had the free-swinging spirit of a lustful teenage girl.

The crowd applauded the spectacle with loud cheers. Leo, grinning with his ten thousand teeth, took a bow and another, and another. When the veterinarian, the goats and their tending ladies arrived at the rail, Leo pulled back the gate and motioned for them to line up behind the starting points chalked onto the dirt track. Mrs Roshiska, trailing pendulously, entered the fenced track last and pushed her walker to a spot behind the veterinarian, the goats and their minders.

The crowd hooted and cheered. The Ringlings, Barnum, Bailey and now Brumsky; the ranks of the greatest showmen of all time had now been joined by Leo, at least in Rivertown.

By now, everyone who was physically able had gone to the fence to watch what might be a race, or bedlam. Leo, ever the optimist, had also chalk-striped lanes onto the track, as if the goats would race in straight lines.

The veterinarian moved across the starting line, unclipping the leashes from the collars of the four goats. The goats remained still.

I shifted to catch the eye of Gregorio. He stared back, but gave no wink acknowledging the ride we'd shared in my Jeep.

Leo raised his hand, put a whistle in his mouth, and blew.

The four septuagenarian lady goat wranglers raised their sticks to the heavens and shook their bells as if summoning down the Greek gods of Chaos.

The crowd cheered louder.

The goats, panicked by the bells and the cheers, took off down the straightaway, precisely as intended.

Despite his easy-going affability, the brown-and-white Gregorio, the largest and longest-legged of them all, quickly took a two furlong lead as the fast-moving pack approached the first turn.

It was then that things went awry.

Gregorio did not follow the turn. He lowered his head and charged the curve in the fence, hitting it full force with his horns. The rails flew up in the air like cheap balsa as Gregorio shot through the new opening and onto the cleared ground beyond the fence.

Whereupon he skidded to a halt.

And then, almost lazily, he turned around to stare insolently back up the track, as if daring any of the four wranglers – Ma or her three similarly poodle-skirted friends – to try to come down to get him.

Gregorio's three apostles wanted no part of any such confrontation. It was lunchtime and they'd sensed there was food around, loose. Charging through the break after Gregorio, they kept on going, circling outside the fence, past the paddock, through the space between the backstretch and the river to the hardened ground where the picnic tables had sat for all time. No one was there; the seniors had left their lunches to move to the track to watch the race.

The three junior goats hit the tables fast, and literally, bucking them up onto their sides, spilling hot dogs and colas and the French fries coated with the yellow stuff Kutz swore was cheese. It stopped them, all that flying food, and the goats set about grazing, all thoughts of escape abandoned.

I looked back at Gregorio, still standing past the section of fence he'd smashed. He was watching us all – the poodle-skirted wranglers, the suddenly silenced crowd, his fellow, foolish goats – with eyes that did not blink. Having established some rapport when I drove him back to the clearing, I guessed that freedom was not his objective. Mastery over any situation, controlling it on his terms, might have been what he was after.

The frozen crowd stared at the goat perhaps staring at them, it being hard to tell because his eyes were on different sides of his head. And though there was no way of knowing for sure what was lurking in Gregorio's mind, it was easy to read the spectators'. They were scared. They stood rigidly along the fence rails, their mouths working in silent prayer, their eyes intent on Gregorio. Even the three rambunctious goats who'd charged the picnic tables had stopped cavorting, sensing the stillness of the crowd, and now stood stiff like statues, though still chewing. They, too, seemed too frightened to move.

And so, for a moment, nothing did. Not the large, muscular, Gregorio, not Ma and her fellow wranglers, not Leo, not any of the crowd, not the other goats. Like a main street in an old Western movie when breaths were held just before a gun duel, the clearing had gone completely and utterly silent.

And then, just as in those old Westerns when the wind nudged a sign hanging on rusted chains, a single thin sound cut into the silence. Something creaked.

It came from no hanging sign, though, but rather the tortured front wheels of Mrs Roshiska's walker, screeching in protest as she put her considerable weight behind them to move forward. Snatching the red leash from Ma Brumsky, she pushed past her four frozen, poodled friends and began moving up the race track, slowly, deliberately, every bit as purposefully as any sheriff who'd ever stared down a gunslinger.

The muscular Gregorio did not move. He stayed in place, holding his ground, watching, waiting.

Mrs Roshiska passed the front stretch halfway mark, both hands firm on the creaking walker, one also clutching the red leash. It occurred to me then that I was no longer seeing a replay of a high-noon movie Western; I was witnessing Hemingway's Pamplona, *el matador* Mrs Roshiska versus the master bull Gregorio.

Mrs Roshiska got to the three-quarter mark. Still, Gregorio did not move. And then, the eye that was closest to me rolled. It did not blink; it did not look up or down. It simply rolled, and I understood. He'd been unable to focus from either side of his head on her face, or her legs, or her walker. The pendulous, free-swinging Mrs Roshiska had trapped his eyes with what rolled beneath her sweatshirt in sympathetic rhythm, up and down, side to side, unmoored and independent of one another.

She wheeled through the break in the fence and right up to Gregorio. He didn't move as she reached out to snap the leash to his collar, turned around, and began leading him back toward the starting line. To my mind, poor Gregorio seemed almost grateful to be led, having now to face only the relative calm of the back of Mrs Roshiska's sweatshirt.

The crowd remained silent as the pair wheeled and walked back up the front stretch toward the waiting hands of the veterinarian, who'd watched the whole drama safely from behind one of the fence posts set solidly in cement. But once he took the leash from Mrs Roshiska, pandemonium broke loose. The three apostles, sensing the drama was over, resumed jumping up and down among the upended picnic tables and began making their frenetic goat noises. Half the crowd raced for their cars.

'Hot dogs are on me!' Leo announced through his megaphone and that stopped most of them. For that crowd, especially the seniors just getting by on reduced fixed incomes, being kicked to death by frolicking goats paled in comparison to enjoying a Kutz-style hot dog for free. Leo raced into the wienie wagon, turned his boom box on loud, and hot dogs on buns began flying out faster than Kutz used to let flies fly in, all to the tunes of his beloved Antonio Jobim. Clutching their free wieners, some began swaying to the gentle sambas and, suddenly, it was Brazilian *carnivale* along the Willahock.

The three apostles, caught up in the merriment of the day, danced and darted in and out as the people shrieked and hollered and danced. Soon, ragged Conga-like lines were formed, meant to herd the goats toward their paddock. Even Amanda's guards, tieless but still dressed like stiffs in dark suits and unseen holstered guns, got caught up in the hilarity of it all, and had linked arms with the other revelers. It was bedlam and it was magnificent.

It took two hours to coral the goats and upright the picnic tables. By then, Leo had run out of hot dogs, French fries, soft drinks, and even the yellow goo Kutz told everyone was cheese. People left laughing, swearing Leo's grand opening was the most fun they'd had in years.

Amanda and I laughed, too, sitting at last at a picnic table with Leo, still adorned with his flame-dyed toque, and Endora, sweat-stained, shiny and elegant. Mock-mortified, Leo cradled his chimney-topped head in his hands, mourning that in all the excitement, he'd forgotten to announce he was now also offering six flavors of ice cream, plus lime gelato.

And then it was time to go. As I started us up the river road, Amanda's guards following fifty feet behind in their Suburban, a massive black Hummer pulled out of the woods in front of us. There were plenty of such massive off-roaders lumbering around

Chicagoland, but this one was tricked out with a solid row of lights above its windshield. Fear bumps danced up the back of my neck. I'd seen that Hummer twice before.

The Hummer slammed on its brakes fifty yards before the turn onto Thompson Avenue. Just as I swung the steering wheel hard left to get around it, a black Impala roared up from behind and ducked between us and Amanda's guards.

Amanda sucked in a breath. 'Damn,' she said, in too small a voice.

I cut the Jeep's engine and jumped out before guns could be drawn.

'It's not a kidnap!' I yelled to Amanda's guards. 'They're here for me.'

FIFTY

I'd guessed right, when I'd addressed the box containing the revolver. It was Raines who got out of the passenger's side of the black Impala, holding up both hands so Amanda's guards could see that they were empty.

'Reaching for a badge,' he called to the guard who'd moved up, jacket unbuttoned, hardware accessible.

I hurried back to stand with Raines, to be doubly sure no one got cranky.

Opening his suit jacket slowly, Raines extracted his ID with two fingers. The guard took a look at it, and then at me, and shrugged. Raines put the ID back and motioned for us to walk up to the Jeep.

Raines bent to the unzipped passenger curtain. 'I apologize for the drama, Miss Phelps, but would you mind joining my associate in that obnoxiously large Hummer ahead? We're having a hell of a time, worrying about how to keep Mr Elstrom here alive.'

By now, Amanda's other guard had moved to the driver's side of the Impala, where Cuthbert was holding out his own badge.

'He goes with Amanda,' I said, pointing to the guard who'd followed us to the Jeep.

Raines nodded, but Amanda hesitated.

I reached in to touch her shoulder. 'Raines is one of the guys who saved my life,' I said.

She nodded, grim-faced, got out and walked alongside her guard up to the passenger's side of the Hummer. It was yet another glimpse of how wearying her new life had become, being constantly reminded of how her great wealth made her an enticing kidnapping target.

'Let's talk,' Raines said, climbing in the Jeep's passenger side.

I got behind the steering wheel. 'Whose is it?' I asked, motioning to the Hummer.

'Miss Phelps will explain later.' He shifted on the seat to look at me directly. 'About your meddling and your muddling . . .'

'Thanks for keeping me alive,' I said.

'It's distracting.'

'How did you know Kopek and Jacks would come for me?'

'We didn't. We, and others, have been watching Kopek ever since he pulled too many strings to get put in charge of the Central Works investigation. He showed too strong an interest. Night before last, we followed him and Jacks to Rivertown, thinking they were taking another run at what you knew and what you didn't. But instead of knocking on your door, Kopek dropped Jacks off by that mess of trees you call a park and then drove away. We stuck around to see why Jacks was hiding across from your home. Five minutes later, you came out, got in your car safely and drove away. Jacks stayed in the park. That made no sense; him there and you gone. We made a snap decision and followed you to that hamburger place. You met Kopek. You left. A moment later, he left, and we followed him to your place, but when he turned off Thompson Avenue, he killed his lights as he approached. We hung back, just off Thompson. We heard gunshots. We intervened.'

I gestured at the Hummer ahead. 'That person intervened, too, like at Central Works.'

'It didn't work at Central Works, did it? You got chased away but didn't stay away.'

'Like the tagger,' I said. 'The witness.'

'We only wanted to scare him, whoever he was, and you away. Tell me about the revolver.'

'It's why Kopek wanted to meet at The Hamburger. He said there was a contract out on me and insisted I take it for protection.'

'You were meant to die with your fingerprints all over that weapon. They'd say you fired first.'

'After that shoot-out in the park, I concluded it was loaded with blanks.'

'A clever precaution, intended for removal after your death. They didn't want you loading it with your own, more lethal rounds.'

'That gun has history?'

'It was used on Walter Dace and his receptionist. Killing you holding that gun would get you blamed for their murders, while eliminating your bothersome investigation.'

'Why would Kopek and Jacks kill Dace?'

He looked away, out the open side curtain. 'The guys beyond Dace—'

'Triple Time?' I cut in, to be sure.

He nodded. 'We think they got worried that Dace lost control of his operation, that the scumbag lawyer, Means, was killed by the scumbag realtor, Sunheim, maybe over money they embezzled. Sunheim, they must have logically concluded, then took off with whatever he stole. Triple Time had already acquired the buildings they needed and thought it best to protect themselves by erasing the rest of the crew. They instructed Kopek and Jacks to kill Dace.'

'And find and kill Sunheim,' I said.

'Of course,' he said, turning back quickly to look at my eyes. 'They were scum, all of them.'

'Not Dace's receptionist.'

'In a war, there's collateral damage.'

He waited, likely for me to ask about Violet Krumfeld. I didn't. I didn't need to hear much more, not truths, not lies.

'Let it go, Mr Elstrom.' He reached for the door handle.

'The kid,' I said. 'I've got to know about the kid.'

He dropped his hand from the door handle and turned around, confused. 'The kid?'

'The kid, in Austin. Calls himself Mister Shade.'

'Ah, Wurder's kid,' he said, nodding. 'Wurder came up with that one, to get you to go to Austin.'

'Why come at me like that?'

He offered up a small smile. 'You didn't scare, Mr Elstrom. You didn't scare at Central Works. One of our associates saw you go to Wurder; we saw Wurder go to you—'

'You kept watch on me.'

'You made no secret of working for Sunheim, but we were unsure if you were involved with Means and Dace, too. We know Wurder from the courts. We spend time there, watching judges set killers free. Wurder wasn't hard to convince after we shot up his front door. The kid was never in danger. You weren't either, not in Austin.'

'Except from random violence.'

'We're all in danger from that, because that's what happens there and here and everywhere. Too many drugs, too many guns, too many kids who can't shoot straight.' He stared through the windshield, his face set hard. 'Why the hell didn't you leave Sunheim there? Why take him? Only a crazy man would do that.'

'Only a crazy cop would have put him there in the first place.'

He didn't answer. He just kept staring out the window.

'Only a crazy cop would take him back,' I went on. 'Only a crazy cop would wrap him in plastic in the first place, like a sandwich for later, saving him to be a message when the timing was right.' I paused, then said, 'Only a crazy cop would pitch a body onto a railcar.'

He worked his mouth, angry, but still he kept staring straight ahead. 'Leave it be,' he said.

'Leave it be,' I repeated, but only inside my head, reminding myself I was talking to a cool-thinking killer and ought to shut up. Reminding myself too that only a crazy cop would ignore a drone lying by the side of a street, or a Jeep parked in the wrong place, that only a crazy cop would ignore another crazy man, out to do something crazy himself.

He opened the door, stepped out, and turned back to the open side curtain. 'The burned bodies have not been publicly identified. How did you know to send the gun to Cuthbert and me, that we were the survivors?'

'You never pressed me about Violet Krumfeld,' I said. 'Kopek and Jacks, they badgered me about her. Not you. That made you for knowing more than you were saying. And it was obvious you knew more about Kopek and Jacks than they knew about you, so that made you for watching them, not them watching you, and that made you for being the last to show up for the gunplay. That made you the survivors.'

'Violet Krumfeld is dead to us all,' he said, and headed back to his Impala.

Up ahead, Amanda noticed. She climbed out of the Hummer, but stopped to lean against the door. Her skin was pale. She was shaking.

Her guard stepped up and held out his hand. She managed a smile and gently brushed it away, and together they walked back to the Jeep. The Hummer pulled away and the black Impala swung out from behind me and followed.

'Amanda?' I asked, as she climbed in.

'Such nightmarish times,' she said softly, and held out her hand.

She was holding a tiny box, wrapped in purple paper and tied with a little purple bow.

'This is for you,' she said.

FIFTY-ONE

'You're sure it's over?' Amanda asked again, early that evening. We'd sat in my kitchen ever since we got back to the turret, seeking closure that didn't want to come.

'Raines insisted on it, at least for me,' I said.

'And Triple Time?'

'Raines is sure it's over for them, too. They know people are watching for them to reappear. And that makes it better to default on the real estate taxes and let their properties revert to the county than to risk setting up another shop.'

'Nobody will ever know who they are?'

'Anonymous, evil men, likely from Mexico or Central America or Russia or any other place.'

'Others like them will come.'

'If they're not here already, but Raines and Cuthbert and their friends are watching.'

'You're conflicted about them.'

'Those two did save my life.'

'Still, cops taking the law into their own hands, no matter how noble their purpose . . .'

'Are vigilantes,' I said.

'Executioners,' she said.

I nodded. We'd worked it over for hours. 'For me, for now, it's done.'

'Except for that,' she said, giving a nod to the tiny box wrapped in purple paper and tied with a purple bow.

'Except for that,' I agreed.

She looked down at her coffee but she was still seeing the person behind the steering wheel of the Hummer. 'A woman meets her sister at a Starbucks right across from a district police station,' she said, needing to go over the story yet another time. 'No place is safer, right? Leaving, the woman heads to her car to drive back to her job. The sister waits for traffic to clear before crossing to the police station, where she's secretary to evidence technicians. A car full of gang-banging boys – very young teens according to witnesses – speeds up, firing wild at another kid who's on that same damned sidewalk in front of that same damned Starbucks, despite the police station that's right across the same damned street.'

She stopped, dabbed at her eyes with the tissue that had been balled up in her hand for the past hour.

'Amanda . . .'

She shook her head. She was going to struggle through the story as many times as necessary, though no sense would ever be made of it. It was a Chicago story and stories like it were told over and over, every day.

'The punks miss the kid on the sidewalk,' she went on, 'but the sister catches two bullets in the head, just down the sidewalk from the woman heading to her car, who's turned to look back at the sounds of gunfire. The woman runs to her sister but the sister is dead. Cops run out from across the street, but the shooting happened so fast, *so insanely*, that no one has seen much of anything. The car is found. It's stolen, of course. The intended victim, probably another gangbanger, has run off to die another day. The shooter boys are never caught.

'The woman confronts a couple of detectives at the sister's funeral – let's call them Raines and Cuthbert, though she didn't say – who work vice, not homicide. She's furious; she wants revenge; she wants to kill the punks that killed her sister. The two detectives say the shooters will never be identified but they mention that some inspector in Streets and Sanitation tipped a cop in traffic about some bulldozing in ruined factory districts – bulldozing that hasn't led to new construction. How the hell does that get the punk shooters? the woman asks. It doesn't, the detectives tell her, but nobody buys so many buildings, and bulldozes so much surrounding ground, without making a grand hoopla about a wonderful new condo development or food store or whatever that they're bringing to an economically depressed area. You're saying they don't want attention because they're setting up to do bad things? she asks them. Drugs, they say, and battles over drugs often make kids shoot from cars. The detectives tell her they've been watching the realtor on the property deals but they want to watch him closer. They think he's susceptible to cheap. They say they've got seized money that never got inventoried for an impound locker, usable for living expenses if she'd care to participate in bringing bad people down. The woman approaches Herbie, offering to work for cash, well under minimum wage.'

'Herbie bites,' I said, 'because he sees himself being out of the office more, working for Triple Time off the books, and he needs to keep up appearances.'

'The woman goes to work for Herbie but she learns nothing. Herbie's regular business is slow, yet he's never around, confirming suspicions that he's working secretively.'

'And then somebody goes out the window at Central Works,' I said.

'Which means nothing to her when it first hits the news, because the property isn't in Herbie's files, which she's searched. The next day, though, her cop friends tell her Herbie won't be returning to work—'

'Implying Herbie was dead?'

'Not in so many words, but she did say they suggested it would be helpful for her to continue, to see who comes around.'

'Which was me, asking about Herbie and the Central Works,' I said.

'And which she dutifully reported to Raines and Cuthbert, who told her they'd already spotted you at the Central Works.'

'She played me like a harp from the first moment I arrived at Herbie's office, keeping Cuthbert and Raines informed about what I was asking and, presumably, what I was learning. She's a tough lady.'

'A *committed* lady, she wanted me to know, because she wants you to understand.'

I looked again at the little purple box. 'Cuthbert and Raines – they're every bit as artistic as the tagger is,' I said. 'They destroyed a cartel's presence here in Chicago, basically with innuendo.'

'And a couple of murders,' she said.

'Beginning with Rickey Means. They set it up to make it look like Herbie killed him, then waited a day and killed Herbie, too. But instead of leaving Herbie where he could be found, they hid his body, making it look like Herbie took off after killing Means.'

'Triple Time's people freaked.'

'But they bought the assumption, because they figured Herbie likely took three hundred thousand of their dollars with him,' I said.

'Did Cuthbert and Raines know about the money?'

'Herbie might have told them, to bargain to save his own life. Obviously, it didn't matter. Cuthbert and Raines and their friends aren't in this for the money.'

'Kopek and Jacks sure found out about the money,' she said.

'Right after Herbie disappeared. Unbeknownst to Dace, Triple Time had those two cops in their pocket. Since the big boys above Dace thought he'd lost control of his organization, and since they already had their buildings, they ordered Kopek and Jacks to clean up and erase any links back to them. Kill Dace; find the money and kill Herbie.'

'Except Herbie was already dead.'

'Thanks to Raines and Cuthbert. And that's what convinced me that some of what Raines was telling me in the Jeep was untrue. He made no excuse for knowing that Herbie's corpse had been left in the Vanderbilt Supply before the building got torched. The likeliest way he would have known that was if he'd put him there himself.'

'I'm still not sure why Herbie hired you.'

'He panicked when he heard a body was found on that boxcar. He knew it was Means, from the description in the news, and was afraid that Dace, on orders from Triple Time, was indeed cleaning house, erasing those links. He must have hoped that by overpaying me to publicly nose around at Central Works, my presence might stop someone from coming after him.'

She grimaced. 'That lasted a day?'

'Cuthbert and Raines were not to be deterred.'

She looked at me then, with arched eyebrows, as if daring me to spin a story. 'Back to that missing money . . .?'

'To be sure, Kopek and Jacks hunted for it, in the faint hope that Herbie had not taken it. They searched his rented room twice; they tried to get Herbie's wife to let them look around her house, and when that failed, they returned to search it when she wasn't home. But, finally, they had to come to the conclusion that Herbie really had taken off with the money, because he simply was nowhere to be found.'

'But then you torched the drug lab, and that same night, Triple Time's other two buildings went up. And . . .'

'Herbie made his grand reappearance,' I said.

'And what did Kopek and Jacks think then?' she asked, like she didn't know.

I shrugged, evading.

'Perhaps,' she said quickly, a frown forming on her lips, 'they became sure that the man who'd been sniffing around Herbie's rented room had indeed found the missing three hundred thousand.'

'Perhaps,' I allowed, because there was no alternative.

'So they hatched the plan to kill you while you were holding the gun that killed Dace, and have a solid look inside the turret before reporting the justified shooting.'

'And telling Triple Time they never could find the money.'

'You're such an idiot.' She got up to open a window. 'About that money . . .' she said, looking out.

'Can you envision your friend in the Hummer towing that railcar down the spur?' I asked, to change the subject.

'It's her Hummer; she's a wilderness hiker. She's quite a lady, so soft-spoken and yet so determined. She would have done anything to make the case more interesting to news folks.'

'She's leaving town?'

'She says she's done with Chicago.'

'Whatever her real name is, she's leaving Violet Krumfeld dead and gone, thanks to that phony assault report Cuthbert and Raines made up.'

Amanda came back to the table, beginning to smile for the first time since the goat ruckus at the clearing. 'You know, I've been wondering about what happened to Herbie's three hundred thousand—'

I cut her off. 'Less the thousand he sent me, don't forget.'

'There are lots of ways that much money can be used, to take back,' she said.

'One can only hope.'

'OK, OK – I'm going to give up asking about the prepaid rent we're going to be enjoying for years to come.' She picked up the little purple box. 'This wrapping paper is lovely. Little flowers, entwined.' She pushed the box across the table. 'Going to open it now?' Her eyes sparkled, teasing.

'I'm never going to open it,' I said.

'But . . . but why?' asked the beautiful woman, pretending to be confused.

'I can tell by its weight that it's empty. It's the outside that matters.'

'Little purple violets.' She smiled, charmed like me.

'The woman who died on a jogging path would never give away a ring her beloved sister made when they were kids. And she wants it to be known that there's nothing to be found beneath the little flower, and would like very much to be forgotten—'

She froze, and held a forefinger to her lips for silence. 'Do you hear?' she mouthed, gesturing toward the open window.

It was a hissing, the sound of a tagger's aerosol can. I'd heard it at the Central Works, on a frightening night. Now, with luck, it might be the sound of closure.

She stood up, about to head again to the window. I got up, quickly grabbed her hand and led her across the would-be hall to the dark part of the second floor. A window there looked out toward the short street that led to Thompson Avenue.

'Don't you want to stop someone defacing your turret?' she whispered, though the window where we stood was closed.

'No,' I whispered back.

'You're crazy,' she whispered.

I nodded, agreeing.

His shadow appeared down below, running hunched toward the short street, bulged at the back by a backpack full of paints.

'He's getting away,' she said, speaking normally.

'Again, thank goodness,' I said.

A john car turned off Thompson Avenue and pulled to a stop on the short street. But in the briefest of instants before its head-lamps were switched off, it had lit the short figure running up onto the grass and into the darkness. And that brief instant of brightness had been enough to show a flash of red – a red I'd first seen on a kid's shoes, a red I'd mistakenly thought to have been dusted on with other designer colors at some shoe factory, but which I now knew was overspray from a tagger's palette of aerosol paints.

I'd been so blind.

'Let's look,' I said.

I grabbed a flashlight from the kitchen and we went out into the night.

It was tiny, done with precision to cover only a single limestone block on the river side of the turret.

'A little yellow smiley face,' she said, grinning as she turned to me. 'A perfect miniature of the huge one tagged on the drug lab after it was torched by persons unknown.'

'Mister Shade is pleased,' I said.

She reached for my hand, to lead us back inside.

'As I will be, too,' she said.